"You just wante

Something changed in her eyes. "What if I did? Could you take more of it?"

"Try it and let's see."

It took her forever to make the move. Then she finally put her hand to the side of his face.

He had to steel himself against a reaction.

Tonight, he was seeing another side to her. Even that resolve in her eyes seemed not about control, but about simple response. Her thumb ran lightly over his jawline, over his chin. The air left his lungs. Then she moved her hand so her index finger could explore his bottom lip. She leaned forward to plant a kiss there. Her lips were a millimeter from his, his parted and waiting for her....

Dear Reader,

When I wrote *Always Florence*, my first Mills & Boon® Heartwarming™ book, I hadn't intended a connected book. I became invested in Sandy's and Hunter's futures, however, and hope you did, too. There had to be a way to unite a woman who is single-minded in pursuit of the life she wants for her daughters and herself, and a man who has enormous personal and financial problems to solve and just wants to be left alone.

I think I found it.

Happy Spring!

Muriel

Muriel Jensen

Love Me Forever

Published in Great Britain 2014
by Mills & Boon, an imprint of Harlequin (UK) Limited,
Eton House, 18-24 Paradise Road, Richmond, Surrey, TW9 1SR

ISBN: 978 0 263 24496 0

33-0514

Harlequin (UK) Limited's policy is to use papers that are natural, renewable and recyclable products and made from wood grown in sustainable forests. The logging and manufacturing processes conform to the legal environmental regulations of the country of origin.

Printed and bound in Spain
by Blackprint CPI, Barcelona

MURIEL JENSEN

lives with her husband, Ron, in an old foursquare Victorian looking down on the Columbia River in Astoria, Oregon. They share their home with Cheyenne, a neurotic husky mix, and a tabby horde (there are only two, but they come in screaming, and she imagines them wearing armor and wielding swords as they eat everything in sight and take hostages for evening TV watching).

They have three children, eight grandchildren, four great-grandchildren, and a collection of the most interesting and generous friends and neighbors. They feel truly blessed!

To Adalyn Saysong Deth,

Tommy and Zoey Erickson,

and to Ashley

CHAPTER ONE

SANDY EVANS FELT DESERTED. The man she loved stood with his broad back to her, his rejection undeniable. Her mother thought she was insane, and her best friend had told her it was just wrong to offer Hunter Bristol thirty thousand dollars to marry her. "He'll throw it back at you," Bobbie Raleigh had warned.

Marriage wasn't the point of the money offer, but—to be honest—she'd have loved it to be the ultimate outcome. So she'd ignored her mother and her best friend, and handed Hunter Bristol a check in that amount. His initial reaction was not promising. White shirt stretched across shoulders that were square and muscular, he'd been silent for about a minute, one hand jammed in the pocket of his gray slacks, the other holding the check between his thumb and forefinger as though it had been smeared with Ebola.

He turned around finally, and she knew Bobbie had been right. Sandy was about to have the check thrown back in her face.

Hunter Bristol was tall and athletic, a man built for action despite having the methodical, meticulous brain of a Certified Public Accountant. His light blue eyes radiated fury and his blond hair, a little too long and roughly styled, almost bristled with his effort to maintain some sort of control. Beyond the glass walls of his office, coworkers glanced their way, obviously wondering what was going on, though they pretended to look busy.

He waved the check at her and demanded, his voice just above a whisper, "Where did you get this kind of money?"

Suddenly tired of everyone's displeasure when all she'd meant to do was ease Hunter's financial problems, she folded her arms and stared boldly into his thunderous face. "I rolled an old lady for it," she said.

He took a step toward her, then apparently thought better of whatever he'd intended and stopped. He glimpsed the outer office and saw that his employer, Nate Raleigh, her friend Bobbie's husband, had come out of his office to talk to Jonni, his office manager, who sat at the front desk. But Hunter appeared to have more of Nate's attention than Jonni did.

"You're lucky," Hunter said, leaning back against a dark wood work table, "that you've got so many witnesses. You want to try that again?"

She closed her eyes with a sigh and perched on his desk, a patch of carpet separating them. "I refinanced the house," she admitted, attempting to sound reasonable. "You're my friend. I'd like to help you get out of debt so we can...you know...be more."

"Sandy!" His temper flared beyond his control despite their audience, and he flung his arms out to his sides in complete exasperation. "Are you totally deaf? We've had this discussion how many times in the months we've been going out? You will *not* pay my debts! I will *not* accept one dime from you."

"It's not out of my monthly income. This is—"

"No. No money from you. Ever."

"Hunter," she continued serenely, "it's not as though you gambled away your money or spent it on women and alcohol. Someone you trusted embezzled from you! This self-imposed penance is unnecessary. Let me help you pay your creditors."

He caught her wrist, pulled his office door open, and drew her after him toward the front door. Nate intercepted them, looking worried.

Nate was a bit taller than Hunter but leaner. The two had been good friends since Nate had moved to Astoria almost a year ago. Hunter had worked for Nate's brother Ben. When Ben and his wife died in a boating accident, Nate, in charge of Raleigh and Raleigh's Portland office, came to take over the Astoria branch and care for Ben's two young boys. Hunter and Nate had grown close as Nate adjusted to life in Astoria.

Nate glanced from Hunter to Sandy. "Where are you going?"

Hunter rolled his eyes. "We're going to sit in her car," he said calmly, "where we might have a little privacy. I *am* tempted to kill her, but you know I won't, so no need to be concerned."

Nate considered a moment, then asked Sandy with a small smile, "Do you want him sitting in your car? I can call his mother, you know."

Sandy had to smile back. Hunter's mother was Nate's housekeeper and nanny. "I feel perfectly safe," she assured him, telling Hunter with a glance that she really did. His attempts to intimidate weren't working. Well, they were, but he didn't have to know that.

Nate stood aside. "All right, then," he said. "Remember you have a client in ten minutes, Hunt."

Hunter ignored him and drew Sandy out into the gray morning. May in Astoria, Oregon, on the northwest coast, did not guarantee spring-like weather. The smell of imminent rain hung in the air.

"I'm parked around the corner." She pointed in that direction, then dramatically favored the elbow he held. "I'll need this at a later date, you realize. I carry Addie in this arm. I mix cookie batter, I scrub the bathtub, I..."

He silenced her with a glare as they walked to her little red Volkswagen Beetle. He opened the passenger side door, pushed her into the vehicle, then walked around to the driver's side and let himself in.

"How true to our whole argument," she joked, turning in her seat to face him as he climbed in behind the wheel. "You have to drive even when we aren't going anywhere. And in *my* car."

He rearranged his long body in the tight space so he could look at her. "I've warned you over and over that it isn't safe to leave the car unlocked. And is it possible for you to be quiet," he asked, anger still in his voice, "and let *me* talk?"

"Oh, sure." She leaned her head against the door and made a face at him. "But there's really no need for you to say anything. I know it all by heart. You intend to pay off the debts resulting from the embezzlement before you let yourself get into a serious relationship. And you won't *accept* help from anyone. I happen to know that Nate made a gift to you in an amount that would take care of all you owe and provide a down payment on a house so that if we *did* get serious, I could move out of my little house and we could get married and buy something bigger together. But you gave the money back to him."

He appeared surprised that she knew.

"Bobbie told me," she explained, "but only because she was excited about it and thought it was great for us. She didn't know you stashed the money away with the intention of returning it to him after you'd earned him some interest." She shook her head at Hunter. "I appreciate your nobility in wanting to get all those debts paid off, how you sold everything and moved into your little apartment to reduce expenses, pay off what you could and meet your obligations. But at some point your nobility is just self-flagellation."

His grim expression made her try harder to understand. "Hunter. Are you just mad at yourself for having trusted the employee who embezzled from you? Because you're not the only person who has trusted and lost. I didn't lose money, but I lost most of the faith I had in men when my father walked away from us and my husband left after Addie was born."

HUNTER LOOKED OUT the front window and rested his wrist on the steering wheel. God, he hated being stupid. Jennifer Riley, his fiancée, had walked away with every penny in his personal and business bank accounts because he'd trusted her and given her access. And she'd taken Bill Dunbar, a tax-season hire, with her.

"You're right," he admitted. "I'm mad at myself because she was my fiancée. I loved her and thought she loved me. Then she stole everything and left with another man."

He hated that he hadn't even seen it coming. Building up his business had been a struggle, but he'd thought he and Jennifer were in it together. He was beginning to see the light when he'd gone to the office early on April 1, three years ago, at the height of tax season, to find she had cleaned him out and disappeared with the rest of his life.

Sandy stared at him for a full thirty seconds. Because she was seldom speechless, he let himself enjoy the moment. When she was quiet, she had an angelic quality about her. She had cocoa brown eyes, pink cheeks and a freckle right on the tip of her nose. She was just a little plump, and in repose, exuded sweetness and gentleness. But when she began to talk and take charge of anything and everything around her, the sweetness evaporated and the gentleness became a warrior-woman fierceness that had to be admired though sometimes strongly resisted.

Sandy drew a breath and the quiet moment was over. "You never told me you *loved* her," she finally said. "I thought she was just an employee. We saw each other for months and you never thought to tell me that?"

They'd been keeping company since a committee meeting Nate hosted in the office's conference room had brought them together seven months ago. At first, he'd thought her interest in him was harmless, but she turned out to be one determined woman. He was learning today just *how* determined.

"It's a sore spot, okay? I…didn't want to talk about it."

"But that's the kind of stuff people usually share."

"I'm sorry. You know me—I don't share well. It was a hard time for me all around."

She looked hurt that he hadn't explained about Jennifer, but she drew another breath and seemed to push the hurt aside. "Did she go to jail?"

"No, she escaped to Mexico, I think. The police lost her trail almost right away. I don't know where she is now. And I don't care. I'd just like my money back."

"So, you don't want vengeance, you just want your money." She pointed to the check. "There it is. Let's put that part of your life behind you and move on to what we can have together."

Hunter closed his eyes against her suggestion, then held the check up and slowly, deliberately, tore it in half. He was running out of ways to make his point with this woman. She was pretty and smart, but she wouldn't accept no for an answer.

When he'd met Sandy, her candor, her lack

of pretense had fascinated him, and her two little girls had captivated him. Time spent with Sandy and the girls over Thanksgiving had deepened his interest, though her need to control everything and her kinetic energy drove him a little crazy. She not only did four things at once, but she also trapped him in her vortex. Which was a problem, because at this point he had to remain focused on his payback plan.

At Christmastime she had mentioned love. Sharing the holidays with her and their friends had been wonderful, but he had to constantly remind himself to keep his distance. Still, her girls liked him, and he liked them. To remain removed from children was hard; he'd never quite accomplished that with Sandy's girls.

"Sandy, please try to understand this." She was looking away from him and he couldn't see the expression on her face, but he could sense her stubbornness. He had little hope of reaching her, yet he tried anyway. "I like you a lot, and under different circumstances, I'd want to see where our relationship could go. But, come on. We've talked about this already. I have things to do before I can consider marriage, and you're impatient to get on with your life."

She faced him finally. "Are you *still* in love with her?"

"Of course not."

"Then, I don't understand. You don't love her, but you don't care about us, either?" She let a beat pass, then shook her head. "So, that's it? We're just over? All those months of you being charming and letting the girls and me think you really cared about us meant nothing?"

"I told you in the beginning..."

"Right, right. Your life is all about staying single to pay off your debts. Money. It's all about money. Well..." Her voice grew louder, further amplified in the tiny car. "I'm trying to *give you* thirty thousand dollars!"

"Well, if all the situation required was money," he shouted back, "great, but it doesn't! I have to do this. My father worked extra shifts to help me get through college. My business was started with my parents' retirement fund. I didn't want to take it but they insisted because they loved me, were proud of me, and trusted me to do something great with it. When Jennifer stole from me, it was as though she took *their* money."

Again Sandy seemed at a loss for words, so he pressed on. He was now even angrier at her because she made him revisit the awfulness that had plagued his life for the past three years and would be with him for some time to come.

"You don't want to understand, because you're trying to buy the life you want. But you can't do that. You can't just decide what to do with my life so that it fits in with your plans."

Her eyes widened with disbelief. "Pardon me, but aren't *you* acting like all it requires is money? Money to pay your debts. Money to support a family. Money before you can decide to actually *live*?"

"Sandy, I need to fulfill a personal obligation. You just want me to fall in with your blueprint. I'm sorry, but a man doesn't let himself get into a mess, then let someone else—particularly a single mother with two little children—bail him out."

"I think you're scared—" she folded her arms, her body language clear "—I am an island in shark-infested waters."

But her voice gentled, despite its brutal message. "You picked the wrong woman once before and you're afraid of doing it again."

"You're absolutely right. And shouldn't *you* be scared? I mean, you believed in your husband when you married him and that didn't work so well. Shouldn't you be careful before *you* go to the altar again?"

Something died in her eyes at his reminder that she'd made a major, painful mistake. He felt almost guilty about that. She sighed, then cleared her throat. "Apparently." There was a moment of loud silence before she asked stiffly, "Would you please get out of my car?"

She was finally pushing him away. This was what he wanted, what he needed. He hadn't expected to hate it. "Sandy, you know where I stand. Eventually, things might be different, but for now…"

"If you won't accept help, won't take that generous gift from Nate, how do you intend to make anything different?"

He said what he knew she wouldn't want to hear. "It'll take time. I've been chipping away at the debt for a couple of years, now. It's a slow process, but I have my self-respect."

"Yeah. Well, I guess there's no arguing with that." She pushed the passenger side door open. "I have to go."

Which was some kind of progress. But they still had to work together. "We have to find a way to be civil with each other," he reminded her. "You're the one who volunteered us to chair the opening of the Clothes Closet. We have to collect the clothes, plan some kind of event. There'll be meetings, reports to Clatsop Community Action…" The Clothes Closet was a new arm of the Food Bank, being set up to provide warm winter clothing free of charge for those in need, and at a drastically reduced price to other shoppers.

"I can be civil," she said. "Just don't ask me to be friends."

He opened his door, too. "Of course not," he said before he climbed out. "That would require tolerance and respect for the other party's opinion."

The moment he got to his feet, she was there to push him out of her way and slip in behind the wheel. The wind whipped up from the river and a light rain began to fall. The atmosphere was perfect for the swan song of a love gone wrong. Or, less dramatically, for a love that couldn't be. At least for now.

She yanked the door closed and he pulled his hand away just in time. He stepped back before she could run over his toes. She drove away in a squeal of tires.

HUNTER STUDIED THE new client in the chair facing his desk. He guessed the man was in his early sixties, and probably financially comfortable. When Hunter took the man's raincoat, he noticed the exclusive label. He looked strong and fit and had lively brown eyes and white close-cropped hair.

Studying the business card the man had given him, he read the name—Harris Connolly. There was a Fairhaven, Massachusetts, address and a cell phone number, but no business name, no lofty title, no email address.

"I came through Astoria on a cruise ship a few years ago," Connolly explained to Hunter as he leaned back in the chair and crossed his ankles. "I loved it here. I fell on the ship and broke my leg." He grinned. "My own stupid fault. Nothing I could sue over, unfortunately. The ship had to go on without me, but the hospital took excellent care of me and arranged to get me a flight to Boston. They even found someone to drive me to the airport in Portland. I couldn't believe how kind everyone was to me. I owe this town."

"It's a great place. We take good care of everyone, tourists included. So, you're back to stay?"

"Maybe. I'm not sure." Connolly had a warm, wide smile, but used it only briefly. He focused seriously on Hunter's face. "I've scraped by for years running a little coffee shop in Fairhaven. Then I developed a new style of whoopie pie. Are you familiar with whoopie pies?"

Hunter laughed. "Whoopie cushions, yes. Whoopie pies, no. Are they a dessert?"

Connolly put a hand to his heart. "Oh, yes. And New Englanders love them. The dessert is basically a cream filling between two cakey chocolate cookies. Some are chocolate coated, some are rolled in nuts, all are scrumptious. But I developed one with cherries in the cream filling, and dipped half in milk chocolate, half in white chocolate."

"Wow." Hunter thought of Nate's wife, Bobbie, and her love of all things chocolate.

"I served them à la mode in the restaurant and people came from as far away as Boston to get them 'to go.' I started shipping them, and caught the attention of Mrs. Walters's Whoopie Pies. A big name among connoisseurs. She finally bought my recipe for a considerable amount of money. I'd like someone to help me manage the distribution of some of that money. I'm not good with figures, and investments just confuse me. I need help."

"We'll be happy to help you, of course. But

we have an investment counselor connected to the firm, Suzanne Corliss. You might prefer to talk to her."

Connolly shook his head. "I want *you* to help me. My aim right now is to give some money to Astoria. I thought you could figure out where it would do the most good."

Surprised, Hunter dropped the pen he held onto his yellow pad and pushed both pad and pen aside. He smiled politely. "That's very kind of you, Mr. Connolly." The unwritten rule was never to let a potential client go for any reason, but he couldn't imagine how this man had found him. Any nonprofit in town would be thrilled with a contribution of any kind, but surely someone in the mayor's office would be more qualified to decide which groups that might be.

Connolly's quick smile came and went again. "You're wondering why I'm here and not at the Community Action office."

"True."

"It's because last weekend I met someone you know and we got to talking; Clarissa somebody. I explained that I was searching for someone who knew about the various nonprofit agencies in town, and she said that you and your friends are active in community service. All that practical knowledge is just what I need to feel my money will end up in the right place."

Hunter nodded. "Clarissa Burke. She's pretty generous with her time, too."

"Also," Connolly shrugged and said with a curiously shy lift of his shoulder, "I'd like to keep this quiet, keep my name out of it. I hate fuss. So, I expect you'd like to do a little research into who needs what and get back to me?"

"I would," Hunter agreed. "And just so that I know what we're talking about here and how to distribute it, can you tell me what you'd like to give?"

"Sure. I was thinking a million dollars distributed among however many agencies you suggest. And if we could work it out so that some of that money is socked away somehow to provide them with long-term funding, I'd be very happy. What do you think?"

"Ah..." Hunter was aware that his mouth hung open. He closed it and swallowed then cleared his throat to reply. "Well thought out, Mr. Connolly," he said, his voice raspy. "I'll do this carefully."

Connolly stood. He leaned across the desk

and shook Hunter's hand. "It's been a pleasure meeting you. I've wanted to for some time."

In the process of getting the man's coat, Hunter turned, surprised at that. "You have? Oh, you mean…since meeting Clarissa?"

Connolly accepted his coat and threw it over his arm. "Yes." He smiled and pulled on a blue plaid cap, then adjusted the bill with a debonair snap. "That's what I meant. I look forward to hearing from you."

"Give me a week."

"Take all the time you need. I just subleased a condo on the river. You know the the building?"

"The Columbia House?"

"That's it. I've written my new landline number on the back of the card, but the cell number on the front still works. Call me when you have a plan and I'll make an appointment."

Hunter walked him to the front door. "It's been a pleasure meeting you, Mr. Connolly." He offered his hand. "You don't run into many philanthropists these days. Everybody's struggling to keep *themselves* afloat."

"I know. But life was generous to me and this town was so kind. I have feelings for Astoria. I'd like to share."

"That's highly commendable."

"Nah. The more I give away, the less I have to worry about. Good to meet you. We're going to do good things together."

"Well, you'll be doing—I'm just fact-finding."

"That's an important part of the process. We want to make sure the money goes where it'll do the most good. I'll wait for your call."

Connolly climbed into a silver Lexus parked out front and drove off.

Hunter strode across the green-oak-furnished office and rapped on Nate's open door. Nate glanced up from the computer. "Yeah?"

"You won't believe this," Hunter began as he took a client chair and told him Harris Connolly's story and what he wanted to do for Astoria.

Nate stared then said finally, "Well, great. If Sandy's still talking to you, you should get her to help you. She knows every group in town."

Running a hand over his face, Hunter groaned. "Yeah, well, I don't think that'll work. She's gone. I have to figure this out for myself."

"She lives in Astoria. How can she be gone?"

"Not gone from town. Gone from my *life*."

"Oh, come on. Don't give up. We all know she has strong opinions on everything." Nate's expression was vaguely superior, Hunter thought, now that Nate had his love life in order. Then Nate's voice became vague as he refocused on the computer. "You'll fix it. She'd do anything for anybody, and you, particularly."

Hunter stood to leave and sketched a wave in Nate's direction. Though Hunter had done his best to discourage Sandy's feelings, he knew Nate's assessment was probably still true. Sandy took care of everyone.

She just had to understand that Hunter Bristol took care of himself.

CHAPTER TWO

DISAPPOINTMENT LODGED like an anvil in her chest, Sandy did what she'd always done in such situations—she got on with her life. She drove to the Maritime Museum, parked her car and walked to the railing to look out on the river. The day was chilly and gray, but she loved it when the weather was like that. Moody and intimate, the air smelling the way she imagined heaven would.

She fought to think positively about other things. She had the rest of the day off and the girls were at daycare. She could finish painting the back porch. She could make goodie bags for Addie's fourth birthday party on Saturday; she could buy gift wrap and treat herself to lunch while she was at it.

She sighed and a strangled little sound came out with the whoosh of air. She put a hand to her chest and breathed in, letting that wood-and-river fragrance fill her up. So she couldn't have the man she wanted. She would survive.

Her father had left without any explanation when she was fourteen, and she'd survived. Her mother had gone into a decline for a few months, and Sandy had kept them going and they had both survived. Her husband had left two months after Addie was born, unable to deal with the tyrannies of parenthood, and she'd come through again. But, every time she'd had to pull it together, she'd felt a little of her soft side erode. She'd wondered what it would be like to have a man in her life who would be there when she turned to him, who would love her forever.

Well, she thought bracingly, that wasn't going to happen today. She inhaled another gulp of Columbia River air and wandered back to her car, considering the virtues of painting her porch against shopping and lunch out, when her cell phone rang. She didn't want to talk to anyone, but it could be the daycare calling about the girls.

The caller ID read A. Moreno. Armando and Celia Moreno and their two little girls were her tenants, living next door to Nate and Bobbie in a little cottage Sandy had inherited from her aunt. Bobbie had rented it before she met and married Nate and moved in with him and his nephews. Because the Morenos had come upon hard times, Sandy charged them just enough rent to cover property taxes and homeowner's insurance. They were embarrassingly grateful.

She answered the phone.

"Sandee!" Celia was breathless. "I took the leaky faucet off the top of the…the sink in the kitchen to try to…to fix it myself and water is like a fountain! I called Mando, but he doesn't answer. They are painting the apartment house by the bridge today." Hunter had gotten Mando a job with Affordable Painting, one of his clients.

Must be one of those days, Sandy thought. "There's a knob under the sink, Celia," she said. "Turn off the one under the cold water. I'll hold on while you do that."

Sandy heard scurrying, mutterings in Spanish, then, "I did, but it doesn't stop!"

"It'll take a second."

"Oh." She heard Celia's sigh of relief. "Just a little fountain. It is stopped."

"Okay. I'll be right there with a new faucet. That one was ready to be replaced anyway."

Celia made a commiserating sound. "I'm sorry. Bobbie says you are having a Sandy day."

She was surprised to feel herself smile. "I am." A pileup of disasters *was* a Sandy day.

After a quick trip to City Lumber, Sandy arrived at her rental house with her tool box to find pandemonium that had nothing to do with plumbing. Celia babysat for friends who couldn't afford formal daycare, did housekeeping and baked goodies for a Mexican bodega on Marine Drive. There were three children under two in a playpen in the middle of the kitchen. They babbled along with a children's show on television, squealing their delight at the antics of a furry puppet. Fortunately Celia's children weren't home yet to contribute to the melee. Her oldest daughter, Crystal, was in the second grade, and Elena, her youngest, in kindergarten.

A loud whirring sound competed with the television as Bobbie sucked up water with a Shop-vac. She waved at Sandy then turned off the machine as two women Sandy recognized as friends of Celia's went through a cardboard box and a large leaf bag on the table. Sandy knew they didn't speak English and simply smiled and offered a friendly greeting.

"They have brought coats from our friends," Celia explained. "In the box, they are good. In the bag, they need sewing. For *el Armario.*" The three women smiled broadly at Sandy. "The Clothes Closet," Celia translated.

"Thank you!" Sandy was thrilled. Except for a few things of her own and her girls' that she'd put aside in a corner of her bedroom, this was the first contribution to the Clothes Closet since the idea was conceived at a Food Bank meeting a month ago. "*¡Gracias!*"

The women nodded and responded in Spanish.

"They are happy to help," Celia said, "because you have helped me."

The women left in a flurry of waves and Spanish exclamations.

"Hi." Bobbie hauled the large drum and hoses away from the sink so that Sandy had room to work. She looked into her friend's face, her sympathetic expression explaining that she'd read Sandy's morning accurately.

Sandy fought with the packaging, finally won and put the new faucet aside. "I am so sorry," Celia said, hanging over her as she cleaned the sink around the mounting.

"It's all right, Celia. No harm done." After putting the faucet assembly in the holes, Sandy crawled under the sink to place washers and nuts on the mounting studs and hand tightened them, then finished the job with the wrench.

"It always surprises me that you're so strong." Bobbie had crouched beside Celia and was watching also. "I can never make a wrench work that well."

"There's a hardware store in my checkered past, remember. I clerked when I was in high school." Sandy pointed to her tool box on the floor in front of the refrigerator. "There's another wrench on top. Would you get it for me, please?"

Bobbie retrieved the tool. "I forgot that. You fixed the john in our dorm room. But, now you're just showing off. Two wrenches?"

Sandy took it from her. "One to hold the fitting and the other to turn the nut on the water supply line." She did as she explained, then told Celia to turn on the cold water, then the hot.

Bobbie looked doubtful. "You want to get out from under there first?"

"No. It'll hold."

Celia did as Sandy asked. There were no leaks.

Sandy crawled out from under the sink and accepted Bobbie's hand up.

Celia wrapped her in a hug. "Thank you,

Sandee. You are the best landlady in the world!" She handed her a check. "Here is the rent. Mando says we must pay you more, but we have no—"

Sandy stopped her. "Celia, we agreed on the rent. It's fine until Mando gets a promotion or you win the lottery or something."

Celia's eyes teared. "I will come and clean your house."

"No, you don't have to do that. When my mother babysits for me, she can't sit still, so she does it. You and Mando are fine here, Celia. You can live here at this rent until the girls get hitched."

Celia repeated her last word uncertainly. "Hitched?"

"Casado," Bobbie provided. "Married." When Sandy looked at her in surprise, she said, "Crystal taught me. Last art class we drew brides, princesses and warriors."

Crystal, Celia's seven-year-old, was in an art class Bobbie taught at Astor Elementary School. Bobbie had learned about the Morenos' troubles through Crystal last Christmas and told Nate, who had called the legal office Sandy worked for to see if anything could be done. Since then, they'd all been allied to make life more livable for the family.

Celia understood her meaning and hugged her again, smiling. "Until the girls are *casado, si.* But Mando will not let them get *casado* until they are thirty. You will wait a long time for more rent."

"It's fine, Celia." Sandy glanced at her watch. "I'll take the box of clothes home with me, run a few errands and be back to make sure the faucet isn't leaking."

Celia nodded. "Then I will send you home with frijoles refritos and flan."

Sandy would have told her she didn't have to, but Celia's flan was legendary. And she put chorizo and onion in her beans.

"That would be wonderful." Sandy picked up the box and Bobbie came to open the door for her.

"You just want to say I told you so," Sandy said under her breath as she passed her.

"Of course I do." Bobbie walked around her to the Volkswagen. "Hunter threw the check at you, didn't he?" she guessed as Sandy beeped the door open.

"No." Sandy placed the box on the back seat while Bobbie held the door. "He tore it in two.

They'd been college roommates at Portland State and since then had supported each other through major life crises. They were dear friends. Bobbie's tone turned from teasing to gently rebuking. "Sandy, he's told you before in no uncertain terms that he won't accept money from you. If you're ever going to have a permanent relationship with him, you'll have to pay closer attention to what *he* wants."

"He wants to never get married."

"That's what every man wants. But he cares about you."

"Yeah, well, caring isn't loving. He wants his self-respect. I guess the girls and I rate somewhere behind that." She closed the door on the Closet's first official donation. At least that was off to a good start.

Bobbie patted her shoulder as they walked around to the driver's side. "You do realize that many men in such a position would be happy to let you solve their financial problems and take care of everything? I think it's to his credit that he won't."

Sandy gave Bobbie a hug. Despite her own anguish, she noted that her friend looked healthy and happy. After battling cancer, falling in love and relinquishing her dream to study art in Florence, Italy, she appeared remarkably grounded and serene. Her dark hair had even grown sufficiently to now curl around her ears. Sandy was happy she was doing so well. She got back to the subject at hand. "Did you know that Hunter was engaged to the woman who embezzled from him?"

Bobbie looked surprised. "No, I didn't. Geez."

"Yeah. And he never told me."

"Maybe he was embarrassed that someone he loved stole from him."

Sandy growled. "Then wouldn't you want to tell everybody how badly you'd been treated? But not him. He keeps his distance." Sandy climbed in behind the wheel. "Thanks for the help. And thank you for coming to Celia's rescue with the Shop-vac."

"I was in the backyard and heard her screaming. I ran over to investigate. I couldn't do the plumbing, but I could get the water up. You know, you're a pretty handy warrior goddess. Did you tell Hunter you can do plumbing? It might change his mind."

"Cute. You can joke about my pain."

"What are friends for? If you have more flan than you can eat, call me."

Sandy drove home and turned into her driveway lined with yellow and orange nasturtiums. Her small, gray two-bedroom on Fifteenth Street had a beautiful view of the Columbia River from the front and a fenced backyard for the girls. Built in the sixties, it was the only single-level house in a block of two-story Victorians constructed around the turn of the Twentieth Century. With the girls already beginning to stretch their personalities, the house was starting to feel too small. Still, it was affordable and, she reminded herself archly that she had just refinanced it, so she had to be happy with it for now.

She carried the box up two steps onto the porch formed by a brick wall with built-in flower boxes. In another month, they'd be filled with purple petunias. She put the box down, unlocked the door then hefted the box again and walked into the cool, cozy living room. Her furniture wasn't new, but after Charlie had left she'd reupholstered it herself, unable to look at the blue-patterned sofa and chairs he'd picked out. She'd repainted the walls pink and chosen a largish lavender-and-white floral pattern for the upholstery. The curtains were lace and the other furniture pieces a motley collection of things from friends—a white spindly bench from her mother, a pair of ginger jar lamps Nate and Bobbie had given her when they'd redecorated after getting married, and an old trunk she used as a coffee table. That had been her grandmother's. She had photos of the girls all over, and a few of Bobbie's paintings.

Bobbie also did calligraphy on handmade paper. When she was still living in Southern California, she'd done a piece of calligraphy for Sandy's birthday that read, "A friend is never known till a man have need." The quote by John Heywood, who lived in the sixteenth century, was on handmade paper with tiny leaves in it, and set in a filigree frame.

Sandy valued the work for more than just its wonderful, esoteric quality, because Bobbie had done it while ill and struggling to get from day to day. She'd said she wanted Sandy to know how touched she'd been that Sandy had left the girls with her mother and flown to Southern California to sit with her for her first chemo session. Sandy always looked at it whenever she walked through the living room.

In her cream-and-yellow bedroom, she dropped the box in a corner, designating that space for the Clothes Closet things. Then she sat on the foot of her bed and let herself plop backward.

So much time had passed since she'd shared this room with anyone. She hadn't forgotten what it felt like to love a man and be loved in return, but the process seemed to have forgotten her.

She wondered if something was wrong with her. Oh, everyone liked her, men were attracted to her, and she had the opportunity to meet many of them in her job at the law office and her work for the community. But she seldom had long-term relationships.

Her mother insisted that Sandy was too competent, but always smiled when she said that. "Thank goodness for your competence. Remember when your father left and I couldn't pay the rent? The landlord was so mean to me, and you went and told him off, though I pleaded with you not to."

She did remember. They were still living in Salem. She'd been mad and scared and had trembled inside, but she knew if they had to leave the apartment, the only place they could go was a shelter or the street. Her mother's depression prevented her from explaining the situation to Mr. Fogarty, the landlord, so Sandy had taken charge. First, she told him how cruel it was for a man who had several businesses and an apartment house to evict a woman and her daughter who were destitute through no fault of their own. Then she told him she'd seen the Help Wanted sign in the window of his hardware store. She said if he'd give her the job, he wouldn't have to pay her until she'd earned the amount of their rent. "I can work weekends and after school," she'd told him.

He'd folded his arms and frowned at her. "You're not old enough to work."

"I'm fourteen." She stood straighter to give herself more height. "I have a social security card and an Employment Certificate from the State of Oregon. I can start this weekend."

And that was how she'd helped get their lives on track again. Her mother had been amazed and grateful.

Sandy remembered those days well and was happy they were behind them. She'd had a part-time job until she graduated from high school with a scholarship. The summer before she went away to school, Mr. Fogarty had given her a raise, full-time work, overtime opportunities and a bonus that provided her with spending money for school. Her mother had gotten a job scheduling appointments and doing the billing in a doctor's office and had even saved a little to help Sandy on her way.

No, competence wasn't the reason men didn't want a permanent relationship with her; most men now realized women could do most things they could do, even those involving muscle. The smart ones appreciated that.

Maybe it was because Sandy had two lively, often loud little girls. Hunter had dealt well with them, whereas even she needed to run for cover sometimes.

No, not that reason, either. It must be something about her personality, not her skills. Life had made her strong and independent. It wasn't her fault that she knew her own mind and recognized Hunter as the ONE. Of course, her mind had once led her to Charlie, and that relationship hadn't been anything to boast about.

The simple fact was that she didn't want anyone halfhearted about her or her girls. If Hunter couldn't be completely committed, she didn't want him—even if he was the ONE.

Okay. That was it. No more agonizing. She got to her feet, put in a load of laundry, straightened up the kitchen, then went back to Celia's. The faucet continued to work beautifully.

Celia sent her off with a casserole and three ceramic cups of flan. Sandy took them home to the safety of her refrigerator, then headed for town and the peaceful, quiet lunch she'd promised herself.

She shopped first, and found a large tube of giftwrap with the *Cars* design patterned after the children's movie of the same name. While Zoey loved princesses in all forms, Addie's passion was Tow Mater, the movie's loveable tow truck character whose greatest skill was driving backward. Sandy's mother predicted that Addie would be the Danica Patrick of her generation, the first woman ever to place in the Indianapolis 500. Addie ignored doll houses and Barbies and loved everything that had wheels, motors and loud noises.

Sandy found *Cars* pajamas, a Tow Mater bank and a bright yellow jacket for herself made from a redesigned sweatshirt.

Her cell phone rang as she was finishing a jalapeño burger at the Wet Dog, a brew pub that was a local favorite.

She saw the name of her employer and answered, thinking someone in the front office must have gone home sick and her free afternoon was about to disappear.

"Sandy!" Darren, her immediate supervisor, said her name cheerfully. "What are you doing?"

"Having lunch," she replied. "What's going on? Somebody sick?"

"No. I wondered if you could come in this afternoon for a quick meeting. I know you asked for the day off, but something's happened that I need to talk to you about."

"What's that?"

"We'll talk about it when you get here. Can you come in?"

She didn't want to, but she did a lot of things she really didn't want to. "Sure. Half an hour?"

"Perfect."

She hurried home to freshen up, trade her jeans jacket for the new yellow one, and wondered what the meeting was about as she drove to the office. It might be scheduling. A new partner had come to the firm several months ago and brought along his secretary. The woman had been remote and superior, and had complained about most things since she'd arrived, but she was good at her job.

Or maybe it was the mundane business of coffee and rolls for the morning meetings. Sandy usually picked them up at the coffee-house when she drove in, but she'd been told not to bother last week, that someone else would handle it.

She walked through the office, smiling and waving at the other women she'd worked with for six years since moving to Astoria with Charlie. His dream of making a fortune fishing had been short-lived when he got seriously seasick and decided he didn't like twelve hour shifts after all. When Charlie left, Sandy's mother had moved to Astoria. Life had been good since then.

Sandy had so enjoyed managing the office, answering the phones, directing clients to the right person to solve their problems, working with various organizations in town to coordinate a client's needs and obligations. Those contacts had made her community work easier.

But the minute she arrived at Darren Foster's office she knew that something had changed. She felt it in the air. Darren, one of the partners, who also supervised the front office staff, was usually lighthearted, eager to make people feel comfortable. But, today he sat focused on the open file in the middle of his desk and barely looked at her except to greet her with a perfunctory smile and invite her to sit down.

Sandy's throat went dry and her heartbeat accelerated. She sensed danger.

"You have been the most loyal, hardworking office manager we have ever had," Darren said, eyes still on the file.

She noticed the past tense. Not *are* but *have been*.

She struggled to remain calm, not sure what was happening. "Thank you," she said.

"Even if I wanted to, I couldn't find fault with your work."

"Thank you."

Darren looked up at her under his eyebrows. "That's what makes this so hard."

Her heart thudded against her ribs. Oh, no. No. She asked calmly, "What is *this*, Darren?"

He closed his eyes and leaned back in his chair.

"Just say it." She sat a little straighter, bracing herself. "It'll be easier on both of us."

He opened his eyes and leaned his forearms on his desk. His gaze held regret for just an instant, then relaxed in that curious manner middle managers in an awkward position acquire. "When Palmer joined us and brought Janice along, we got a sort of twofer. She's a trained legal secretary, and she's good on the phone and..." His voice seemed to lose power. "We think she can manage the office."

Sandy was out. Jobless. That was her new reality. She laughed nervously. "Darren, she bought oat cakes and herbal tea instead of donuts and mochas for the office meeting. You said you hated that." Of all the examples Sandy could have brought up in her defense, that one was pathetic, but she wasn't at the top of her game at the moment.

He nodded grimly. "The people who count thought it was innovative and appropriately considerate of our good health."

She knew Kevin Palmer had been brought in because Jim Somerville was in his late seventies and finally thinking it was time he retired. Palmer was an impressive litigator and had clients in Portland, Seattle, and several in Hawaii. His billable hours had been a lot of his appeal.

"It's business," Darren said, firming his voice, clearly unwilling for the meeting to go on longer than necessary. "Things have been a little tight for us the last few years. We bill a lot of time, but we don't collect on a lot of it."

"Everybody's broke."

"The economy's picking up."

"But...you just said things are tight."

He frowned at her challenge. "It's picking up where Palmer's clients are, but not here. Not yet. Maybe if things turn around…" he began.

She stood, unwilling to listen to him tell her they might want to bring her back. Hunter had dangled the same nebulous promise in front of her, too, as though the future might somehow improve her appeal. "Do you need a couple of weeks?"

He stood, too. "No. You're free to go today." He reached into his middle drawer and handed her an envelope. "Severance. Two extra weeks and your vacation pay." He drew a breath and asked in a rush, "Can I have your key?"

She accepted the envelope, desperately trying to hold on to her dignity. She struggled to get her office key off the ring and finally resorted to using his letter opener to hold the ring open while she pulled the key off. Then she handed the key to him.

"Thank you." He looked embarrassed for a moment then seemed to harden himself against her distress. All the years she'd gone above and beyond to do her job well counted for nothing in the face of a tight cash flow.

"Goodbye, Darren." She angled her chin and forced a smile.

He nodded. “Bye, Sandy.”

She intended to take the photos of her girls and her mother off her desk, thinking she would pack up her other belongings later, but Vi, who had the desk beside hers, already had everything in a document box.

She handed it to Sandy, her eyes brimming. “I’m going to miss you.” No one understood office politics like the worker bees.

Sandy leaned forward to touch her cheek to Vi’s with a quick thank-you, then turned to leave. All eyes were on her. She smiled, waved and left before she fell apart.

CHAPTER THREE

LORETTA CONWAY OPENED her back door and smiled at Sandy in surprise. Sandy's mother, her hair all gray but worn spikey, was a small-framed woman in her fifties who still looked great in jeans and a sweater. "Hi, sweetie! I thought you had the day off." Her eyes went over Sandy's new jacket with approval. "New duds? How pretty." Then her gaze settled on Sandy's face and she grew serious. "What?" she asked anxiously.

Sandy threw her arms around her and just held on. She allowed herself a spate of tears, then pulled herself together.

"I just had the worst day off in the history of the world. Can I have a glass of wine?"

"Of course. Come in."

Sandy followed her mother into a huge kitchen with a giant work island, high stools pulled up to it on all sides. Loretta had been a sous chef in her youth and loved to cook for friends and family. Her house, with two bedrooms upstairs, was small otherwise, but she often said she'd bought the cottage, which had belonged to an Astoria restaurateur, for the roomy kitchen.

Hiking herself onto a stool on a corner, Sandy watched her mother pour wine into two tulip glasses, then place one in front of her. "What's happened?" her mother asked.

When it took Sandy a moment to answer, her mother sat at a right angle to her and said softly, "I was right about Hunter and the check, wasn't I?"

Sandy swiped away a single tear. "You were right about his reaction. I still think I was right about the situation. But, he yelled, tore up the check, and we broke up."

"Oh, sweetheart. I'm sorry. Your offer just had disaster written all over it." After that bit of frankness, she added bracingly, "Of course, part of your charm and your life success is that you jump in, whatever the prevailing opinion, and do what you think is right. And it's served you well many times."

Sandy sighed, thinking about her job and trying not to succumb to panic and more tears. She said with an attempt at humor, "Well, it hasn't served me well today. I got fired."

"What?" Her mother responded with flattering indignation. "Why? And who will they ever get to show up on Sundays to meet clients and get signatures on whatever those lawyers enjoying their weekends need signed but aren't willing to drive over to the office for and get signed themselves?"

"Apparently, it was an economic decision. The new partner's secretary is a two-fisted talent, so I'm told, and she'll be doing my job *and* hers."

"For the same money?"

"Well, she earns more as a secretary, but I doubt she'll earn more for doing my job as well, because then the move would no longer be economical."

Her mother waited a beat then asked gently, "Have you had time to think about what you'll do?"

"No, actually. It just happened." Sandy took a long sip of her wine, felt it trail warmly down her throat into her stomach, then shook her head over the day. "I wonder if anyone else has ever lost the love of her life and a job she really enjoyed in the same day. While fitting a plumbing job in between."

At her mother's look of concern for her mental stability, Sandy explained about Celia's call for help.

"Ah. She's such a good housekeeper. She did this place in three hours flat last week."

"You hired her?"

"No." Her mother looked surprised. "She said you paid her to do it. You didn't?"

Sandy rolled her eyes and took another sip of wine. "She's always trying to pay me back for letting them rent Aunt Lacey's house. Honestly. She's been trying to clean my house, but I told her you always clean it when you babysit, so I guess she thought she'd be sneaky."

"Well, she was thorough. I recommended her to some friends and I think she's picked up a couple of jobs."

"That's great. Maybe she'll get big enough to hire *me*."

"Oh, honey, you don't have it for housekeeping."

Sandy would have been offended had it not been true. She kept the house tidy enough, but her preference for playing with the girls or taking them to a movie often compromised her attention to detail.

"If worse comes to worse, you and the girls can always move in here. I promise not to kill you, if you promise not to kill me." Her mother was right about the potential for disaster. They were alike in many ways, but completely incompatible in sharing living quarters.

"I do have thirty thousand dollars, so I'm not immediately desperate."

"Yes, but letting that get eaten up on monthly bills would be criminal. Have you considered selling your aunt's house?"

"No. I promised the Morenos they could live there forever, and I'll do anything before I take that away from them."

"I know you have a wonderfully giving nature, but you have a right to consider yourself and the girls first."

"I just keep imagining myself in Celia's shoes. Being so short of money that your husband steals cash from a store, goes to jail, and you have to somehow support two young girls. If it hadn't been for my firm responding to Nate's call for help on Bobbie's behalf..." She stopped short. It was no longer "her" firm. "Anyway, thank goodness the little house was empty when Armando got out of jail and they had to leave their old apartment."

"I worry a little about you being involved with a...a criminal."

"Mom. He didn't use a gun—the clerk went to help a customer and left the register open and unattended. Armando couldn't feed his family and felt desperate. Anyway, booting the Morenos out is not an option."

"Right. Well, there's got to be a solution. Maybe you'll find something in the classifieds. Want me to pick up the girls from daycare and bring them here so you can relax a little tonight?"

"No, thanks." She sipped more wine and was beginning to feel steadier. Not better, but steadier. "I'll take them to McDonald's. They never fight when we eat out. Then, after they go to bed, I'll check out the want ads. There has to be something in Astoria for a hardworking, fund-raising—" she slid off the stool and quoted her mother "—'wonderfully giving' woman."

"I'm sorry you've had such an awful day, Sandy," her mother said, walking her to the door, "but I have complete faith in your ability to work things out. You did it for us when your father left and I wasn't much help for a while.

You survived Charlie leaving. And the girls are smart and happy. Which is quite an accomplishment for a woman having to do it all herself."

"I'll be fine," Sandy assured her mother. She kept her worry about the dearth of jobs in Astoria to herself. "Thanks for the wine and the shoulder."

"Anytime."

DINNER AT MCDONALD'S was peaceful. Turning off her concerns about the day, she watched Zoey, who looked and generally behaved like a princess, talk about one day marrying Sheamus Raleigh, Nate's nephew, who was eight. The girls saw a lot of him and eleven-year-old Dylan when Bobbie and Sandy exchanged babysitting.

Platinum hair in a messy ponytail she'd made herself, Zoey held the sock monkey wearing a tutu that went everywhere with her in one hand, and a glittery magic wand that Nate and Bobbie had brought her back from Disneyland in the other. She put down the wand to pick up a nugget of chicken. "Where's Hunter?"

"He's—um—working tonight."

"Taxes?" Delicate eyebrows rose over bright blue eyes as she asked the question.

Sandy was astonished. She was sure Zoey

had no idea what taxes were, just that Hunter and Uncle Nate had worked hard because of them the past couple of months.

"No." She pulled extra napkins out of the dispenser and wiped a smear of ketchup off Addie's mouth. "Tax season is over. That's when they work really hard to get everything done on time. This is just regular work."

"Sometimes Hunter wishes he was a cowboy." Zoey examined a French fry, then snapped off a bite.

"How come?"

"They only have to count cows. Counting money is a lot of trouble."

Sandy swallowed hard. Zoey quoted Hunter all the time, a reminder that when he was with the girls, he talked to them, enjoyed them, saw that they were never left out of the conversation. He'd never kept the distance from them that he'd kept from her. He would have been a good father.

Addie, about to be four, and smaller than her sister but already giant in personality, leaned over on her elbows toward her mother. Her hair, the same color as her sister's, was wild and stuck up out of a tiara, also from the Raleighs' trip to Disneyland. Addie's dark blue eyes were alight with intelligence. "Hunter's coming to my birthday!" she said.

Great, Sandy thought. But she smiled at that news. "That's nice."

"She told him he had to bring a present," Zoey ratted, sounding disgusted.

Making a face at her youngest, Sandy said, "It isn't nice to ask for things, Ad. Even when it's your birthday. When did you see Hunter?"

"He brought stuff to Rainbow," Zoey replied. Rainbow was the daycare center. "We were having lunch and Addie ran to see him. You're not supposed to leave the table."

Sandy knew that Raleigh and Raleigh did the books for the daycare center. In the tradition of small towns, Raleigh staff often delivered reports or payroll to their clients.

"Grandma's going to make your birthday cake," Sandy said, trying to divert the conversation. "And it will have Tow Mater on it."

"Sweeet!"

Sweet was Addie's new favorite word. Especially when drawn out, the way the Raleigh boys said it.

"When I grow up," Addie said seriously, "I'm gonna have a tow truck."

Sandy smiled supportively. She was raising

a grease monkey. While other little girls were dreaming of horses, Addie wanted a tow truck. Sandy hoped that somewhere out there another mother was raising a young man who could fall in love with an unconventional woman.

On the way home, the girls sang "The Wheels on the Bus" song until Sandy turned into the driveway. They did all their usual evening things—watched television, had a snack, took their baths—then Sandy tucked them into bed.

Now, with a thick black marker in one hand and a cup of decaf in the other, Sandy sat at the kitchen table, opening the *Daily Astorian* to the classifieds section. She scanned the Personals, the Lost Pets, all the interesting things for sale, then zeroed in on the Help Wanted columns.

There were all kinds of ads for workers with skills she didn't have—pipe layer, concrete finisher, licensed insurance agent, bus driver. A logging company was looking for choker setters and rigging slingers. She lingered over that ad. She would have loved to choke or sling someone.

Discouraged, she circled the hotel housekeeping ads in Seaside and Cannon Beach. Tourist season was coming and housekeepers were always in demand. Her mother was correct about

Sandy not keeping her own house spotless, but she could certainly do it for someone else—particularly if she was being paid.

Waitressing was not an option because she simply didn't have the skill to carry three plates on each arm. Cannery work was out because of a similar lack of dexterity and the lethal nature of those filet knives.

Tomorrow she'd prepare a résumé. There. She felt better. Nothing like being proactive.

Her positive attitude lasted about a minute, until she remembered Hunter. No amount of proactivity would help her with him. How unfair, she thought, that irresponsible, obnoxious men were out trolling for wives, but charming, thoughtful men wanted no part of marriage.

That was fine. Life went on. She kept reading.

Business Opportunities. She leaned closer to read the column of franchise offerings and businesses looking for investors. Then she spotted a block highlighted in yellow, which meant it was a new ad in today's paper.

"Coffee Cart for sale. Money Maker with established clientele. Great location. Fully equipped, big inventory, helpful staff. Priced to sell quickly. Owner headed for Chicago. Call Crazy for Coffee." The ad listed a number.

Sandy felt a jolt of excitement. Crazy for Coffee! The cart just off the Astoria-Megler Bridge was where she bought coffee most mornings on her way back from dropping the girls at daycare. Bjorn made the best caramel-vanilla latte she'd ever tasted. She always had to wait in line, so "money maker" was probably not an exaggeration.

A coffee cart! She felt another jolt of excitement, then drew herself back, thinking logically. Long hours on her feet; early, early start to a day that involved children and a daycare that didn't open until seven o'clock; and… She couldn't think of anything else negative.

The positives. She could afford it. She could learn to do it. She could set her own hours. She could handle the long hours on her feet by wearing comfortable shoes. Maybe her mother would help her with the girls in the morning.

She had to know more. Pushing her coffee aside, she dialed the number.

HUNTER SAT AT his mother's kitchen table, sorting through her tax receipts. Stella Bristol made a space in the middle of the piles he'd created and set down a cup of black coffee.

"How's it going?" she asked.

He dropped the stack of brokerage statements in his hand and leaned back in his chair to frown at her. "It's a good thing I filed for an extension for you, Mom. I can't believe that the woman who encouraged me to be an accountant, who helped put me through school, who works for my boss, also an accountant…" His voice rose. "Would keep her tax documents and receipts in a shoe box!" He'd been sorting for three hours, and he barely had her paperwork organized enough to assess where to begin. "This is the bad joke of all accounting offices. Didn't I buy you an accordion folder last year?"

"I'm sorry," she said, but the apology didn't ring true. "I do have a full-time job, you know. I haven't had much time to get organized. And it's not a shoe box. An elegant pair of candlesticks came in that box." She pointed to a low table behind the sofa, where they stood with yellow tapers in them. "And I have recipes in the accordion folder."

Of course. "Mom, you're missing the point."

"No, I'm not. I hired you to do my taxes because I don't have a brain for numbers. Therefore, I don't have a brain for organizing the things in which you put numbers."

He thought about that a moment, and when it still didn't make sense, he shook his head. "You *hired* me? You mean I'm getting eighty dollars an hour for this? Because that would make the job much easier to take."

She patted his shoulder as she walked away. "Don't be silly. You're doing this because you love me."

He caught her wrist to prevent her escape. "Not so fast. Tell me about these checks to Toads and Frogs. Is it a bar? A conservation group? What?"

She sat down opposite him, her manner suddenly defensive. "It's a yarn shop. Why? I had a little extra from my investments so I decided to bet on a friend."

Looking at her blankly, he repeated, "Toads and Frogs is a yarn shop."

"Yes. A toad is a knitting project you really wanted to do but never finished, and frog means you've quit a project. Like "I frogged that hat because the pattern was too hard."

A moment of silence followed, then he asked patiently, "So you've invested your hard-earned money in a woman who named her shop using two words that suggest failure?"

"No! You know Glenda. She was my neighbor when I first moved here after your father died. That little rental on Alameda? She's really very good at what she does. Her goal is to provide a place where customers won't give up on projects, because she's there to help them figure out how to complete them. So, you'd go to Toads and Frogs to succeed, not to fail."

Glenda. He had met her a couple of times. A formidable woman with a single gray braid. Made a great banana bread, as he recalled.

Drawing a breath for patience, Hunter nodded. "Sometimes, you scare me, Mom. But, okay. So these checks are investment in a business?"

"Yes."

"Are you a partner?"

"No. Just a sort of…capitalist. I give her capital when she needs it."

"Does she pay you back?"

"She will when she's on her feet."

"Does she have a business plan? Something that tells you when that might be? Do you two have a contract?"

"A verbal one. We're playing it by ear." She smiled in the face of his disbelief.

"You don't play business by ear, Mom."

"Maybe in banks and accounting offices, you don't. But in yarn shops, you trust your friends and play it by ear."

He sat back in his chair, frustrated with trying to protect her financial interests. "Don't you have any sense of self-preservation? You worked hard to get some financial stability after Dad died. Now you keep giving money away. You lent me money to resettle here after I closed the business."

She sat across the table from him and covered his hand with hers. Her joking responses suddenly took a serious turn. "Hunter, you can get your debts paid without putting your entire life on hold. You know, the guilt you feel is completely unnecessary. No one blames you for what happened. I understand that you feel responsible to your father and me because we wanted so much to help you. But, if your father were here, he'd be the last to criticize you or to regret giving you the money. Please, please, let yourself be happy."

"I'll be happy when I've paid all my debts and returned your investment."

She growled and punched his arm playfully. "You are so much like my father. Stubborn through and through."

"Mmm. I think he passed that quality on to you, and that's how I got it."

"Okay, let's go with that. Stop thinking like an accountant. Toads and Frogs is a wonderful place to put my money, and you know why?"

She required an answer. He looked up. "Why?"

"Because while money is a sometimes-you-win-sometimes-you-lose investment, love invested is always a win-win. Glenda is always there for me." She put a hand to his face maternally. "You are a bean counter, darling. You have to start counting—I don't know. Flowers. Stars."

She patted his cheek and turned toward the kitchen. "You need a sandwich." She disappeared and left him with her scary accounting.

Count flowers and stars. Good Lord.

By the time he had the rest of her paperwork organized, all the things he couldn't fix at the moment he pushed to the back of his mind.

He decided the world was lucky Stella Bristol had chosen to invest in a yarn shop. Anything more serious and she could have undermined Wall Street in a week and a half.

By nightfall, he'd finished a Reuben sandwich, had agreed to fix a sticking cupboard door and was setting the water heater in the basement up a notch because the stairs were steep and his mother didn't feel safe on them.

She provided him with a large envelope to put her documents in so he could take them home. "You're sure you don't want something more to eat before you go?"

"Thanks, but no. I've got to get some sleep."

He had one foot on the porch when she said his name. He knew the tone. Reluctance overcome by the lioness-guarding-her-cub syndrome. This would have to do with Sandy. He'd been so close to escaping.

He stopped reticently and faced her. "Yeah?"

She put up both hands to ward off the protest she seemed to think was imminent. "I'm just worried and want what's best for you, so I have to ask."

How many times in his life had he heard her say that?

"You're sure you're right not to let Sandy help you with a little money? Especially since you won't take help from me, and you gave Nate his money back."

He was a hairsbreadth away from a primal scream. But he replied calmly, "It wasn't a *little* money, it was thirty thousand dollars. And, who told you…?"

"Loretta and I talk."

"That's nice." Great. All he needed was his mother and Sandy's collaborating. "Mom, I'm not getting involved until I have my bills paid. Sandy does well on her own. She doesn't need to be mixed up in this." He kept going when his mother tried to interrupt him. "I know you and Loretta both have our best interests at heart, but, for now, anyway, Sandy and I are pretty much over. Just give up on whatever happily-ever-after scenario the two of you had going."

His mother frowned.

"Mom, she refinanced her house to help me pay off my debts. I'm not letting her do that, so she's mad at me."

"Do you know that her husband just walked away when Addie was born? And that was after her father left them when she was just a teenager?"

"She told me. But, Mom it's more complicated than just all the debris in my life. It's her.

Sandy doesn't understand anything that isn't part of her plan. Which seems to consist of putting a responsible man in her life because the others have flaked out on her."

"And you're not that man?"

"No. At least not now. And she's an immediate kind of woman. She wants what she wants, and she doesn't want to wait for it. Usually, I'm not a man to be talked over, ridden over or shoved over. Jennifer managed to do that to me when I wasn't looking, but nobody's going to do that to me again."

"Hunter. You're not comparing Sandy with Jennifer."

He was now exhausted. "Of course not," he said wearily. "But Sandy is pushy, and I'm in no mood to be pushed right now. Good night, Mom. I'll run your numbers through the computer and let you know what comes up."

Her voice followed him down her front walk. "Then how will you do the Clothes Closet opening together? It's already been announced in the paper."

Several bad words raced through his mind. "We're adults," he replied over his shoulder. "And neither one of us cares about *us* anymore.

We'll be able to focus on the project. Good night."

Depression sought to pummel him as he drove home, but he fought it off. He would pay off his debts and start over. He figured getting square with the world would take him another five years. Thirty-nine wasn't too old to pull his life together.

His apartment on Grand Avenue was dark and cool when he got in. He flipped on lights, then turned on the television in the small living room furnished with a brown tweed sofa and chair from his old place and a coffee table he'd gotten from Goodwill. He went into the kitchen to nuke a cup of coffee. The landlord had called the kitchen small and efficient, everything within easy reach, when he'd shown him the place. Hunter should have realized it was a warning that he'd always be slamming into a cupboard door he'd left open or banging his knee on a drawer. But the rent was reasonable, the other tenants pleasant and quiet. He could do this for five more years. He looked out his window to the lights on a freighter at anchor in the river and the nostalgia of early evening overtook him. Leaning against the window molding, he felt as though his stomach had caved in.

Five years was a long time to be lonely.

CHAPTER FOUR

SANDY STOOD IN the middle of the dark, overcrowded box that was Crazy for Coffee and, inexplicably, felt her small world open up. She smiled at Bjorn, who watched her a little worriedly. He was in his early forties and going home to Chicago to help his parents manage their deli because his father was in poor health. She bought a caramel-vanilla latte from Bjorn a couple of mornings a week, and he was a client of the law firm she used to work for, so she knew him fairly well. They'd had a long talk on the phone the night before.

"What's the matter, Sandy?" he asked. "Are you claustrophobic? Because if you are, you'll go nuts in here."

"I'm not claustrophobic," she assured him. She held up the folder he'd given her with the last two years' tax returns and several other financial reports. "I'm very, very interested."

"Okay, I don't mean to be nosy, but how will the law office get along without you?"

"Easily, I think. They let me go. So, I'm looking for something else. Be nice to be my own boss for a change."

Her research showed that a coffee cart had relatively small operating costs, an easily sold product, and a good profit margin. She figured that with careful management and hard work, she could do this, and do it well. She had confidence in her ability to make anything work. Well, she didn't seem that great with relationships, but she could make everything else work.

He laughed at her. "Owning your own business definitely has its perks, but you're It in a crisis. Or any other time, really. There's no one else to turn to when you have a problem. Are you ready for that?"

She shrugged. "It's just like parenting, or owning a home, or living your life. You're It, the last word. I have a lot of experience being It." She looked around herself and nodded. "I'd like to buy Crazy for Coffee, Bjorn." Since Hunter didn't want a future with her, she'd set out bravely on her own.

"You would?" He appeared surprised, then probably realizing that was not good salesmanship, added quickly, "Don't you want to see the books? Talk to my accountant? Sales *are* up about 12 percent since I bought the business two years ago."

"I did a little research on you and the business. And whenever I come for coffee in the morning, I'm usually fourth or fifth in line, so I know you have the customer base. And you can't beat the location, on a concrete slab allowing access on both sides, right on 101 and just off the bridge." She gazed at the supplies, the bottles of syrups, the refrigerator filled with cream, milk, fruit and other necessities. "Does the price include the inventory?"

"No. But I can tally that tonight when I close and give you a final figure in the morning." He excused himself to respond to a honk at the north window, quickly prepared a mocha grande, handed it out the window, then dropped a few bills and a handful of change into the register.

She held out her hand. "So, we have a deal?"

"We have a deal." He took her hand and shook it. "Great." Then he looked troubled. "My lawyer is one of your bosses. Your *former* bosses. Are you okay with meeting me there tomorrow to draw up the papers?"

"Sure. I'll have a check for you. When did you want to turn it over to me?"

"The first of June is in eight days. Does that work? What about employees? I do mornings, and two high school girls come in in the afternoon. They're pretty reliable and from the feedback I've gotten, they make good drinks. They just have to be reminded not to chat too long with friends driving through. Since school shuts down for the summer in two weeks, you can schedule them earlier in the day instead of just afternoons."

"Great. I'll keep them on if they want to stay. Think I can learn the ropes in that short a time?"

"Of course you can. But you realize how it is. You won't officially know it all until you've worked it for a couple of months."

They agreed to meet at her old office the following afternoon as soon as his staffer came on after school.

Sandy had dropped the girls off early at daycare, and went home to take a quiet moment and make a list of all she should do today. At home she sat down at the kitchen table and wrote: "acquire a couple of pairs of jeans and shirts to work in, transfer money out of savings, buy something pretty" (since it would probably be the last thing she'd be able to buy herself for some time to come), "tell Mom and Bobbie that I now own a business and see if Mom will help with the girls, take a long walk and appreciate that freedom." There would probably be precious little for a while.

For Zoey and Addie, this would be the same as when she worked in an office all day—possibly even a little better, because she'd be home slightly earlier. Of course, she'd have to leave earlier to be ready to open at five o'clock.

A loud knock on her front door startled her out of her strategy planning. She pulled the door open, thinking it might be UPS with the *Cars* bedspread and pillow she'd ordered for Addie's birthday.

It wasn't UPS. It was Hunter.

HUNTER WASN'T PREPARED for the pretty picture she made against her blue door. Her red hair was caught up in a knot, long, straight strands of it falling to her chin. Her cheeks were flushed, her brown eyes alight as though something had already brightened her day. She wore a white sweater, and white always made her look somehow molten.

"Ah..." He had to think a minute. He'd come over because he required some information from her, but he hadn't expected her to look so...cheerful. He was getting the distance from her he sought, but it put him in a pit of depression. He really missed her. Why was *she* happy? "I know I'm the last person you want to see today, but the Food Bank called me at the office this morning and wanted a date for the opening of the Clothes Closet. And the *Daily A* said they could get us sponsored advertising, but, again, we need a date. We have to talk about these things."

"I suppose we should." She sounded halfhearted. "But, I'm sorry, I have a lot going on today, and I..."

"Sandy, come on. I have to be able to depend on you for this. You're the one who volunteered us. The Food Bank said they couldn't reach you. What's happening? If you're going to pout about the breakup, tell me now so I can make other plans." He was sure that would get her. She couldn't stand accusations of a childish display, couldn't stand being disconnected from the goings-on.

"I am not pouting," she denied, a little royal indignation in her attitude, "and I'd like to help, but you'll have to cut me a little slack. I've had a slight change of plans."

"What plans?"

"You know. Life plans."

"How so? I have another big project I could really use your help on." He hesitated, plotting how best to approach her about Connolly's gift. "What kind of slack do you need?" he asked at the same moment that she asked, "What big project?"

"You first," she told him. "What big project?"

"Astoria has a benefactor," he blurted, sure it topped her news.

She focused on him more intently, suddenly interested. She even stepped out onto the porch. "What do you mean? Who?"

He explained about his client, the man's previous visit to Astoria when he'd been treated so kindly, then his sale of the dessert product for big money and his retirement to Astoria. Honoring Connolly's wish, he kept other details to himself.

"That's wonderful," she said. "But what does that have to do with me?"

"He wants me to distribute a million dollars to our nonprofits. I thought since you've raised money for most of them at one time or other, you'd be a good resource for the project."

Her mouth fell open. It was a lovely, supple mouth. He could almost feel it on his own. But—then—words would come out of it and ruin everything.

"A million…?"

"Yes. Do you want to help or not?"

She cocked her head and scolded, "Who wouldn't want to help since you asked so nicely?" Then her look became troubled. "But my situation's changed a little and I…I'm not sure if I can."

"So you said. But, how? What's changed?"

"I just bought Crazy for Coffee!" she said, appearing a little surprised by her own news.

He was stunned. Bjorn Nielsen was his client. So, she was the caller Bjorn had told him was interested in his coffee cart. Hunter had gone into the office at four in the morning to run off reports he then delivered to Crazy for Coffee.

Sandy was changing her life? He was no longer involved with her so that shouldn't bother him, but he knew how she was—headstrong and impulsive and impervious to suggestion. Small business was a killer of dreams ninety percent of the time.

"Have you thought this through?" he asked.

Immediately her expression turned defensive. She folded her arms. “Of course I have.”

“What if you lose everything?”

“Thank you for your expression of faith in me,” she replied. “It’s so nice to know that after all we’ve meant to each other…”

He held a hand up to stop her. He was a little amazed when it worked. “What I meant was, have you investigated the business?” He knew Crazy for Coffee was sound, but that could change in a month with careless management. She’d never be deliberately careless, but things could happen she might not be prepared for. “There’s a lot to…”

“I saw his tax returns, his P&L and balance sheets.”

“Good. What about lease assignments?”

“What?”

“Lease assignments. Bjorn happens to be one of Raleigh and Raleigh’s clients. I handle his account. As I recall, he leases a few things. You’re responsible for taking those over. That’ll add to your monthly expenses.”

“Oh.” Her eyes narrowed. He suspected she hadn’t thought of that. “We’re meeting at my old office tomorrow. I used to work for lawyers, remember? They'll make sure everything's covered."

He raised an eyebrow. "*Used* to work for lawyers? You mean you've already quit?"

"No, I mean they fired me."

"What?" His annoyance at that news matched her mother's and made up a bit for the "what if you lose everything" remark. "Why?"

"It's a long story that involves the economy, office politics and a new partner's secretary who can do her job *and* mine. Hence, the coffee cart."

"I'm sorry," he said sincerely. He knew she'd loved her job and had done it well.

"I'll survive. I always do." Deep in her eyes, he saw a suggestion of fear, then she drew a breath and it was gone.

"About the coffee cart. Do you have help?"

"Help?"

"Hired help. Employees. Or do you plan to work seven days a week, twelve hours a day?"

"Yes, I have help. Two high school girls in the afternoon."

"Do you know how to do payroll?"

Telling when she was truly annoyed was never hard. The pink in her cheeks flamed, and her eyes ignited. "Don't treat me like an idiot,

Hunter. I know what I'm doing. If you don't want to be part of my vision for my future, then I'm taking it in another direction. And you have nothing to say about it."

She'd done this with the money she'd tried to give him, the money from refinancing her home. Before he could say that buying the coffee cart was reckless, possibly even ill-advised, she turned around and walked back inside.

He took a step forward as she prepared to close the door on him. "Tomorrow in my office," he said. "What time can you be there? We'll set a date for the Closet opening and make a plan for the money for the nonprofits."

"I'm meeting with Bjorn to sign papers tomorrow."

"Can you meet Monday?"

"That's Memorial Day. Aren't you and the Raleighs going to Fort Stevens for the Civil War reenactment? I'm working with Bjorn."

"That's right. Tuesday, then?"

"I'll call you. The way my life is right now, we may have to do it over the phone."

That was what he should want—dealing with her over the phone rather than sitting across a table from her or side by side in a restaurant booth. It would simplify his life.

"All right. But, I promised the Food Bank an answer by Friday."

"I'll phone you in the middle of the week." She started to close the door.

"Incidentally..." The single word stopped her. "What about the girls?"

"What do you mean?"

"If you have to open at 5:00 a.m., what about the girls?"

There were sparks in her smile. "I thought I'd sell them into slavery for some operating capital."

He groaned at her. "I meant, daycare doesn't open that early."

"And how would you know when daycare opens?"

He waited a beat. "Rainbow Daycare is my client. I know a lot about them."

"Well, it was a stupid question, Hunter. When have you known me not to consider my girls? I have to go. Goodbye." She closed the door.

He stared at it for a moment, thinking he might *want* to simplify his life, but it didn't seem to be happening.

SANDY CALLED HER MOTHER from the sidewalk in front of Toni's Boutique, an elegant clothing store for women on Commercial Street, absentmindedly noting the colorful resort wear in the window.

"You did what?" her mother exclaimed after Sandy told her about Crazy for Coffee.

"I needed employment, so I bought a business so I could hire myself. Makes good sense to me."

"Oh, sweetheart. Working for yourself only means more bills, not necessarily more income."

"Mom, Hunter just did his best to discourage me. Come on. I need positive input. And Toni's is having a sale. If you'll watch the girls for me in the mornings between 4:30 and 7:00, when you'll to take them to daycare, I'll buy you an outfit."

She heard her mother gasp. "Four…?"

"And a jacket," she added quickly. "Just until I can hire someone for those hours. And a pair of shoes."

Her mother was silent.

"And a car!" Sandy continued with theatrical extravagance. "Mom, I realize it's a lot to ask…"

"Okay, Okay," her mother said finally. "You're lucky I'm an insomniac. I'll do it. But it better be some car."

CHAPTER FIVE

LORETTA SEPARATED PAPER plates while Sandy placed squares of cake on them. Bobbie added scoops of vanilla ice cream and Stella delivered to the crowd of little children gathered around two picnic tables in Sandy's backyard. The yard sounded like Times Square on New Year's Eve!

Bobbie scooped heroically from the two-gallon tub. "Who'd have thought such a big noise could come out of such little children?"

Sandy glanced up in surprise. "I don't even notice noise anymore. The girls are always giggling or shrieking. My head rings continually." She turned toward Stella, who stood in the yard near one of the tables and held up two fingers. "Okay, guys. Two more, then maybe *we* can have coffee and a piece of cake."

Grateful for the rare sunny day in the coastal Oregon spring, Sandy smiled at the sight of her daughter and her daycare and neighborhood guests wearing their jackets and the plastic superhero capes she'd provided. She had fashioned the capes out of tarps she'd cut to shape, Bobbie had painted familiar superhero symbols on them, and all they'd had to do was convince the children to turn the capes around to the front when they sat down to eat.

Dylan, Bobbie's eleven-year-old nephew by marriage who was helping keep order by tossing balls and leading races around the yard, frowned at Sandy. "Now those superhero capes are just bibs," he accused.

Sandy whispered back, "Yes, but no one's noticed yet, so please keep it to yourself."

"Hmm. Trickery. Sweeet!" Dylan was clever and observant, and surprisingly patient with the younger children, unlike Sheamus, who found them childish from his lofty eight-year-old perspective.

The doorbell rang. "I'll get it." Dylan ran off while Sandy went out into the yard to investigate a sudden scream that rang out above the din. By the time Sandy reached a boy and girl throwing punches while rolling over each other in the grass, Stella was pulling them apart.

"What happened?" Sandy asked, drawing the boy toward her and dabbing what looked like a smear of blood on his forehead. Mercifully, it was only frosting.

Towheaded and freckled, Danny Hankins jabbed a finger at the sturdy girl with blunt-cut dark hair who was fuming. "She kissed me!" he shouted in disgust.

Stella bit back a laugh. Sandy, relieved nothing worse had happened, tried to sound reasonable. "But a kiss is a nice thing. Why would you punch her?"

"Because when I wouldn't kiss her, too, *she* punched *me*! I was just offending myself."

*"De*fending yourself. Molly." Sandy leaned over the little girl, whose eyes betrayed hurt under the anger. Considering her own situation, Sandy felt a certain sympathy for her. "It isn't nice to hit. And you can't make somebody kiss you. They have to want to."

"Well. You do understand that." A taunting male voice made Sandy straighten. She looked up into Hunter's smile. He wore jeans and a dark blue T-shirt with the Raleigh & Raleigh emblem on the pocket.

"Hello, Hunter." Her tone was polite but stiff. She noticed a giant package held against his side. "What on earth…?"

He swung a red kiddie car, large enough for

a child to ride in, out from under his arm. His smile developed an edge. "If you can tolerate me long enough to let me wish your daughter Happy Birthday, I promise not to stay."

"Wow!" Danny put a pudgy hand up to stroke the car's bumper.

"That's mine!" Addie declared with four-year-old vehemence, arriving at his side in a flash, wearing her tiara. She looked up at Hunter, avarice in her eyes. "Isn't it?"

"Yes, it is." He put it down on the grass, having to urge the growing circle of children around them to back up. Addie climbed right into it and uttered a little scream of delight. "My car!" she squealed, and heartlessly ripped off the rainbow-striped bow stuck to the windshield.

"Your car." He squatted to point out the controls to her. Then he indicated the walkway that ran all around the yard and protected the flowers growing against the stockade-style fence. "It'll work best on the walkway. You can't go out of the yard with it or it'll stop working. Okay?"

Sandy had to appreciate his instructions. He turned to her, his expression neutral. "Can she take it for a spin?"

"How fast does it go?"

"Two and a half miles per hour."

"Then, yes."

"Okay." Hunter lifted Addie out and she squealed in protest as he carried the kiddie car to the walkway. She ran behind him and climbed back in the moment he placed it on the stone strip. "Please be careful with the flowers. And watch when you get to the corner so you can make the turn. That's what real drivers do."

Addie was off, the mob of children deserting their cake to follow her, screaming their delight at this new excitement and pleading for their chance to ride. Hunter turned to greet his mother, then Loretta and Bobbie. "Good afternoon, ladies. Addie invited me."

Bobbie indicated Addie behind the wheel of her car. "Addie's thrilled that you're here, and it's *her* party, after all."

Addie did three circuits of the yard before she stopped, her eyes sparkling and her cheeks flushed.

"Do you want to let your friends have a ride?" Sandy asked, already knowing the answer.

"No." Addie's reply was clear and concise.

"But they're your guests."

"No."

"Everyone brought you presents. It would be nice if you let everyone..."

"No."

"When you go to their houses," Hunter said, "they'll let you play with their stuff if you let them play with yours today."

Addie thought about that. "No," she finally said.

Danny hung over her. "You can have my spy nightscope for a day if I can ride your car around the yard just one time." Danny could often be seen in front of his home after dark, night goggles on, their pop-up spotlight activated. Addie lusted after them. Sandy had a mental image of the two of them off on a spy mission in Addie's car and with Danny's goggles.

Addie thought again, then looked into his face, her expression fierce. "Promise?"

"Promise." He crossed his heart and held his palm up in an oath.

She climbed up and shouted orders as Danny climbed in. "You can't hurt the flowers, and you have to go slow there." She pointed to the corner.

Danny rode off, the children running the perimeter with him.

"That was good, Addie," Sandy praised, though her daughter had made the good choice out of greed, not generosity. But, truth be told, Sandy still made some of her own decisions that way. "Look at how much fun your friends are having."

Addie caught up with the crowd of cheering children as Danny navigated the turn, slowing as instructed, before heading toward the house.

"Well." Stella patted her son on the shoulder. "Nice present, Hunter, but we'll need some help organizing the children into a peaceful taking of turns. Otherwise, we'll have to call in the National Guard."

"Sure." He beckoned Dylan and Sheamus, who were watching the scramble from the middle of the yard. They ran to him.

"You guys up to helping me organize the little guys into having turns in the car?"

"Sure." Dylan did a stair-step motion with one hand. "We can line them up by size and let the smallest ones go first. They make the biggest noise when they don't get what they want."

Hunter patted him on the shoulder. "Great idea." He smiled at Dylan's mother, his eyes sliding over Sandy without appearing to notice her. "You ladies take a break. We have this handled."

Doubtful, Sandy remained where she stood. "Ah..."

Stella caught her arm and pulled her toward the house. "He can do it. Let's go have some coffee."

In the kitchen, Loretta lined up four brightly striped mugs and poured while Bobbie pushed Sandy toward the table and cut four pieces of cake.

"Your son seems good with children," Loretta said as she placed a steaming mug in front of Stella.

Stella added a dash of cream to her cup and looked up, a smile quickly banishing the hint of sadness in her eyes. Sandy knew she longed for grandchildren. She must know by now, that her son had little intention of giving her any.

"That's because he hasn't entirely grown up. Oh, he's responsible in many ways, but he has a side that will probably never mature."

Bobbie distributed cake while Loretta followed with scoops of ice cream, then sat across from Sandy. "The best people have an active inner child. Sandy does." She grinned across the table at her friend. "Right, Sandy? Didn't you just take the world's most impulsive action by buying a coffee cart?"

"I heard about that!" Stella looked up from a bite of cake. "What are you going to call it? It's Crazy for Coffee now, isn't it?"

"It is." Striving to show the good cheer she felt only occasionally now, rather than the panic that overtook her in the silence of midnight, Sandy nodded with manufactured confidence. "I'm going to keep the name—at least for now. I've got lots of cups, napkins, stirring sticks and bags with the logo on them. It'll be nice to not have a rebranding expense right away."

Stella nodded approvingly. "That's sensible. What time will you be opening in the mornings? I mean, you have to be ready for the really early crowd, right?"

"I do." Sandy sighed. "The current owner opens at 5:00."

Everyone groaned.

"I know, right? Mom's going to help me with the girls in the morning."

"That's so good of you, Loretta," Bobbi said. "You deserve another scoop of ice cream."

Loretta caught her hand to prevent her from getting up. "Thank you, but I'm stuffed. The mac and cheese and hot dogs were quite a feast." She patted a flat stomach, then smiled fondly in Sandy's direction. "Sandy's been a pretty special daughter. I owe her."

"My son does my taxes," Stella said, her chin on her hand. Her eyes twinkled with amusement. "So, he's pretty special, too. And I do my best to make it an experience for him. His accountant's mind wants the world to be orderly, and I try to show him another way. When he can't create order, he blames and punishes himself."

"Are you talking about the embezzlement thing?" Bobbie asked.

Stella nodded, anger now betraying the amusement in her gaze. "Mostly. He loved that woman. She cheated on him and ran off with everything he had. I have a detective on the case, but don't mention it to Hunter. He can't afford one and he didn't want me to spend my money on one. All part of that doing-it-all-himself thing. When I think about Jennifer, I get mad enough to murder. Hunter is trying not to have revenge distract him, just to get everything paid off. I have no such compunction."

A shriek rent the air, followed by the sound of sobs and Dylan came running toward the house. Sandy went out to meet him, with her mother and friends behind her.

"Kaylee Palmer from up the street rode over Addie's foot," he said, following as Sandy raced toward the knot of children. Hunter stood in the middle, kneeling over her daughter. He had Addie's pink tennis shoe off and was gingerly manipulating her toes and instep. Kaylee stood a step away looking frightened and defensive. "I didn't do it on purpose."

"I'm sure you didn't," Sandy said, putting her hands at Addie's waist to take her from Hunter. "Are you okay, Ad?"

Addie brushed her hands away, keeping a death grip on Hunter's arm, clearly upset by the interruption in her party. Her tiara was crooked.

Fighting a severe case of hurt feelings and complete annoyance, Sandy stepped aside as Hunter lifted Addie off the grass. He held the small foot out for Sandy to examine.

"I think it's okay," he said, rubbing a thumb over Addie's instep as Sandy's fingertips probed. She noted absently that his thumb was as long as the width of Addie's foot. "She seems able to move it with no problem. I don't think anything's broken. Probably just bruised."

Zoey, standing beside Hunter, reached up to

touch her ever-present wand to her sister's foot. "Make it better!" she ordered the universe.

As though responding to instant intervention, Addie wiggled her toes.

"Can you walk on your foot, sweetheart?" Sandy asked, holding on to Addie's hand as Hunter put her down. Except for a slight hobble because she had one shoe on and one shoe off, she appeared fine. She even pushed Kaylee aside, straightened her tiara, and climbed into the car.

Sandy stopped her before she could take off. "No. No more car for the moment. Let's finish our cake and play some games. Come on, Kaylee. Everything's okay. Let's go back to the table."

"But I want..." Addie tried to wriggle away, pointing to the bright red car.

"No," Sandy said firmly. "Not right now. Hunter will park it in the garage with my car, and you can ride it later. Did all the kids get a turn?"

Hunter nodded. "Kaylee was taking a second turn, Addie was chasing her down and that's how it happened."

"Okay. Come on, girls."

Liking the idea that her car would live in the

garage beside her mother's, Addie went peacefully back to her cake. Kaylee followed.

HUNTER PICKED UP the car and carried it through the kitchen, into Sandy's garage. Sandy and her friends were now settling the children back around the tables and his mother was taking photos.

Hunter opened the door to the garage and flicked the light switch. Nothing happened. With the smells of mustiness, laundry detergent and fertilizer in his nostrils, he sidled carefully around Sandy's Volkswagen to the tool bench, where an emergency light hung from the rafter above. He switched it on, bathing garden tools and storage tubs in a harsh light.

Hunter went to the stationary tub between the washer and dryer on the other side of the car, pulled a handful of paper towels from the rack above it and wet them under the faucet. He wiped sticky fingerprints and smudges off the red plastic car, then placed it on the built-in workbench. He couldn't help but smile at the messy toolbox that stood on one side of the table. He'd given the toolbox to Sandy last Christmas.

She had amazing skill with tools. He didn't

consider women less capable than men in any aspect of life, but in his experience, most women were happy to let a man fix house things if one was available. He'd watched Sandy tackle plumbing, simple wiring and basic carpentry on her own, to great success. But she'd kept her tools in a basket. Sure the tools would be offended, he'd given her the toolbox.

The only thing she'd needed help with was her car. The internal combustion engine baffled her.

He'd liked that she had that vulnerability. She was so bright. To be able to do something for her was gratifying. Which reminded him of the garage light. He couldn't imagine that she loaded the girls in and out of the car in a dark garage. Not that she couldn't change a bulb. There must be a reason she hadn't. He scoured the shelves for lightbulbs and finally found several boxes on a top shelf near cleaning supplies.

The light fixture was directly above her car, but he thought if he placed the ladder right beside it, he could reach the light provided he stretched sideways. Not OSHA approved, but it should work.

He climbed halfway up the ladder and was able to reach the burned-out bulb at the farthest reach of his arm. He unscrewed it, placed it on the ladder's bucket shelf, then put in the new bulb. He climbed down again and went around the car to flip on the light. The roof of her red VW gleamed under it.

Satisfied, he folded up the ladder and was leaning it against the wall when the door to the kitchen opened. Sandy stood in the doorway in jeans and a yellow sweater, her hair caught back in a functional ponytail for the busy day's activities. She glanced around in puzzlement, as though not sure what was different, then she realized the overhead light was on.

She smiled widely. "You changed the bulb!" she said, pleased.

Making sure the ladder was secure, he returned her smile. He'd been concerned that his help would annoy her. "You're welcome. How did you get the girls in and out of the car in the dark?"

She shrugged as though it were simple. "In the morning, I back out first and load them into the car in the driveway, and at night, the headlights stay on until I get them into the kitchen. I should have changed the bulb long ago, but every time I thought about it, it was the end of the day, the car was already parked and I was too pooped to move it. It'll be nice not to have to do laundry by the emergency light." She laughed. "Thank you. That was thoughtful. And thank you for Addie's car. She couldn't be more thrilled."

"How's her foot?"

"Bruised, but fine."

"Good."

Not brilliant conversation, but then they were in a garage that smelled of fertilizer, with a bulbous vehicle between them. The fat little car made of metal and fiberglass seemed to exemplify the sturdy, crash-proof nature of all that stood between them.

On the other side of the vehicle, she looked a little tense, in a state of suspension, as if she read his thoughts, understood his regrets. Suddenly his need to escape was desperate.

"Thanks for letting me take part," he said, again sidling carefully around the car until he reached the doorway where she still stood. Yellow was a good color for her, he thought. Her hair glowed and her brown eyes took on a golden quality. He'd always thought her pretty, but since he'd made a point of keeping distance between them, she appeared even more so. It wasn't like him to be so contrary.

"Sure." She held out a plate he hadn't been able to see in her hand when the car was between them. "Here's a piece of cake. My mother made it. It's wonderful."

The piece was a generous, lushly frosted portion decorated with what appeared to be buckteeth and a smile.

"That's Tow Mater," she explained, seeming uncomfortable. "From the *Cars* movie. Addie loves him best. Well…" She backed up several steps so that he could get through the doorway.

"Thanks." He held up the plate. "I'll bring it back to you when we meet this week. Remember I have to have a date by Friday."

"Okay."

"Okay. Bye."

"Bye." She followed him as he went out to his car. Mothers were arriving to pick up their children. He turned to wave, but she was already occupied with a woman she was ushering inside.

He climbed into his ancient but reliable blue BMW, placed the plate on the passenger seat and turned the key in the ignition. Home to his apartment to work on his mother's taxes? Or to the office, to locate the problem that nagged him in the Buehler Farms report the bank wanted?

He'd have given anything for a third option. Barring one, he pointed the car toward the office.

CHAPTER SIX

SANDY STUDIED HER reflection in the bathroom mirror. It was four-thirty in the morning, June 2. The house was silent, she'd eaten a cup of raspberry Greek yogurt for nourishment, drunk half a cup of Yorkshire Gold tea for the caffeine. After eight days of working a variety of shifts with Bjorn and his staff, she was ready to take on her new role as the proprietor of Crazy for Coffee. She'd caught her hair up in a loose knot at the back of her head, was wearing jeans and one of the shirts she'd had made with a crazy cartoon face Bobbie had designed with spinning eyes and electrified hair. It seemed to exemplify the Crazy for Coffee name. If she could just stop shaking, she could look like a woman who knew what she was doing.

She'd introduced herself to her suppliers by phone, and taken her two-member teenaged staff to dinner at the Urban Cafe to get acquainted. They were lively and even adorable from a grown woman's perspective, but Terri, lanky and brunette, talked constantly, and Callista, plump and blonde and half a head shorter than Terri, kept trying to tell Sandy what to do. At this point, Sandy was mostly grateful for the girl's self-confident instructions. The girls didn't always get along but, according to Bjorn, except for a little sniping, their work was unaffected.

Sandy had spent half the night wondering what on earth she'd been thinking when she'd decided to embark on a new career, and the other half reminding herself that she'd had no choice. She could have kept looking for a job that required her skills and paid reasonably well, and that might or might not have become available before she had to dip into her refinance money.

But it made sense simply to use that money now to put herself in business making the best coffee anyone in Clatsop County had ever had.

"Ready?"

Sandy's mother's voice startled her.

"Hi, Mom," Sandy said.

Standing in the bathroom doorway, her mother looked her over and asked sympathetically, "Scared?"

Sandy seldom admitted to fear, but this was her mother. They'd been through fearful times together. "I am. Why did I think I could run a coffee cart?"

"Because you're always taking the next step," Loretta replied, edging out of her daughter's way. Sandy turned off the bathroom light. The two women went down the hall toward the girls' room. Peering in, Sandy saw they were fast asleep, Zoey clutching her sock monkey ballerina, her wand on the floor beside her, and Addie holding a teddy bear, her tiara hung over the bed post.

"They're good," her mother whispered. "I just checked."

Sandy pulled the door closed softly and gave her mother a hug. "Thanks again, Mom. I really appreciate your help so I can do this."

"Sure. I'm car shopping," her mother teased. "And I'm looking for all the extras."

"As soon as I can, I'll get it for you."

They headed for the kitchen and the door to the garage, stepping over Matchbox cars, dolls and Lego toys.

"Don't clean that up for them," Sandy said, pointing to the kid debris. "They're supposed to pick up after themselves before they go to bed. I forgot to get on them last night."

"Right." Her mother opened the door for her and said bracingly, "This is going to be good for you, Sandy. You were a great office manager, but stuck in an office all day when you're so full of ideas and dreams isn't the best thing for you."

Sandy had to laugh. "Now I'll be stuck in an eight-and-a-half-by-twenty-eight-foot coffee cart all day."

"But you'll get to see other people besides stuffy lawyers and I have every confidence you'll have a ten-cart chain in no time."

More horrified than excited by that prospect, Sandy hugged her mother again and stepped into the dark garage. She flipped on the light Hunter had fixed and went to her car. Every day she thought about how nice it was to have the light working again.

She hit the garage door opener, backed her car out, then closed the doors, wincing against the noise. The neighborhood was in darkness, silent except for the stirring of new leaves on the trees in the early morning breeze and the bark of a neighbor's dog.

Then she drove out of the driveway, headed

for her new life. An image formed in her brain of Hunter among the children at Addie's party, Hunter holding Addie's tiny foot out for Sandy's inspection, Hunter standing in her garage, looking as though he belonged there. But he didn't.

She closed her eyes against the image, then decided that wasn't wise when she was driving down the hill toward town. She opened her eyes and willed away all thoughts of Hunter Bristol. Her new life did not include him.

THE INSIDE OF the coffee cart reminded Sandy of the galley on a boat; there wasn't an inch of wasted space. A three-spigot coffee machine stood in the front of the cart between the two service windows. On the left was a sink with a spray hose and on the right, the cash register. Underneath the counter sat a wide refrigerator that held milk and other perishable products, and there were cupboards on either side of the service windows, where backup cups and bags for pastries were stored.

Along the right side of the cart ran a counter for food preparation, with cupboards above and below; there was also a stand-up fridge, with juices, yogurt, a freezer with ice cream for the milkshakes.

On the left side there were more cupboards, a metal paper towel dispenser on which she'd stuck a magnetic frame with a photo of the girls in their snowsuits, taken last Christmas, and one of her mother the newspaper had run when her church circle sold Norwegian desserts at the Scandinavian festival. There was also a basic coffee pot for the simple coffee addicts, and a plug-in tea kettle for tea drinkers. A 54-quart stainless-steel beverage cooler under the counter held ice cubes.

The ninety flavors of syrup to make fancy coffees were everywhere, with triples of vanilla, hazelnut and raspberry because of their popularity.

Her heart hammering out of control, Sandy took one last look around, decided she was as ready as she would ever be and turned on the Espresso and Open lights.

As though someone had been waiting for signs of life, a white Chevy Blazer pulled up to the window on the left side.

Sandy leaned out the window with a wide smile. "Good morning," she said cheerfully. "What can I get you?"

The large man in a red-and-blue flannel shirt and a Mariners baseball cap frowned up at her.

The magnetic sign on the side of his vehicle said Dave's Maintenance. He stared at her suspiciously from behind wire-rimmed glasses, and demanded anxiously, "Where's Bjorn?"

She held on to her smile. "He moved back to Chicago to help his parents. I'm Sandy."

Knowing her name didn't appear to ease the man's distress. She understood. A person's first cup of coffee of the day was important and not to be trusted to just anyone.

"Can I get you something?" she prompted.

"Ah…well…can you make a white chocolate caramel mocha?" he asked.

Suddenly more comfortable because his order suggested he wasn't the toughie he appeared to be—she'd have figured him for an Americano—she nodded confidently. "Sure can. Eight ounce? Twelve ounce?"

"Sixteen," he said. "With a white chocolate bean."

Every coffee drink was served with either a white chocolate– or a dark chocolate–covered coffee bean.

"One pump of white chocolate?"

"Two, please."

Ah. Hard-core. "Coming up," she said.

Hands trembling, she went to work. After

placing the small glass measure under the spigot, she turned on the espresso maker. She steamed milk, added mocha powder, all the while keeping an eye on the espresso. Bjorn had insisted that it be poured and served within ten seconds of being done, to maintain the integrity of the flavor profile. Mercifully, everything ready within the prescribed time, she added caramel and then two pumps of white chocolate. She put a lid on the cup, stuck in a straw, added the comfort collar so that he didn't burn his fingers, put the white chocolate-covered bean in the little depression on the lid and handed the coffee out the window.

"Four twenty-five," she said.

He gave her a ten-dollar bill and she surreptitiously kept an eye on him while she made change. He sipped, tasted, leaned his head back—apparently to analyze—then sipped again.

She passed him his change. "How is it?" she asked.

He nodded. "A little too much caramel," he said, then added grudgingly, "but passable. I'm Dave."

She leaned over to offer her hand. "Nice to meet you, Dave. I'm Sandy."

He switched his mocha from hand to hand and shook hers. Then gave her a one-dollar tip. "Have a nice day," he said and drove off.

Sandy expelled a sigh of relief. Though passable was hardly a compliment, she had a feeling it was high praise from Dave. Anyway, how could you trust the opinion of someone who thought there was too much caramel in anything?

The morning was a blur. She moved from one window to the other, preparing drinks, making change, struggling to keep supplies handy, thinking excitedly that this might be a profitable venture after all. If she could just keep up.

She was moving milk from the stand-up refrigerator to the cooler under the counter in the front when she heard a shout. "Hello?"

She leaned out the left window and recognized Hunter's BMW.

"Hi." He leaned out his window. His customary good looks were even more striking today with the collar of a light, black leather jacket turned up against the morning chill. "I need four drinks. Do you have time?"

"Of course."

"Great." He rattled off a series of drinks, one

she recognized as a favorite of Nate's. "And can we have four scones with butter and jam?"

"Absolutely."

Preparing the order took her longer than it should have. She dropped two scones and had to toss them, dumped over the box of straws when she tried to extract four, tore several napkins and dropped the Americano and had to make another. She finally passed the bag of scones and the coffee carrier out the window. "Sorry about the delay. Still getting the hang of everything."

"Not a problem," he said. No smile, but his tone was sincere. He handed her several bills. "Things going okay?"

"Yes, thanks." Four cars sat lined up behind him. She hated to think what might be at the other window. She made his change and handed it back.

"Did you check on the contract assignments?" he asked.

"I did." Annoyed that he'd brought up something he'd been right about, though she would never admit it, she said with cool politeness, "Thanks for stopping by, but could you move on? I have a line behind you."

Obviously annoyed also, he pointed to the beanless lids on the coffee. “No beans?”

“Oh, sorry.” Wanting to kick herself, she poured half a dozen white and dark chocolate beans into a small cup, put a lid on the cup and stuck it out the window.

“Rookie mistake,” he said and drove away.

HUNTER’S COWORKERS RUSHED him when he walked into the office with their morning coffee.

“How’s she doing?” Jonni asked immediately. Nate’s office manager was a pretty, middle-aged blonde with a professional bearing who knew everything about all of their clients. She kept the office humming while still saving time to harass Hunter. She sipped at her raspberry mocha. “Yum. How’s yours?”

Hunter handed Nate his Americano and Karen, who filed and updated data on the computer, her vanilla latte. Nate nodded over his as he walked back to his office and the ever-efficient Karen shouted over her shoulder as she carried an armload of files toward the conference room and the file cabinets, “Delicious!”

“She seems to be doing all right,” Hunter replied to Jonni’s question. “She took a little longer than Bjorn would have, but then, this is her first day alone. She's getting a lineup, but if people are patient, she should be fine." He sipped at his ordinary mocha. It was delicious. She'd even given him only half the usual whipped-cream topping—she'd remembered from the times they'd driven through Crazy for Coffee when Bjorn owned it.

"Hunter!"

Shaken out of his thoughts, he turned to find Nate standing behind him in the kitchen. "What?" he asked.

"Your phone's ringing, and a client's waiting in your office. Everything okay?"

"Who's waiting?"

"Jill Morrow from Community Action. She said Sandy told her to get in touch with you." He gave Hunter a knowing look. "Call me if you need help fending her off."

Hunter sighed, dispirited. "Nice of you. I'm on my way." He pushed past Nate and dragged his feet toward his office. Hunter had worked with Jill to get the Morenos help with fuel last February. Jill had been eager to assist. In fact, her eagerness had been somewhat of an embarrassment.

Bobbie had noticed it first. "She's always

touching your arm or your hand," she'd pointed out. "Are you sending signals?"

"No," he assured her. "No signals. She's pretty, but a little scrawny for my tastes."

"She's gorgeous."

"I know. I've seen her a couple of times at various events. She has two ex-husbands and a boyfriend. I think her flirt factor is on automatic pilot. She can't help herself. And while I admire her brain and her civic conscience, I don't want to get involved."

Jill, however, seemed determined to change his mind. She stood when he walked into his office, handed him an armload of manila folders and used the possibility of his dropping them as an excuse to hold on to his forearms.

"Hi, Jill." He took a step back and dropped the folders on his desk. "What is all this?"

She appeared surprised that he didn't know. "Sandy Evans told me to bring these to you. Budgets, operational data, plans for what we could do if we had more money." She leaned closer on the excuse of sharing a confidence. "Are we getting more money? And if we are, what do you have to do with it?"

He smiled and turned her gently toward the door. "I can't tell you about it yet, but thank you so much for being so prompt with all this information." Sandy could have given him a heads-up that Jill was coming. She knew the woman drove him crazy. "I'll call you as soon as I learn anything."

Jill leaned closer as she waited for him to pass through the doorway with her, forcing him to bump into her. He groaned inwardly.

"Well, give me something to go on, Hunter. Have you found a way to make a nonprofit profitable?"

Hunter walked her toward the front door and opened it. "Then we'd both end up in jail."

"Oh…" The single-word reply was quiet and suggestive. "Would we get to share a cell?"

"Thanks for stopping in."

She looked at him over her shoulder as he nudged her out the door. "Will you call me if you need anything else?"

Not on your life, he thought. Aloud, he said, "Of course. Thanks again."

Jonni stood behind him when he turned to lean against the closed door with a sigh of relief. She smirked. "That's what you get for being such a love god."

He made a face at her. "I'm in no mood, Ms. Thomas."

She pretended disappointment, handing him a purple folder and an email printout. "Fine. Women's Resource Center sent you a bunch of stuff in the mail, also at Sandy's request, and I forwarded you this email from CASA so you can open their attachments. More of the same, I think. Anything I can do to help the process?"

Now he pretended shock. "You want to help *me*?"

She put a hand to her heart. "I'm serious. My payrolls are done for today, I'd be happy to help."

All right. He had just the job for her. "Can you do a spreadsheet of income and expenses so we can see who makes best use of their funding, then draw up a wish list for them and calculate how much money it would take?"

The smirk became a smile. "Sure." She socked his arm. "Not because it's you, you know, but because it's such a worthy cause."

Jonni walked back to her desk. "Oh, and Hunter? Mr. Connolly phoned. Wondered if you wanted to have lunch tomorrow."

"Lunch? But we're just starting to collect information."

"Yeah. He said he wasn't rushing you about the project, just wanted to get together."

"Hmm."

"Yeah. That's what I thought. Who'd want to get together with you?"

CHAPTER SEVEN

"I REALLY LIKE HIM, but he's like this total brain freak. He knows everything about everything. Before school was out, Mr. Barker in history was telling us about Alexander the Great and couldn't remember the name of his horse. Ryan knew. And when the Wi-Fi was messed up in the library, he fixed it. I mean, I get by okay in school, but I'm not a brainiac."

Terri had come on duty at two o'clock. It was now 2:20, and she hadn't stopped talking since she'd arrived. But in jeans and a Crazy for Coffee T-shirt, a lot of makeup and a heart pendant around her neck, she could still serve two customers to Sandy's one.

Now, after three weeks of operation, Sandy was beginning to feel more comfortable in the confined space and wasn't always colliding with the girls when in a hurry. She now reached for products instinctively without having to think about where they were.

Scooping ice cubes made of coffee into a cup, she opened her mouth to offer Terri some advice, but the girl was still talking.

"He's like this Drama Club genius, too. He's working with the Astor Street Opry Company this summer. Should I ask him if he wants to come by for a mocha?"

This time she waited for an answer. Sandy poured hot coffee over the coffee cubes, which would prevent dilution of the flavorful brew, then replied as she squirted in cream and put a lid on the cup, "Of course. We need all the customers we can get. And it would be good for him to see you at work." She added a straw. "He'll be impressed." She handed the drink to Terri, who passed it out the window and took payment.

"What if I mess up?"

"Everybody messes up sometime. I'll bet even Ryan does. We all understand that about one another. Just don't forget there'll be other customers besides him. Don't give him *all* your attention."

"Right. Calli will be here early tomorrow, anyway."

"Good. Okay, if you've got this, I'm going home. Please don't forget the two raspberry mochas and the caramel-vanilla latte for the fire department. Somebody will be by to pick them up around 4:45."

Terri indicated a note she'd attached to the register. "I won't. Have a good evening."

"You, too."

Feet sore and brain frazzled from the long day, Sandy would have loved to stop at the Urban Cafe for a piece of chocolate cake and a glass of white zinfandel, but she knew her mother would have picked up the girls at day-care half an hour ago and was probably eager for some peace and quiet. So Sandy headed home.

She sang to Garth Brooks as she made the turn onto Fifteenth Street. The day had been a good one all in all, despite her sore feet and her whirling brain. She was making a small fortune, she thought with quiet delight. She looked forward to sitting down with the books after the girls were in bed tonight and getting a picture of how she was really doing.

Judging by the activity at Crazy for Coffee, she was doing wonderfully well; she just wasn't sure how income weighed against expenses at the moment.

She was enjoying herself more than she'd

expected to. Panic had set in just before she'd signed the contract, and she'd worried about whether she was doing the smart thing. But, skeptical Dave now stopped twice a day, on his way to work, and on his way home, and called her by name. He'd retracted his "passable" judgment on her white chocolate caramel mocha and now deemed it "superior." She was flattered out of all proportion.

She'd acquired other regulars after just a few weeks of operation, she had a good working relationship with her two-woman staff and she was beginning to feel she knew the ropes. Maybe she hadn't done the smart thing, but she'd done the right thing.

Keeping a distance from Hunter seemed to be restoring a certain balance to her life. She didn't think about him all the time—well, she did, but pushing him out of her mind was easier. It also helped that he, apparently, was trying to stay away from her.

Jonni had been making Raleigh & Raleigh's morning coffee run. Sandy managed to get all the nonprofits on their list to report to Hunter directly so that she didn't have to serve as go-between, and deliberately choosing a time when she knew Hunter would be too busy to answer his phone, she left him a message about having checked the city's calendar of events, and suggested the last weekend in July for the opening of the Clothes Closet.

When Jonni had made the pick-up this morning, however, she'd told Sandy that Hunter wanted her to look over the spreadsheet with the competing nonprofits' incomes, expenses and proposed projects. Sandy had rolled her eyes. "Can you bring me the spreadsheet?" she'd asked Jonni.

Jonni hung out her window to take the coffee carrier and bag of scones and handed Sandy a twenty-dollar bill. "He wants to talk them over with you. Phone me and I'll make sure his schedule's clear."

So, maybe she'd lost that one.

Sandy noticed Bobbie's truck parked in front of her house as she pulled into her driveway. That was nice. She could always use a dose of Bobbie.

And besides, if she had to see Hunter she could do it. She was on her way to being a successful businesswoman, and was now too busy to long for him anymore. She was done with that.

The girls came running out as she turned

off the engine and opened her door. They had colorful smears of paint up to their elbows and paint all over their faces. "We're painting flowers with Bobbie!" Zoey announced.

"I see that!" Sandy smiled as her friend walked out of the house. "Hey, Bobbie! What's going on?"

"Gramma had a emergency!" Zoey announced.

"Oh, no." Sandy's beleaguered brain forgot everything for a moment to worry about her mother. "Is Mom all right?" she asked Bobbie over the top of the car as her friend waited on the steps.

Bobbie nodded. "I think so. She just said she was feeling kind of punk and didn't want to give the girls or you anything. You can't afford to be sick."

"Did she see a doctor?"

"Yes. He thinks it's just a bad cold complicated by allergies. He told her to lay low and stay out of crowds. She'll be better in a week."

A week. Genuinely filled with sympathy for her mother, Sandy still couldn't help fretting about how she would handle her domestic logistics for the next week. Her mother was right. Sandy couldn't afford to be sick. But—

selfishly—Sandy couldn't afford for her mother to be sick, either.

She pulled herself together. "Thanks so much for stepping in, Bobbie. Where are the boys this afternoon?"

"I'd just taken them to Karate Class when your mother called. I don't pick them up until 5:30."

Sandy gave her a quick hug as they stepped inside the house. A wonderful aroma drifted from the kitchen. Sandy sniffed appreciatively.

"Spaghetti sauce," Bobbie said. "I took the liberty of starting dinner for both of us if you don't mind lending me a bowl to take some home. I brought the makings, but forgot a container."

Sandy hugged her again. "You are an angel."

"I've been thinking about what you can do in the mornings until your Mom is well."

"Thanks, but that's not for you to worry about. I'll figure out…"

"You should call Stella," Bobbie interrupted.

Sandy didn't want to frown except she couldn't help it. Stella was a lovely woman, yet her proximity to Hunter…

"I know," Bobbie went on. "But she's a consummate professional where kids are concerned. Like another mother. And she probably won't even mention Hunter to you."

"Probably?"

"Well, you know, she's his mom and she thinks he's pretty wonderful. We all do."

Wanting to sidestep any discussion of Hunter, Sandy asked, "But what'll *you* do without her? The kids are out of school. You won't get any painting done if you…"

Shaking her head to stop Sandy, Bobbie went to the stove and stirred the contents of the large pot. "I'm taking the boys to Southern California to visit my father for about ten days. We won't need Stella until I get back." She dipped the spoon into the sauce, held a hand under it and offered it to Sandy.

Sandy gingerly tasted the sauce and found it garlicky and wonderful. "Excellent. Good thing I don't have a boyfriend. That sauce will keep vampires at bay. You'll have to make sure Nate eats as much as you do so you won't offend."

Bobbie laughed. "It'd take a twelve-foot stone wall to keep us away from each other. And even then, Nate has rappelling experience."

Sandy envied her friends their love for each other, which nothing could deter. She wanted that kind of love; she just didn't seem able to find it—or to inspire it in someone.

"Thanks so much for today, Bobbie. I owe you big. And I'll phone Stella right after dinner."

"Good." Bobbie pointed to the corner of the kitchen where she had the girls do their painting on a tarp. "I hope it was okay to use that. I found it in the garage. And good job on getting the light bulb changed, by the way. It's nice to see what you're doing in there. When I helped you put your Christmas decorations away, I thought I'd kill myself."

"Hunter replaced the bulb," Sandy admitted, "the day of Addie's birthday party."

Bobbie's expression was unreadable. Sandy guessed that was deliberate. "Well, he's always the gentleman. I'm sorry we slopped over onto the floor with paint, but it's water-based, so it should wash up fine. I'll clean it before I go."

Sandy dug a bowl out of the cupboard and spooned spaghetti sauce into it. "You'll do no such thing. I'll handle it. I already owe you… what?" She cast a glance at Bobbie as she fit a lid onto the container. "What could possibly pay you back for all the help you've been to me?"

"Oh, I don't know. I'll think of something

big." Bobbie gathered car keys and cell phone, then accepted the bowl Sandy had covered with a lid and wrapped in a towel.

Sandy walked her to the door and down the steps, then stopped her to say seriously, "Truly, Bobbie. There are so many times when I don't know what I'd do without you."

"Oh, Sandy. You flew a thousand miles to spend the day with me when I had my first chemo session, you got me the commission for your office and rented me your little house so I could come to Astoria to do the work. It's time you got a little payback. Will you open the passenger door so I can set this down?"

The spaghetti sauce safely stowed on the floor, Bobbie turned to give Sandy a hug. "How's it all going at the coffee cart? Are you glad you bought it?"

Sandy was able to answer honestly. "I am. It was the right thing. I'm checking income and expenses tonight so I can figure out how I'm really doing."

"Good. I'll call Stella and give her a heads-up."

"Great. Thanks."

Sandy waved Bobbie off then went back inside to admire the girls' artwork, which they had posted all over the refrigerator with magnets. "And, Mommy, come see!" Addie caught her hand and dragged her toward the garage. "I painted my car!"

Sandy flipped on the light and immediately spotted the red kiddie car on the workbench. Addie had painted Tow Mater's signature prominent teeth on the front of her car, and a daisy on the side. Bobbie's hand in the expert rendering of the teeth was easy to see.

"Bobbie helped her." Zoey held up her wand. "And we made my wand brighter. 'Cause, you know, that makes it better."

Smiling, Sandy admired the car and the wand with glitter added in the center, appreciating her friend even more than she had. After escorting the girls back into the kitchen, Sandy led the cleanup from their painting. The girls set the table for dinner while she dialed her mother.

"Hi, Sandy," her mother said in a quiet, croaky voice. "I'm so sorry."

"Don't be sorry—no problem here. I have everything handled. But I'm sorry you're sick. It came on suddenly."

"Tell me. One minute I was fine, the next I had to phone Bobbie to pick up the girls. She's such a doll."

"I know. Mom, do you need something for dinner? I can bring you eggs, or cottage cheese, or..." She began rummaging through cupboards, hunting for sick people food. "How about chicken noodle soup?"

"Thanks, but I have no appetite whatsoever. And I've got a few things. I'll be fine. You just stay away and keep the girls away so nobody gets this. You don't have time to be sick, and if the girls get sick, you'll get sick."

"I'll drive over and look in on you Sunday."

"No. Keep your distance. I'm serious. I'd feel terrible if I gave you my germs. I'm going to sleep a lot and just take it easy. Doctor's orders. I'll phone you when I'm feeling better and we'll all do something together."

"Mom..."

"Sandy, I mean it. If I know you're worrying about me, I'll worry about you, and that isn't good for either of us. I'll check in by phone every day, I promise."

"Okay."

"Will you take the girls to work with you?"

"No. Stella might be able to help us. I'll talk to her tonight."

She heard her mother's sigh of relief. "That's good. So, they're all right?"

"They are. They want to say hello. Hold on." She gestured the girls to the phone. They told their grandmother about painting the car and the wand with Bobbi, and about riding in Stella's car. "It has something in the seat that warms your bottom!" Zoey said.

Addie giggled and asked Sandy, "How come we don't have that?"

"Because our car isn't that fancy."

"Well, let's *get* a fancy one!"

Absolutely. Right after your college education and a furnace that actually works.

The girls finally said goodbye and Sandy added a quick, "Call me if you need me!" as her mother hung up.

Sandy served dinner and listened again to the same stories they'd told her mother.

It was almost nine before the house was quiet. Sandy spread out her bookwork on the dining table but was interrupted by the telephone. It was Stella.

"Bobbie told me about your situation," Hunter's mother said with her customary good cheer. "I'm sorry your mom's not well, but I'd be happy to help until she can take over again. I'll come by just before you leave the house. What time do they go to daycare?"

Sandy explained the routine and promised Stella she would have most of the day to herself once she dealt with early morning. Sandy suggested a generous sum in payment. It would be only for one week, and she couldn't imagine what she would have done had Stella not been so understanding and willing.

"It sounds workable," Stella said.

"Thanks for being a friend, Stella."

"That's what it's all about, sweetie. See you at 4:00."

Relieved that such an enormous problem had been so easily solved, Sandy focused again on her paperwork. She studied receipts, determining to get everything entered into the computer as soon as she had a moment. Her cash registers were programmed to separate all sales into categories, but she still had to enter all other purchases and expenses. She had looked into contracts as Hunter had suggested and that had been good advice. It gave her a heads-up on the Porta Potty that was two hundred dollars a month, which she hadn't considered in her initial plan.

The paperwork for the cart insurance she'd intended to take out as soon as possible fell out of the folder in which she kept all her notes. She put the insurance quote aside, hoping she could write a check for it tonight, as soon as she'd figured how she was doing. And Jonni had phoned to tell her she'd emailed Sandy the payroll calculations for her two employees. Sandy had to write those checks tonight, too.

Preparing payroll was a monthly expense she intended to handle herself as soon as she had a moment to breathe. Jonni promised to help her through the first time. Right now, having it done for her was a convenience that smoothed out her first month in business.

An hour and a half's review of her figures proved that she was holding her own. Covering all her start-up costs had eaten up considerable income, so she wasn't doing quite as well as her nonstop busyness suggested, but tourist season should help her further improve business. She had enough income to cover her business expenses, meet payroll and pay her personal mortgage and utilities, but cart insurance, she realized, would have to wait until next month. Being without it made her uneasy, but at least she wasn't *driving* the cart, and there wasn't a lot that could go wrong in something that size.

She also worried a little about the continuing expense of daycare. But she put that out of her mind right away. It wasn't a problem yet, and she refused to borrow trouble.

HUNTER GAVE THE HOOD of his mother's old Saturn a final swipe with the chamois and stepped back to check his work. He walked around the car to make sure he hadn't missed a smudge.

"Beautiful!" Stella praised from her doorstep. "You want some lunch?"

"No, thanks. Try not to get stuck in a slough again, okay? Not good for the undercarriage."

She made a face. "Sound advice. I wish you could do for my shoes and black linen pants what you did for the car. Walking—rather, *slipping*—out of the slough wasn't good for my undercarriage, either. That's what I get for trusting the GPS."

"Yeah. Well, it's always smart to watch where you're going, even with GPS. Especially when you're guiding a ton of steel."

"My heavens, but you're *full* of sound advice this morning, aren't you? Want to come in and see what Glenda sent you to help stock the Clothes Closet?"

"Sure." He curled up the hose onto the reel, gathered up the chamois and bucket.

She held the door open for him and he noticed that she looked tired. "Not sleeping?" he asked. She had an occasional problem with arthritis in her knees.

"No, I'm fine. I'm just helping Sandy for a few days. It's only Tuesday and already I'm pooped. She keeps terrible hours. I don't know how she does it."

"Why are you helping Sandy?" he asked, dumping the contents of the bucket into the sink and rinsing out the bucket. "And how?"

"I'm watching the kids when she goes to work until daycare opens."

"I thought *her* mom was doing that."

"She has a cold…and allergies. Doctor told her to lay low for a week."

"And Sandy called you?" He placed the chamois to dry over the side of the sink and washed his hands. Somehow, he couldn't imagine Sandy calling his mother for help.

"Bobbie called me to tell me what she was up against, and I called Sandy."

"Well…" He wasn't sure what to say. He didn't like the two of them working together, getting cozy—talking. "That's nice."

She handed him a towel to dry his hands and led him into the living room. "We're not conspiring against you, if that's what you're worried about. The subject of you never really comes up."

That was a relief, if a little hurtful.

He wound his way after her through the bright yellow kitchen into the pink-and-gray living room filled with flowers, knickknacks, and bamboo furniture. He'd always thought his mother's living room looked like it belonged in Florida. Because his father had died at fifty-five after a long career as a cop, it was probably the closest she could get to their dream of retiring to the Sunshine State. The sunny room always ground in his guilt at letting them give him their nest egg to start his business.

"Everyone in each of Glenda's classes did something for the Clothes Closet. The beginners made scarves and simple throws, and the advanced people made sweaters, fancy blankets, and baby stuff. Look at this!"

Stacked all over the sofa and two chairs were colorful piles of knitted and crocheted work. He smiled as he fingered a scarf in a soft purple with a beaded fringe. Sandy had a shirt that color. "Would these have been their toads and frogs?" he teased.

"No. There's nothing halfhearted or unfinished about these." She unfolded a masterfully created blanket made up of different colored and patterned squares sewn together. "Look at this. The woman who did it could have gotten hundreds of dollars for it in Glenda's retail shop. You have to write the women a note. Or, better yet, pay them a visit and tell them how grateful you are for their contributions."

Pay a visit to a yarn shop. He'd rather be audited. He smiled noncommittally. "I'll make sure they know how much we appreciate this."

"The shop's in Warrenton. Not very far."

"Mom, I wouldn't know what to say to ladies in a yarn shop. It's all so…female. I'll write them."

"Stop being such a chicken. They've also collected a monetary donation for you. They got customers to contribute and they want to present you with a check. It's probably not four figures, but it's from a bunch of women who love to see their hard work go to a worthy cause. The money was one of her students' ideas because she and her little girl wouldn't have survived without the Food Bank and the warm clothes the Saint Vincent de Paul Society gave them."

She drew a deep breath and stared him in the eye. "I told them you'd be by to thank them.

So Glenda's having all her classes come to the Thursday night meeting. 7:00."

He closed his eyes and counted to three, but that wasn't nearly high enough, so he kept going. The money donation was extremely generous of them, but what would he say?

"They were impressed," she went on in a coaxing tone, "because most of their sons' interests lie in basketball games, bars, monster trucks and loose women. They think you're pretty special."

He groaned loudly. "You want me to do this so you can show them you can still push me around. I'm not going. Like I said, I have no idea what to say to a group of women who knit. I'll write or I'll call. You're welcome for the excellent job I did washing your car." He headed for the door, then he turned to ask her grudgingly, "Can you store all this for a while, until we get the Clothes Closet ready?"

"Yes."

"Thanks."

She closed the door on him. That was happening to him a lot lately.

He needed a month in Bermuda. Away time to clear his mind of the vision of Sandy in the purple shirt that matched that scarf with the beaded fringe.

Generally, he was doing just fine without her. His evenings and his weekends were free. No one challenged everything he said or did—well, except for his mother, and he didn't see that changing anytime soon. No one wanted to know what he was thinking, or the feelings behind his thoughts.

He was enjoying his freedom. He ate whatever he wanted without concern for clogging his arteries, and he could watch cop shows without someone beside him muting the violent parts.

He didn't have to clean the apartment against drop-in visitors, didn't have to worry about whether the toilet seat was down, or whether he had anything in the fridge but sardines and hot sauce.

He headed for home and the Mariners-Yankees game. He had a frozen pizza in the fridge and a dozen date bars Bobbie had made. He looked forward to a quiet evening—until he noticed Sandy sitting on the bench in front of his simple old brick apartment building.

Mild panic formed in his chest, but he kept reminding himself that it was over between them, and though he often thought of her and even sometimes longed for her, he was sure she didn't long for him. So her heart wouldn't beat faster as he approached, so it would be deadly to let her see that his did. If she had any idea at all that he had moments of regret that their relationship was over, he'd be dead meat. Like the gazelle at the watering hole.

He parked and climbed out of the car with a friendly smile. "Hi, Sandy." He was happy to hear the polite, uninvolved sound of his voice. "Are you waiting for me?"

She looked more tired than his mother had. And if he wasn't mistaken, her face appeared just a little thinner. She studied his expression as though trying to read his thoughts. He kept them carefully hidden and continued to smile.

She picked up a manila folder that sat on the bench beside her and stood. She wore black jeans and a black long-sleeve T-shirt. The black made a torch of her hair, which was caught up in a fat, curly ponytail. He noticed instantly that her hips had a little less curve. He kept his smile in place and the concern from his eyes.

"These are my recommendations for the mystery money. I didn't think you'd appreciate me bringing them by at 3:45 in the morning, or 10:00 at night, so I thought I'd drop them off when I had a minute. Terri's manning the cart. However, I have to get right back."

"But you haven't seen the spreadsheet."

"Actually, I did." Her cheeks pinked. "I stopped by late one afternoon to see you at the office." She glanced away at that admission and he could only guess she'd stopped by when she knew he wouldn't be there, probably checked first with Jonni. "You were at a client's and the spreadsheet was on your desk. I took some notes and...voila."

He didn't recall ever seeing her look embarrassed. *"Voila?"* he asked.

The pink in her cheeks deepened. Maybe her heartbeat was accelerating. She shrugged and smiled. "I tried a lavender latte today. I'm feeling French."

He accepted the folder from her and resisted the fragrance of her, which was part honeysuckle soap, which he was used to, and part coffee cart—a complex smell that combined strong coffee, milk chocolate, and something citrusy.

"How's it going at Crazy for Coffee?" He kept the question casual.

She nodded. "Decent. I'm getting more comfortable with it every day." She took two steps down the sidewalk, then turned and said reluctantly, "I've been meaning to thank you for the heads-up on the assigned contracts. Found one I hadn't thought about and it was good that I did."

He felt mild elation that she thought that, but went to great pains to remain casual. "Happy to help."

"Well..." She pointed toward town. "I'd better..."

"Do you knit?" he asked abruptly, walking after her as she started for her car.

She turned to him with a blink of surprise.

"Or crochet?" He kept talking, hoping to keep her there. "Thanks to my mother's nosey parker interference—or assistance, however you want to view it—her partner in a yarn shop sent us all kinds of scarves and blankets and things for the Clothes Closet. She had all her classes working on it. Mom told her I'd stop by to thank her and her students, but I'd feel like, you know..." he shrugged, groping for the right word and finally settled on "...stupid. Way out of my element."

She clearly was trying not to smile. "I used to knit when I was younger. When Bobbie and I were in college we shared a booth at a craft fair. She sold small paintings, and I sold hats and scarves. I haven't had time in ages. But...

how nice of them to do that for us. Needlework takes time and attention."

"Do you want to come with me to their meeting Thursday and tell them that?" he asked. "I don't know what to say. But you know what work goes into that stuff."

"No," she said simply—and now she did smile. "I'm sorry you're uncomfortable, but I have so much to do—I'm trying to learn payroll, and get my books on the computer and spend some time with the girls."

He nodded his understanding, hid his disappointment. "Of course. I understand."

Laughing lightly, she started to walk away. "They'll realize how much you appreciate their help. Women always relate to your charm and your sincerity."

He had to laugh, too. "*You* didn't," he reminded her.

She'd reached her car and unlocked it with the remote. "That's because you weren't thanking me for anything, but instead raking me over the coals for attempting to do something *for* you." She pulled her door open. "They'll love you. Just be yourself. Tell them how many children and babies we have among our clients. How many old people, and how much more comfortable the gifts will make them. Appreciation generates affection. Gotta go."

She drove off with a tap of her horn. Hunter watched the little red car disappear around the corner toward town and refused to dwell on how relaxed she appeared around him. That had to mean she didn't care. She'd been as casual as he'd had to pretend to be.

Actually, that was better all around. He didn't have to be so guarded around her. Weird, though. Now that she was behaving in a way that allowed him to direct his own life, he missed her interference. He needed counseling.

He climbed the steps to his apartment, the game, the pizza and the date bars suddenly holding less appeal than they had a few short minutes ago.

CHAPTER EIGHT

"No, no, no!"

Sandy stood with her hand on a barely cold two-liter bottle of whole milk in the stand-up refrigerator. No. This couldn't be. She moved her hand along the half dozen bottles beside and below it, and they, too, were only moderately cold. The cart's harsh overhead light usually kept the 4:30 darkness outside, where it belonged, while Sandy prepared to open. This morning, however, the darkness was invading her being.

Anger at a fridge that would allow its contents to grow warm was ridiculous, but she felt precisely that as she struggled to push the big case away from the wall to determine how it had become unplugged.

She gasped at the sight of the plug still firmly in the socket. The refrigerated case was simply not functioning. It was broken. Required a repairman. Had spoiled several hundred dollars' worth of everything she needed to open for business this morning!

Feeling panicky, she went to the refrigerator under the counter in the front to check how much product she had there. An unopened two-liter carton of nicely cold, whole milk and a half-empty carton of two percent. No fat-free. That wouldn't last her an hour with all the latte junkies who were now her regulars between six and eight o'clock.

She groaned and made a quick list of what to buy and how much the fridge could hold. Fat-free milk, two percent, whipped cream. She took the money she would have used to pay her cable bill, flipped off the light and ran to her car. Thank God the nearby Safeway was open twenty-four hours.

She purchased just what she needed to start the day and thought she might be able to impose on Bobbie in the middle of the morning to run to the store for her. She raced back to the cart, was stopped for speeding by a police officer who was sympathetic but still gave her a ninety-four dollar ticket.

Biting back tears, she put everything into the low refrigerator, found her list of repair people Bjorn had used and left a message for P & L

Johnson Mechanical, stressing the urgency of her situation. She turned on the lights at 5:01 and greeted Dave with a smile.

At ten-thirty, with little milk left, she phoned Bobbie and had to leave a message. When Bobbie hadn't returned her call by ten forty-five, she phoned Stella and had to leave a message there, too.

When no one had phoned her back by eleven o'clock, she did the only thing she could think of. She called Hunter at the office.

"This is Hunter," he said in his professional voice. "How can I help you?"

"Hunter!" she said with what she knew was too much enthusiasm, but she didn't care. "Thank God!"

"Sandy?" He sounded confused.

"Yes."

"Did you mean to call me?"

"Yes!"

"What's wrong?"

She sighed. "I got a speeding ticket this morning, but right now, that's the least of my problems. Listen! I need a favor. If you'll do this for me, I'll go to the yarn thing with you."

"Really?" She heard his voice brighten. "It's tonight."

"Okay."

"Then, sure. What do you need?"

She explained about the refrigerator and all that had gone wrong. "I could only buy as much as would fit in the fridge under the counter and I'm almost out of everything again. If I call Safeway, give them my order and my credit card number, would you pick it up? Please?"

There was an instant's silence. In her desperation, it felt like five minutes.

"You won't back out on the yarn shop meeting?"

"I will not."

"Then, I'm on my way."

She placed her order at Safeway while preparing chai tea for a customer.

Fifteen minutes later a rap sounded on the door of the cart. Mercifully between customers, she ran back to let Hunter in. He carried a large box filled with two-liter bottles of milk, a six-pack of whipped cream cans and four bottles of juice. She tried to take the box from him, but he held on. "Where does this stuff go?" She pointed to the front.

He ate up the small space in four long strides and placed the box on the counter.

"Snickers Frost!" someone shouted from

the window on the left. Sandy peered out and smiled at an unfamiliar face. "Coming right up!" she said.

Then, without thinking, caught up in the swift and easy solution to what had been a giant hurdle to business just half an hour ago, she wrapped her arms around Hunter's neck and hugged him.

"Thank you, thank you!" she said.

With a gentle hand to the middle of her back, he held her to him for just a moment. "Sure," he said, then retreated a step.

Curiously, in the tight confines of the cart, standing toe-to-toe, her lips inches from his throat, their eyes locked in surprise. She thought she could hear his heartbeat, feel the rhythm of his body's power train—blood flowing, lungs expanding, thoughts humming.

"Snickers Frost!" the voice said again.

Sandy pushed Hunter away and grabbed one of the milk cartons out of the box. She poured some milk into a blender carafe, added something slushy out of a container, a generous dollop of ice cream and snapped the container onto the blender. She turned on the machine, held it in place with a hand on the lid. It whirred for several seconds, then she poured half the contents into a clear cup, put a bubble lid on it, fit the tip of a whipped cream can into the hole in the top and pushed. Cream filled the bubble, and as she removed the can, a tiny dollop popped out of the hole. She inserted a straw and handed the cup out the window. "Four dollars and fifty cents, please."

Hunter heard "Keep the change," and the purr of a motor as the customer left.

Sandy put the money in the register, then poured the rest of the mixture into another cup. "Want cream on it?" she asked Hunter.

He tried to demur. "Oh, thanks, but I'm not much for really sweet…"

She shot cream into it. "Because you've never tried this." She put a straw in it and handed the cup over.

Obligingly, he took a sip—and was instantly converted. The drink was probably diabolically laden with calories, but it was the best thing he'd ever tasted, smooth, sweet and just like a Snickers bar liquefied and frozen. She grinned. "I keep wondering what it would be like with crème de cacao in it."

"Yeah." He sipped again. "We definitely have to try that after hours."

He half expected her to remind him that they

wouldn't be together after hours, but that line of talk would be futile now and she probably knew it. When she'd needed help, she'd called him; when she'd wanted to thank him, she'd used her arms rather than words; and she was now smiling at him as though a barrier was down.

He tried to make himself relax, but his body was rioting. She was still only inches away from him and he could feel the heat of her, smell that complex honeysuckle-coffee fragrance that now defined her for him, and the energy coming from her made him think of photos he'd seen of lightning forking out of the sky in a jagged string of power and the earth reaching up to meet it. A charge moved between Sandy and him that hadn't been there before.

He was going nuts. All this sugar was sending him over the edge. He had to get out of there.

"Thank you. This is incredible." He saluted her with the cup before turning toward the door. "The meeting's at 7:00 in Warrenton. I'll pick you up at 6:30."

He let himself out of the cart, ran down the three portable steps that were pushed up against it and drew the first even breath he'd taken since he'd heard her voice on the phone.

He headed for the Urban Cafe, thinking that he had to get something to eat to temper his mood and all the sugar in his body. They had a beef, cheddar and veggie quesadilla that was to die for.

As he walked in, Nate was walking out with an aromatic paper bag and a coffee cup. "Call Connolly," Nate said as they passed, forced to keep going by a crowd in front of the building. "Wants to talk to you this afternoon."

"Right." He'd forgotten to return Connolly's earlier call. What was wrong with him?

"And your mom phoned."

Just what he needed. "Okay, thanks!"

He called his mother from a table in back while waiting for his lunch. "Hey, Mom. What's up?"

"Well…" She sounded uncertain, unusual for her. "I'm not sure. But something odd."

He pulled in a breath to maintain patience. "What, specifically?"

"I took the girls to daycare this morning. Then I went grocery shopping at Fred Meyer." She hesitated, probably for some assurance that Hunter was listening.

"Yeah?"

"Guess who I saw?"

"Who?"

"Loretta Conway. Hunter, she did not look like a woman who is ill, and she was struggling with a man."

He straightened. "What do you mean, struggling?"

"Well, she was trying to walk one way and he was pulling her another."

"Maybe...she just wanted to go to another department."

"They were arguing."

"Everybody argues. Did she yell for help? I mean, with all the shoppers who had to be in Freddy's, someone would have come to her aid, if that was what she wanted."

"Did you know she was seeing a man? I didn't, and we talk often. Has Sandy ever mentioned that her mother has a man friend?"

Hunter wondered about his mother's concern. "Mom, are you jealous?"

She made a sound like a quashed scream. "I am not jealous! I'm trying to make you see that something's strange. Loretta loves Sandy and the girls, and she wouldn't just abandon them to someone else's care for no good reason. Or lie about being sick. This guy had his arm around her in a sort of death grip. I'm wondering if he's some criminal or something and is hiding out at her place. Honey, please go over there. Take the police."

He put a hand over his eyes and almost matched her quashed scream. "Mom, I'm sure you're imagining this." But she wouldn't allow him a moment's peace unless he did what she asked. "But I'll stop by there."

"You have to go inside."

He ignored that. "I'll let you know what I find out. Meanwhile, try to relax, okay? Sandy's having a rough day. Her stand-up fridge broke down and I picked up some stuff for her. She'll need the girls to be mellow tonight."

"You helped her?" She sounded thrilled. "Oh, Hunter. That was nice."

"It doesn't mean anything, Mom, except that she needed help and called me, and I did what I could as a friend."

"Friendship is a good thing. Don't forget to phone me."

"I won't. Bye, Mom."

Hunter called Nate and told him he had an emergency. Then he went to the counter to tell Casey, the pretty, dark-haired waitress, to pack his lunch to go. He noticed that the soup of the day on the menu board was chicken noodle. If that didn't give him an entrée into a presumably sick woman's home, he wasn't the conniver he thought he was.

Hunter drove toward Astoria's South Slope and Sandy's mother's place. He parked out front and, carton of soup in hand, strode up the walk and knocked on the door. Loretta's white sedan sat in the driveway. It took a moment, but he finally heard footsteps, then the door opened a few inches and he saw Loretta peer out inquiringly.

She smiled in recognition and opened the door just a little more. He glimpsed a tailored red jacket over a white T-shirt and jeans and suede boots. She certainly looked well put together for a woman who was ill. And, he thought wryly, if some man had forced her to go shopping, as his mother suspected, he'd let her apply makeup first.

As far as Hunter knew, Loretta was not romantically involved with anyone. Of course, that didn't mean she couldn't have a relationship she simply didn't talk about. Even to Sandy.

He held up the bag, trying to conceal his concerns. "Hi, Loretta. My mother said she was watching Sandy's girls while you were ill. I thought you might like some chicken soup."

That sounded lame. She appeared to think so, too. "Well...that was nice of you, Hunter." She reached out a hand for the bag. He could hear the television in the background. The sounds of automatic weapon fire and male screams floated in their direction. Okay, that was strange.

He felt obliged to plump out his story, now determined to get inside. Loretta had the same aversion to violent TV programs and movies that Sandy had. He felt sure she wouldn't be watching whatever that was if she was alone. "I was having lunch at the Urban when I talked to Mom, and she suggested I bring you something soothing."

She nodded and cleared her throat. "How nice of the two of you to worry about me." She smiled a bit wistfully. "It's not like we're family anymore. Well, we were never actually family, but you know what I mean. I was hoping."

He smiled at that. Not too sick—or distressed—to be a mom.

"Can I do anything for you? Do you need anything at the drugstore?"

"Thanks, no. We— I," she corrected, "went shopping this morning."

Hmm. We? He had a thought. "Loretta, may

I use your phone, please? I have to call a client." He smiled winningly. "My next stop, and I left my cell at the office."

She was clearly reluctant to let him in. "Well…the house is kind of a mess…"

"I promise not to run anything by the white glove test. It would just help me a lot to use the phone. If that's all right?" He put the onus on her. "Give me a good reason I can't—particularly since you just expressed a wish that we were still 'family.'"

She looked over her shoulder, then back at him. Finally, with obvious reluctance and a suggestion of fear that sharpened his senses, she opened the door wider and let him pass. He went to the breakfast bar where she had the cradle for the cordless phone.

"You've got to get a cell phone," he said, trying to distract her while he dialed the weather and glanced around surreptitiously for signs of another occupant in the house. "It's cheaper than a landline, depending on the program."

She smiled back, looking a little uncomfortable while she put the soup down on the coffee table, picked up the remote and aimed it at the television to silence it. "So I could leave it behind and have to use someone else's landline?" she teased.

"Touché," he said, then pretended to answer the phone. "Hi, Mr. Connolly, it's Hunter. I got your message earlier, but I've been tied up. I was hoping to stop by this afternoon. Does that work for you?" He waited a moment, as though listening to a reply. "Okay, well, I'll come by, and we'll talk. About half an hour? Great. Yes, thank you. Bye." He replaced the receiver, thinking he really did have Actor's Studio potential.

Loretta watched him with a curious, almost amused expression he couldn't quiet interpret. She went into the kitchen to fill the sink with sudsy water, quickly placed dishes in it, but not before he saw two plates and two cups. The kitchen smelled of bacon. Apparently the cold wasn't affecting her appetite.

He went to the sink to thank her, mostly so he could glance out the kitchen window into the yard. Nothing to see there. Unless a man was hiding behind her little garden shed. Hunter had mowed her lawn enough times in the past to know there was no room for anyone *in* the shed.

"Thanks, Loretta. I appreciate it." He lowered his voice and asked, "Are you okay?"

She cleared her throat again and turned to him, wiping her hands on a tea towel. "No, I'm not okay."

His nerves tingled and he prepared to accept her confidence, braced for action.

"I have the a cold," she said.

His bristling senses collapsed. He was convinced something was wrong, but since she refused to confide in him, he was unsure what to do. About ready to grab her by the arm and force her out the door and into his car to get her away from whatever the threat was, he stood frozen in place when the basement door squeaked open suddenly, and a rifle barrel appeared, aimed directly at him.

Adrenaline pumping, he grabbed the barrel and thrust it toward the ceiling. Then he yanked the man who held the rifle into the room.

Brown eyes stared at him in shock and disbelief. "Bristol!" the man roared.

Hunter stared back, then demanded, equally disbelieving, "Mr. Connolly! What are you doing here?"

Loretta sank onto a kitchen chair with a weary but taunting grin. "Good question. Especially since you just talked to him on the phone."

CHAPTER NINE

HUNTER TRIED TO make sense of the scene. The man who was giving Astoria money was staying in Sandy's mother's house. With a rifle? He pulled it out of the man's hand. "Why on earth are you threatening me with a rifle?"

Connolly rubbed a hand down his face and used it to muffle an expletive. "I wasn't threatening you," he denied, exchanging a surprisingly resigned and intimate look with Loretta. Hunter glanced from one to the other in confusion.

Connolly dropped onto a chair beside her at the work island. "I wondered if she still had the rifle my father had given me. She said she thought it was in the basement. I was coming up to show her I'd found it..."

"You may as well get the whole story." Loretta pointed Hunter to the chair at a right angle to her. "Please sit down. But you have to promise to keep what you learn here to yourself."

Confusion made him a little cross. "I'm not promising anything. At least, not yet."

"If you can just listen to us with an open mind."

Connolly sighed. "A *really* open mind."

Hunter regarded Connolly's face and for the first time saw features that were familiar to him—the cocoa color of the eyes, the contentious angle of the chin, a note in the voice that rang clearly, though at a much lower register than the voice it reminded him of.

Oh, no. "You're Sandy's father," Hunter said. He had a bad feeling this was going to mean trouble for him, though he wasn't sure why.

Connolly nodded approvingly. "I am."

Hunter willed himself to relax. "She's a lot like you, though I didn't see it at first. Why on earth are you here without telling her you are?" His voice rose with each word as he posed the question. There would be hell to pay, and somehow he would be right in the middle. "She remembers you leaving with such…" He stopped himself.

Connolly squared his shoulders. "Say it."

"Okay. Pain. She remembers with great pain you leaving her and her mother."

Lowering his head, Connolly groaned. "I

can't believe I let this happen. I staked out the town for a month before I even came to see Loretta. I wanted to make sure she hadn't found someone else. Then, we've been so careful, going out only when we were sure Sandy was at work, trying to stay away from places she frequents. I know. I know. Sheer avoidance, but I needed to talk to her mother first, to see..." He shook his head against whatever was on his mind, as though finding words for it was difficult. He turned toward Hunter as Loretta placed cups of coffee in front of each of them. "So, Sandy's told you about us?"

"Some."

Loretta placed her hand on Connolly's. Well, peace had been made there.

She smiled at Hunter with an expression of apology. "I'm sorry you and your mother were worried."

"You said you were ill," Hunter reminded her. "Then my mother saw you at Freddy's with a man who was trying to pull you one way when you wanted to go another. We thought you wouldn't lie to Sandy lightly."

She drew a deep breath and rolled her eyes. "I realize I'm going to pay for this. But I didn't know what else to do. I should have told Sandy the day Harry came to see me, but she'd just bought the coffee cart. She was up to her neck in learning new things and seriously working herself to a frazzle. Telling her that her father had returned home didn't seem the right thing to do at the time. And our tug-of-war in the store was simply that he wanted to get ice cream, but I didn't want to until just before we were ready to check out."

Everyone looked so strained. Hunter tried to relax the atmosphere. There was a lot he wanted to know. "What brought you home, Mr. Connolly?" he asked.

"Please call me Harry." Connolly grinned at him. "If we're going to be in deep dung together, we may as well be on a first-name basis."

"Yeah. And thanks for putting me there, by the way."

"Sorry. I was a complete jerk all those years ago. Loretta and I were working opposite shifts at the same restaurant, never saw each other, the money we made wasn't covering all the bills. Sandy was growing up and needing things. We had to think about college, but there was never money left for anything extra, much less savings. The pressure was so strong that eventually we couldn't hold a civil conversation." Harry's eyes lost focus as he thought back, apparently seeing his troubled family past in his mind's eye. "I didn't know what to do, so I just left."

"He..." Loretta began, but he covered her hand with his and she stopped.

"I left. It was selfish and thoughtless and I should have been shot for it, but that's what I did. I moved east to Fairhaven, Massachusetts, where I'd lived as a child, and I got a job at a little diner. For a long time, I just got by, then when the owner decided to retire he let me buy it without a down payment. As the owner, I had more freedom to try new things."

"He was always a genius in the kitchen," Loretta put in for him.

"I developed a couple of recipes people came back for over and over. When I took charge of the place, I added some special new things to the menu of old favorites and we did well, even when the economy tanked. But thoughts of Loretta and Sandy began to haunt me. I tried to call a hundred times. When it came down to it, though, I didn't know what to say."

"Hunter..." Loretta tried again to say something, but Harry kept talking.

"I wanted to come home so badly."

"Did you really visit Astoria?" Hunter asked, recalling Connolly's story about being on the cruise ship.

"I did. But that was four years ago. I was going to visit Loretta and Sandy and see if I could do anything to draw us back together as a family." He shook his head in fatal acceptance. "Would you believe that was the weekend Addie was born? I just couldn't burst in on that. So I went back to the boat, bitterly disappointed. The stairway to my cabin was well lit, but I was completely distracted and fell and broke my leg. It's true that people were so kind to me I'll never forget it. The ship left that night while I was in surgery, having my leg pinned. I was in the hospital for a few days, then the nicest woman—her name was Barbara Stapleton—I'll never forget it—was responsible for discharge planning—and she arranged for a ride for me to the airport in an ambulance, got me on a flight with no stops and arranged for me to be picked up at the airport in Boston by a medical van that took me home. I couldn't believe it."

He stopped for a sip of coffee. Hunter was beginning to wish his own had been laced with brandy.

"I cooked on crutches with a very hardworking and supportive staff. My old boss even came back to help until I could take over completely again. So—to help myself forget that I'd failed in my mission, I started working on a dessert recipe Loretta and I had tried together." He squeezed her hand, then put an arm around her, as though unable to be that close without holding her. "Remember the whoopie pie recipe I told you about?" Hunter nodded. "It reminded me of how good things had been in those days—before it all got so…hard. We'd had a problem with finding a way to thicken the cherry juice without making it pasty. I finally solved the problem. Got rave reviews in gourmet magazines and had patrons coming from all over New England to try the dessert." He smiled. "À la mode, the pie was absolutely incredible. So Mrs. Walters's Whoopie Pies eventually approached me about selling the recipe, and when I balked, they offered a price I'd never have imagined in my wildest dreams. I've returned home to share that boon with my family. Or to see if we can be a family again."

Harry's story had exhausted Hunter. He smiled at Loretta, who had a look in her eyes never there in the time he'd known her. She seemed suddenly elevated somehow, as though something had been restored to her.

"It appears a part of your family is back together," Hunter said. "I'm happy for you."

"We needed time to talk." Loretta linked her fingers in Harry's and held tightly. "We had to have time alone together, so I told your mother and Sandy that I was sick. As I said, I couldn't tell her the truth with all she was going through, and at that point we weren't even sure where all the talking would lead us. We had a lot to get over." She turned to Harry with a tortured expression and he gazed at her with such love that Hunter had to look away.

"We've come to terms with each other," Harry said with a big sigh. "Now all we have to do is figure out how to tell Sandy."

Hunter understood their concerns, and though he couldn't claim he understood Sandy, he felt fairly sure she'd be furious to find out that her father was home and no one had told her.

"I'd say, just do it." He sat forward, looking Harry in the eye. "She's a formidable woman. And my guess is that she'll be upset, but she'll come around. I'm sure she'll understand when you explain how you felt."

Harry frowned. "Who could understand a parent just leaving?"

Hunter thought about his own father, who would have died in an instant for his mother or him and would never have left for any reason. But seeing inside someone's heart, understanding what had brought Harry to the point of leaving, was impossible.

"If she understands that you returned to make up for that, to be a grandfather to her children, and the father she missed so much, she'll come around." Now he thought about the hardheaded, single-minded, demanding woman he knew, and prayed that the softhearted angel he sometimes saw in her would hold sway and understand her father's regret.

"So…you know her pretty well?" Harry's question had a new depth. "You…love her?"

Hunter shook his head and bit back a laugh. "Our relationship is complicated."

"Loretta's mentioned a little about it." Harry leaned forward, arms stretched out on the table. "And about you. She told me before I even met you that you've been good for Sandy, that she's been happier since you've been part of her life. Until lately. Your debts have become an issue, haven't they? What if I gave you a small loan to get you out of debt so you two can...?"

Hunter pushed away from the table and stood. "Thanks, Harry. That's very kind of you when you don't really know me, and I appreciate the generosity with which you've made the offer, but I have to do this my way."

Harry stood and offered his hand. "Well, it's gratifying to learn you're as stubborn as she is. Give her a run for her money."

"Yeah. I'm pretty sure she'll find a way to blame me for this."

"She doesn't have to know that you know. And..." he turned to Loretta for confirmation "...we're going to tell her right away."

Loretta agreed.

"I'm glad. Well, I'd better go. And—off the subject—we have that nonprofits list firmed up."

"Perfect. I'm eager to spread my good fortune around. Sure you don't want just a little?" he asked as he opened the door for Hunter.

"Thanks, but I'm fine. You can give that much more to the Women's Resource Center. Where's your Lexus? I didn't see it in the driveway."

"In the garage. I didn't want Sandy to notice

a strange car in her mother's driveway on the chance she drove by."

"Right. Good luck."

"Thanks. To you, too."

Hunter drove back to the office, parked on the side street, and sat there in the silence, thinking through his visit with Sandy's parents.

So much for Loretta having a mysterious affair or a dangerous abductor. Either of those possibilities would have been simpler to deal with than the return of the man who'd abandoned his family all those years ago but now seemed determined to right his wrong.

Hunter called his mother.

"What do you mean you can't tell me what she told you?" she demanded. "You can't keep an affair a secret forever. Did you see *him?*"

"All I can say is that it isn't what you thought it was at all. And it'll be explained soon. Until then, please don't say anything to Sandy about having seen her mother out and about when she's supposed to be sick."

"Because she isn't, is she?"

"No. I can assure you that Loretta is fine and you don't have to worry."

"But, Hunter. You can't even give me a clue about what's going on?"

"No. It's none of our business, Mom. So please honor that. She's fine."

"And you're sure we shouldn't tell Sandy?"

"I'm positive. Sandy's up to her eyeballs right now. Just be quiet about it. Like I said, it'll all be revealed soon."

"Okay. *Revealed.*" She repeated his word, savoring it. "So it is a mystery?"

"Sort of."

"Well, you'd think the woman who discovered it should be let in on it."

"Mom…"

"All right, all right. Will someone call me when it's all *revealed?*"

"I'll let you know myself."

"I'll hold you to that."

"Of course you will."

"Okay, Mom. Love you. I'm going back to the office."

SANDY TOOK THE GIRLS along on the trip to the yarn shop meeting in Warrenton. It was a way to keep her promise to Hunter without risking another moment like the one she'd experienced in the middle of her cart when she'd forgotten that he didn't want her and remembered only how much she'd once wanted him.

She was over that now, of course, but her brain seemed to operate in some kind of loop that always brought her thoughts and her needs back to Hunter.

Zoey and Addie were thrilled to be in his company, and he accepted their presence with a grace she'd always appreciated in him. He welcomed them warmly, helped her put their seats in the back of his car, and popped in the *Lion King* CD he still kept in the console. The music kept the girls happy on the fifteen-minute drive.

He seemed softer, sweeter tonight, not his usually quick-tongued, witty self, eager to plant himself in the path of whatever suggestion she tried to make or point she tried to prove. His gaze turned on her several times during the drive with a compassion he didn't always display. Was he finally beginning to see her point of view?

THE LADIES GOT TOGETHER in the basement of a church that smelled of incense and freshly baked goods. A lace-covered table on one side of the room was laden with several cakes, different kinds of cookies, a fragrant banana bread, a hot pot filled with coffee and a teakettle on a hot plate.

By the time they had been there five minutes Zoey had a cookie in each hand, and Addie had found a toy box in an adjoining room sometimes used for childcare. She had placed a rag doll upside down in the back of a large yellow plastic dump truck she rolled across the tile floor on her hands and knees.

Sandy caught Hunter's eye as the dump truck collided with his ankle. He laughed. In conversation with two white-haired ladies, he swooped down to gather Addie up in his arms. Had Sandy done that, Addie would have kicked in protest, but the little girl settled comfortably against him.

Sandy ran quickly to rescue the toys but was intercepted by a large woman with a long gray braid, who introduced herself as Stella's partner in Toads and Frogs, Glenda Barrows. She put an arm around a pretty teenager beside her with buzz-cut blond hair, jeans with holes in the knee and a red sweater off one shoulder.

"Sandy, this is Belinda, my granddaughter. Blin, this is Sandy Evans, a friend of Hunter's, who is the son of my partner, Stella Bristol."

The girl smiled and offered her hand. "Blin can keep an eye on the girls for you while we have our meeting," Glenda said. "She does this for me during my evening classes. Helps her with her Family Dynamics class."

"If you really don't mind watching the girls, I'm sure it'll make the meeting a lot easier for everyone."

"I don't mind." Belinda went to collect Addie from Hunter, then held a hand out to Zoey, who put one cookie in her mouth so she could take the offered hand. They disappeared into the room with the toys. Hunter followed with the dump truck and the doll doing yoga.

"We're so happy to have Hunter and Sandy with us," Glenda said a few minutes later when they'd begun the meeting. She spoke to thirty or so women, who'd pulled folding chairs into a circle. They made up Glenda's four needlework classes. "They're chairing the Clothes Closet project that we donated many of our class projects to. They've come to say thank you."

Glenda held a hand out to Hunter. He rose, looking uncomfortable, and smiled around the circle with a kind of shyness Sandy had never seen in him. Charmed, the ladies melted with affection.

"I can't tell you," he said with a sincerity that captured everyone's attention, even Sandy's, "how grateful we are to have such a strong and beautiful start to our collection of warm clothing. The hardest part has been resisting the impulse to take that beautiful blanket with the colorful squares for myself."

A small, plump older woman with knitting needles stuck into a white bun at the back of her head blushed while everyone around her patted her on the shoulders.

"Was that your work?" Hunter asked with respect in his voice.

The woman's blush deepened as she nodded.

"Well, it's wonderful. Thank you for donating that to us when there must have been other, more...profitable things you could have done with it."

She offered a shy "You're welcome."

He went on to mention that he was leaving tax deductible receipts that they could fill out themselves according to the IRS accepted remuneration schedule, which he'd brought along because he was an accountant and accountants had to think about those things. The ladies giggled. "Thank you from all those in need in the county and from the hearts of all of us working to ease their way."

Sandy wondered why on earth he'd thought he needed her. The entire gathering was totally impressed and probably already planning to contribute more.

Hunter turned to Sandy. "This is Sandy Evans, who works on almost every fund-raising effort in Clatsop County. You saw that she's a busy mom and runs Crazy for Coffee, the best coffee cart in three states, but she finds opportunities to give her time and effort anyway. Sandy?"

She got to her feet, smiling and wondering what on earth she could say. She couldn't improve upon Hunter's thanks, but she could certainly heap on more gratitude.

She told them how much everyone appreciated the effort and expertise that went into their donations and that everyone was humbled by their generosity. "You sent so many beautiful things. I'd like to invite all of you to come to the opening of our refitted Food Bank and Clothes Closet on the twenty-sixth of July. We'll be sending out formal invitations, but we'd love it particularly if you could come. Thanks so much."

The ladies applauded and Hunter nodded his approval. Then Glenda handed him a check. "This is from all our customers and all of us.

Even in charitable work, a lot has to be paid for, so hopefully, this will help."

The ladies swooned a little when Hunter hugged Glenda.

After they'd socialized and sampled the treats, Sandy and Hunter received hugs and good wishes for the Clothes Closet project and promises to come for the opening.

The two of them and the girls finally left with a foil-wrapped plate filled with goodies and a smaller one specifically for Stella. Sandy left payment for Belinda that Glenda tried to refuse. Sandy insisted she keep it.

"Belinda is nice!" Zoey said on a yawn as they drove home. "We can call her Blin, but we can't call her Belly."

Sandy could see that. She grinned at Hunter as they crossed the Youngs Bay Bridge to Astoria, the pink sunset yielding to darkening skies. A ship coming in over the bar had its lights on and looked majestic as it made its steady progress toward Astoria. "When I was a kid," she said, "they used to call me Creepy Connolly."

He glanced at her in surprise then turned back to the road. "No. I don't believe that."

"Yes. Well, I had this horrible hair. Or sometimes it was Red Rover."

"I get the red because of your hair, but Rover?"

She laughed lightly. "Really? You don't get the obvious rover/dog implication?"

"Oh," he said, realizing he'd misinterpreted the term. "Frankly, my brain went to the Mars Rover rather than a dog's name, so I didn't get the connection. And I still don't. I can't imagine you weren't beautiful even then."

He spoke so sincerely, that she felt a sudden tenderness toward him.

"Well, I had a lot of attitude in those days. My father had left, my mom was in denial, or in hiding, or in some sort of escape fantasy of her own, and I was trying to be the adult and hold things together. I wasn't always very nice to the kids who had normal families and grumbled about their petty problems. Hair that wouldn't curl right, or a measly two-pound weight gain. I've been fighting an extra fifteen pounds since I became a teenager."

HUNTER HADN'T KNOWN that about her. He was aware of a little discord between her and her mother, but there was some between his mother and his sister also. He thought what they all experienced was a natural mother-daughter antagonism. As far as the fifteen pounds she worried about, they seemed to him elegantly distributed.

He focused on the traffic roundabout on the Astoria side of the bridge. He knew it well, but some other driver was always getting confused about which turn to make and ending up in oncoming traffic.

"I'm sorry," he said, glancing in his rearview mirror. Both girls were sound asleep. "That must have been difficult for you. I mean, I knew your father left, but I didn't realize you had to step up for your mother."

"She came around pretty quickly." Sandy sat forward and sighed. "And she's been so much help to me since I bought the coffee cart."

Right. He was reminded of his visit to her mother because of his own mother's fears, and hadn't detected any suggestion in Sandy that she thought her mother might not really be sick.

"How is she?" he pumped gently.

"I call her every day. She doesn't want me to go see her or take her anything because she's afraid the girls or I will get sick, too. She says she's feeling better and might be well by Monday."

"That's good."

She pointed out the window as they passed

Crazy for Coffee. "There's the cart." It was dark except for the neon closed sign and a light over the door at the top of the portable stairs.

"I'm considering stringing lights to outline it," she said, looking over her shoulder as they drove on. "What do you think?"

"Who's going to do it for you?"

"I can do it. Bobbie's going to help me."

"Do you have a ladder that tall?"

He could sense her instinctive impatience. "Hunter, you changed the lightbulb in my garage using my ladder. That ceiling is no taller than my cart. You always manufacture problems."

"I don't manufacture them, but figuring out where problems could appear when you attack a project is only good sense. So, now we know you're prepared."

"I *already* knew I was prepared. You just presume I'm reckless and will forget things."

"Not at all. I was merely trying to help."

She sighed heavily. "I don't want to fight. It's been a lovely evening."

"You don't want to fight? Maybe I should rush you to urgent care."

SHE BACKHANDED HIM in the gut. Oddly, it was a pleasurable experience. He laughed and caught her hand. "Just teasing. And slugging the driver while the vehicle is in motion is not a great idea. I think it's even illegal."

"Then pull over so I can do it without breaking the law."

He surprised himself by easing into a McDonald's parking lot. The front of the lot near the restaurant was parked up, but this end was empty, except for two motorcycles in the slot next to them. He switched off the motor, undid his seat belt and reached down to free hers.

He had no idea what he was doing. He wanted this—he didn't want this. He might not understand himself, but he was clear about one thing: he wanted Sandy, hardheadedness and all. He didn't care about the confusion he felt. He didn't have to comprehend what was going on between them, he just had to have some... contact.

He faced her, the girls still fast asleep in the back.

"Yeah?" he challenged. "So, we're stopped. What was it you wanted to do to me that might get you arrested?"

Her eyes shone in the shadowy interior of the car, wariness visible in them. She was as surprised as he was that he was acting on her playful remark.

"I'll have to keep that to myself," she said softly. "We've finally found a way to be in the same town and not kill each other..."

"That's not entirely accurate. You just punched me in the gut."

"You as much as called me argumentative. You had it coming."

"I think," he replied, the air around them alive with their unresolved issues, which didn't seem to matter right now, "that you just wanted an excuse to touch me."

Something changed in her eyes. The wariness vanished and a sudden bright resolve replaced it. "What if I did? Could you handle more of it?"

"Try it and let's see."

It took her forever to make the move. He'd even begun to think she'd changed her mind, when finally she lifted her hand to his face.

He steeled himself against reacting, as he remembered how her hardheaded determination to have things her way had eroded happy memories of all the times they'd been casually affectionate in the months they'd spent together.

Yet tonight, he was seeing another side to

her. Even that resolve in her eyes seemed not about control. Her thumb ran lightly over his jaw, his chin. Then her index finger explored his bottom lip. The air left his lungs in a rush. She leaned forward to plant a kiss there. Her lips were a millimeter from his, his parted and waiting for her—

"Mommy!" Addie stirred fussily.

Sandy started and put a hand back between the seats to her daughter. "It's okay," she said. "We're almost home."

Her mouth was still just a hairsbreadth from his.

He closed the tiny distance and kissed her soundly, one hand cupping the back of her head to keep her near, the other hand entangled in her silky hair. Her lips were cool and pliant. She moved her hands to his shoulders and held on, as though she needed support. He kissed her again, taking his time, feeling a lively passion in her response.

When she drew back, a small smile played on her lips.

Now Zoey was awake and noticing the McDonald's sign. "I want a strawberry sundae!" she said, her voice clear despite her having just awoken.

Sandy seemed to have to tear her gaze away from him. She turned to tell the girls, "We're on our way home. Hunter just had to stop the car to…check something."

"What?" That was Zoey.

"Something."

"What?" She was a child who liked answers.

"Um…he was checking how much gas he had left."

A lame answer, but Zoey bought it. Addie, however, the car aficionado, pointed to the gas meter. "It's there. Just like on my car."

The smile of a moment ago gone, Sandy looked so unsettled he tried to tease her back to equanimity. "The moment they hit third grade and multiplication tables, I'll teach them to do taxes. They don't miss anything."

Sandy smiled feebly. "Yeah. Well. We'd better go. Calli's going to open for me in the morning so I can get some supplies for the cart. But I still have to be there at six. The coast guard cutter is picking up a big order Calli will never be able to fill by herself and take care of the windows, too."

"Right." He pulled out of the parking lot and wound his way to Fifteenth Street. In the short distance, the girls fell asleep again. Sandy carried in Addie, and Hunter took Zoey. When they got into the house, he did as he had done when he and Sandy were going out: he tossed blankets back, put Zoey in the top bunk in the girls' little room, pulled her shoes off, and covered her. Sandy did the same with Addie. She would change them into bedclothes before she went to bed.

Sandy walked him to the front door.

"Anything I can do for you before I go?" he asked from out on the steps.

She stood in the doorway with that wary look. "No, but thanks for helping with Zoey. She's starting to weigh a ton."

"She's grown an inch or two."

"Two and a half. And Addie's brain is outdistancing her body growth."

"Yeah. She's like a hobbit genius."

Sandy laughed at that, which made him feel a little better about leaving her. He wasn't used to her looking so unsettled.

He was surprised by how much it hurt to have to go. He waved.

She waved back and closed the door.

CHAPTER TEN

OKAY, SANDY THOUGHT, so she was a little short this month to pay all her business and personal bills. So the girls had come home with a letter announcing that the cost of daycare had gone up. No need to panic. She'd lost a lot of product when the stand-up fridge had failed, and the fact that it couldn't be repaired but had to be replaced turned out to be a considerably bigger blow to Crazy for Coffee's economy than she'd anticipated.

She pulled into the Safeway parking lot at just after five o'clock, daylight inching out the early morning darkness. The large colony of sea lions living on the East Mooring Basin docks barked noisily. She sat for a moment to enjoy the dawn and try to ignore the din. She understood the noisy sea lions drove the neighbors crazy, but Sandy related to their insistence on letting the world know they were there.

Concerns about money again intruded into her moment. Though she told herself not to panic, her body was tired and responded with a will of its own. A dark cloud of depression threatened. Even when the breadwinners in her life had abandoned her, she'd always paid her bills. She'd made that deal with their landlord when her father left, and she had a job when her husband walked away. She'd had to budget to the last penny, but she'd made the money stretch.

The cash from refinancing her house had seemed such a fortune. But once she'd bought the business, including the inventory, paid all her first month's bills, met her payroll and attended to her personal bills, she'd had an alarmingly small amount left. Then the fridge had failed, costing her several hundred dollars' worth of product plus the cost of a new one, and that small amount was gone.

And she still hadn't paid for insurance.

She pushed her car door open and stepped out into the wet but delicious morning air. It smelled salty because the Columbia flowed into the ocean just over the Columbia River Bar not too far from where she stood. The fragrance of flowers and pine mingled with that of fish and diesel and salt to make a perfume that was definitively Astoria.

Dark clouds crowded the slash of light on the

horizon. Hard to tell what that would mean for her day. Sometimes rain meant fewer customers, but often hot coffee provided warmth and comfort on a wet day.

Hoping for that scenario, she breathed deeply, shouldered her purse and ran for the market, trying to turn her thoughts around. She had to stop thinking about having too little money, and start planning ways to make enough extra to cover everything.

She caught the handle of a cart from the long lineup in front of the store, pushed inside as the doors parted for her and headed to the cooler in the back. She had a clear path. At this hour, no one seemed to be in the store but her—and the restocking staff.

'Think, think!' she told herself. The traditional cost-cutting measures wouldn't work. She opened the cooler and pulled out a carton of coconut milk for one of her customers who was lactose intolerant, then a carton of almond milk for another who didn't like coconut milk. She smiled at the realization that she could save a little by not catering to every customer's needs and preferences, but she was into their stories now and attached to their struggles.

Kate Loughman was keeping her alcohol demons at bay through teaching an exercise class and running. She was in her early thirties and raising a little boy alone because her husband died in Afghanistan two years ago. She always accepted her raspberry latte with coconut milk with a greedy, grateful look in her eyes.

Brody Benson had lost three rental houses and his job in construction when the economic downturn put his boss and most of his friends out of business. He lived in a friend's basement and delivered two early morning routes for the Oregonian newspaper to earn some income while taking classes in welding at Clatsop Community College. He placed his order with a smile every morning at five forty-five. Sandy could only imagine what that smile cost him and tried to make an absolutely superb double mocha with the almond milk he preferred.

She couldn't operate without either Terri or Calli, though payroll had so many costs she hadn't considered when she went into business. She was just grateful she had only two part-time employees.

Daycare was a killer cost, but the girls were well cared for there and loved the friends they'd made.

She picked up a blueberry Greek yogurt, a

package of Double Stuf Oreos, and a bag of sweet potato chips. Breakfast and lunch.

Think, she told herself again, wandering along the produce aisle, heading for the large tower of bananas. The girls loved them and they were only thirty-nine cents a pound this morning.

She circled the display, looking for the perfect bunch while mulling over her problem, when she collided with someone.

"I'm so sorry!" she said to the back of a man trying to tear a plastic bag off a roll.

He turned to her with a smile of apology—and the world dropped out from under Sandy's feet. She gripped the cart, felt her mouth fall open and a small, startled cry escape her throat. Her surroundings swirled and swung, while a loud rattling sound filled her ears. Then there was silence and the world seemed frozen in place.

For one instant, joy rose in her like a geyser and she wanted to reshape her mouth into a smile and shout, "Dad!"

Then the geyser collapsed as quickly as it had sprung and in its place was the emotional cavern her life had been after her father had left, the struggle to regain her self-worth, the dark months her mother had endured trying to find herself again. And the long, long expanse of time without a word from him.

She wanted to hit him. She wanted to hurl angry words at him. She wanted to scream until they heard her in Outer Mongolia. Unwilling to risk a crack in her slipping self-control by doing any of those things, she simply glanced at her watch and said quietly, "Huh. Sixteen years, three months, and four days. Wow. Long time. Well. Got to run..." She tried to push the cart around him to escape, but he caught her arm.

"Sandy..." There was tenderness in the sound of her name, in the depths of his eyes. That almost made her feel tenderness toward him, and *that* made her furious. She suddenly did all the things she'd thought she shouldn't do.

With an angry, wailing scream she pushed him away with all her strength. He scrambled for balance. And then she let him have it.

"You horrible, *horrible* man!" she shrieked at him, words tumbling through her brain, firing out of her mouth, propelled by years of thinking them and having to hold them back. "Do you have any idea what Mom went through when you left! Do you have any idea what I...what I..." She swallowed in an effort to hold back the sobs crowding the back of her throat.

"I *loved* you," she said, to her horror. That hadn't been in her brain at all. It had to have come from the heart he'd broken. The sobs erupted. "You just walked away as though we were nothing! As though all those years of you being such a good father, and…and…" She had to gasp for air, clutching at her heart. It wasn't failing, just thumping like something gone wild.

He glanced around worriedly, probably wondering if the market had defibrillation paddles on hand.

"Sandy…" He caught her arm again and when she tried to yank away, he dropped it. "Sandy, please. Let's talk…"

"*I am* talking, can't you hear me? What are you *doing* here? Why are you shopping at dawn?"

He looked uncomfortable. She liked that. Otherwise, the part of her brain not occupied with emotional havoc noticed, he seemed to have aged well and with a certain style. His hair was white and nicely groomed, his jeans and blue sweatshirt casually youthful.

"I…ah…" He drew a deep breath, expelled it with an expression of acceptance and dread, and replied, "I've been home for about a month.

And I didn't want to run into you, so I came shopping early."

"You've been home for about a month." Her voice sounded computer-generated.

"Yes."

"And you've been hiding from me."

He sighed. "Yes."

"So. Even when you're in the same town, you don't care that you have a family."

"Sandy…"

"Why are you *here*? If Mom runs into you… She's been sick and this could kill her."

He shifted his weight, folded and unfolded his arms. "Actually, she's been staying with me. I…have a condo on the river."

"What?" The word was loud and shrill in her head, but came out with quiet threat. Sandy caught a glimpse of a young man in a white apron working nearby on a display of water-melons and looking in their direction.

"Can we go somewhere to talk?" her father asked. "Please."

"You want to go somewhere with me?" she shouted at him, aware she was being a complete shrew. But long held *stuff* was surfacing and demanding relief. "Where have you been for the past sixteen years?" She calmed herself and made herself ask in a lower voice, "Why is Mom staying with you. So…she isn't sick?"

He closed his eyes and nodded, as though to himself, apparently accepting participation in a conversation he didn't want to have in the produce section of Safeway. "I've had some good fortune and returned to see if I could…pull our family back together."

He looked into her eyes, searching, she imagined, for some sign she was willing to understand. She gave him nothing. He went on intrepidly.

"I wandered around in Astoria for a while, trying to determine what your situations were. I called your mother first and asked if we could talk. I picked her up and…we've been talking for days. I helped her pack some things and now she's staying with me."

Sandy was feeling that geyser again, but this time it was steamy anger. "Oh, and did both of you forget you had a daughter?"

"I was reluctant to get in touch with you," he said patiently, "until your mother and I had worked things out. She wanted to talk to you, but I kept finding reasons not to."

"And how do you work out abandonment?"

He hunched a shoulder, searching for the

right words. "It can be done. It was done. I was about to come to you..."

"Really?" She pretended gratitude. "How nice. Mom made me think she was sick so she could work things out with you while I try to keep life going like I always do, like you *forced* me to do when you left, until the two of you have the time to let me in on..." She walked around in her agitation, flinging her arms out as she shouted, fury seeming to lengthen her stride, widen her reach. Her hand connected with a pyramid of apples and there was a terrible clatter as it collapsed and apples flew to the floor and rolled all over the aisle.

Sandy threw herself at the display, arms protectively outstretched, in an attempt to save the remaining apples. It was too late.

"Sandy," her father said gently. He moved to push back the apples teetering on the lip of the display. "Let me help you."

"Help me?" she demanded, abandoning her efforts with the apples, and turning to push her father away. More apples fell and rolled. "Help me! Where were you when I really needed your help?" She pushed him farther back as she shouted into his face. "I..."

She was stunned when a strong hand closed

over her arm and pulled her away from her father. She looked up in surprise into the face of a police officer. "Are you all right, sir?" he asked her father solicitously.

Had Sandy simply stood still, it all might have ended there, but hearing the officer ask her father if *he* was all right after what he'd done to *her* was hard to take. She tried to yank out of the officer's grip just to tell him her side of the story. That was when he hauled them both off to the police station.

HUNTER COULDN'T QUITE believe his ears. It was Sandy's voice, but first—he couldn't believe she'd called *him*, and—second—"You're *where*?"

"In jail!" she enunciated, her voice choked and angry. "Well, technically not *in* jail, but at the police station. Please come and get me."

His question was instinctive, though irrelevant at that point: "What did you do?"

"I accidentally dumped a display of apples." She sniffed. "At Safeway. He said I was throwing them at him, but I wasn't."

"Who said that?"

"The police officer."

"Throwing them at who?"

"My father."

Oh, no.

"I'm sorry to bother you, but Bobbie's out of town, I'm not speaking to my mother, and *your* mother has my girls and I don't want them to remember that they picked up their mother at the police station."

"I'll be right there."

Sandy was a sight to behold. She wore her jeans and her Crazy for Coffee T-shirt, and appeared exhausted. Her face was red and puffy from crying, her eyes were a little crazy—like the figure on her shirt—and her hair looked like a red octopus caught in a rubber band. It reached out in all directions and seemed to move. Rain beaded in it contributed to the underwater beast metaphor.

"Hi." He spoke quietly. She reminded him of a clutch of dynamite with a quarter inch of fuse.

"Hi." He put a hand up to smooth her hair and try to pinch off the fuse. Blocking his hand to stop him, she surprised him by catching it and keeping a grip on it in her two.

"Can I go now?" she asked of the tall, fair-haired officer Hunter recognized. Scott Richardson. Hunter did his taxes.

"Sure." Richardson held his office door open.

"Sorry about the trip down here," he told Sandy, "but the 911 call said a wild woman in the produce aisle was throwing apples."

She drew a breath, apparently for patience, and said as though she'd said it several times before, "The apples fell. I was angry, made a wide gesture and my hand hit the pyramid of apples. Why do they pile them up that way, anyhow? It's just begging for disaster."

"Thanks," Hunter said to Richardson, his hand still caught in Sandy's. He led the way to the door. Rain now fell in sheets.

"Where's your father?" he asked before they went outside. "Does he need a ride?"

She gave Hunter a withering look. "My mother's coming for him."

"Sandy..." Feeling as though he should do something to plead her father's case, he started to explain that he'd met him, but gave up when Loretta appeared around the building, holding up the hood of a dark blue rain jacket. She stopped short when she saw Sandy and him. Loretta opened her mouth to speak, but Sandy dropped his hand and covered her ears.

"Please don't, Mom. I don't want to hear it right now." She ran to his car. He tossed her the keys to unlock it and she got inside.

"Thank you for coming for her." Loretta, too, looked as though she'd been crying. "Is Harry all right?"

"I didn't see him, but I think so." Hunter took Loretta's elbow and drew her in the doorway under cover. "I'm not even sure what happened, except that it involves apples."

"Yes. According to Harry, they bumped into each other, and she was furious to discover that he's been here for a month. And that I'd been staying with him. Well, you can imagine."

"I can. I thought you were going to tell her right after we spoke."

"We were, but Harry was scared. And justifiably so, it seems. Will you stay with her today? Bobbie's gone and she doesn't want anything to do with me."

"Don't worry. I'll take care of her."

Giving him a wry smile, Loretta pushed the buzzer that rang at the dispatcher's desk. "Good luck with that," she said to Hunter, then added when the dispatcher answered, "Loretta Conway to pick up Harry Connolly."

"My car's in the Safeway parking lot," Sandy said when he got in behind the wheel. "Please take me there. I have to go to work." She still didn't seem at all like herself, except for the inclination to issue orders, which was probably etched into her DNA.

"No," he said, backing out of the parking spot and turning onto the street. The windshield wipers tried to clear his view. "We'll pick it up tonight."

He felt her face him as he waited to get onto the highway. "I want to have it now."

"Sorry." There was a brief opening in the traffic and he took his chance.

"Hunter!"

"We're going to the beach."

"What? I have to go to work!"

"I phoned the cart and Calli's doing fine. She's quite a kid. She says she can manage. She called Terri in to help her."

"The Coast Guard placed a huge order. The girls can't watch both windows and get extra drinks made!"

"Calli says she can."

"She's sixteen!"

"How old were you when you worked after school and weekends at the hardware store?"

They were passing Safeway and he kept his eyes on the road. It was now almost eight o'clock and the morning rush was on. She made a sound of impatience as the sight of the store disappeared behind them.

"Hunter, I don't have time to go to the beach. And neither do you." She waved a hand impatiently at the rain outside. "And look at the weather!"

"I spoke with Nate before I came for you. I have the day off. And Oregonians don't let the weather prevent them from doing what they want to do."

"Well, aren't you efficient. That's fine when you're organizing *your* day, but this is mine. I have to go to work."

"It's now *our* day. You invited me into it, so it's no longer just yours to organize. Think you can deal with that?"

She let her head fall back against the headrest. "Great. I wish I had dumped the watermelons. I could be doing hard time by now."

"Good," he said. "A sense of humor is good. Just relax. You need a break."

"Hunter, I don't want to spend the day with you."

"Then, why did you call me?"

"I told you. Bobbie's out of town, and I'm not speaking to my mother. And I thought you'd just take me back to my car."

"That's what you get for presuming. Have you had breakfast?"

"No. I picked up some chips and cookies, but...I never got to...check out."

He heard a crack in her voice and glanced at her. Her eyes were wide and hurt and—seldom seen in her—fearful. "I *have* to go to work," she pleaded.

"No," he said, comfortable at taking over. "We're going to breakfast."

"If I don't have something to do..." She caught the shoulder of his sweatshirt. "I...I'll fall apart."

"You're entitled." He removed her hand from his shoulder and brought it to his lips. "You're exhausted, you've been dealt a hard blow, and you're so used to always being in charge that you don't know how to react from just your gut."

She sank wearily against the back of her seat. "I did that today. I was screaming like a madwoman. And there were apples all over the floor of Safeway as a result."

"I'm sure everyone will survive that."

"I hate that I lost it like that."

"He probably expected you to be angry."

"I was *horrible*."

Hunter laughed lightly. "You're often horrible and we're all still here."

She began to cry as he pulled into the almost full parking lot of the Pig 'N Pancake. He parked in the back, turned off the motor and pushed the seat back as far as he could. Then he turned to her and beckoned her to him.

He'd been prepared to have to reach for her, not certain she'd want to cooperate with an offer of comfort, but she flew into his arms despite the cup holders and console. He drew her close, settled her into the tight space, and held her while she wept out the shocking morning.

He rubbed her back and told her quietly that everything would be all right.

She clung to his neck with one arm, and he could feel her other arm wedged between them, her hand in a fist.

"I hate him!" she sobbed. "How can it ever be all right?"

"You hate him now. But I know it's going to be all right because you always find a way to make things happen that don't seem possible at first."

"But…when I saw him…" She stopped to cough and sniff. "All I could think about was…

how good it was to see his face. How much I... used to love him."

"If you can admit that to yourself," he suggested gently, "it's something to build on."

"I can't."

"Then there might be another way to make it work."

"I don't want it to work."

"But...if he and your mom are back together..."

She raised her head off his shoulder, her tear-filled eyes roving his face. "How do you know they're back together?"

He should tell her the truth, that he'd seen and talked to them and had known for a few days that her father was in town, but he couldn't contribute to her considerable pain at the moment, and, selfishly, he didn't want anything to move her soft, pliant body from his.

"You told me your mom was staying with him," he replied easily. "Remember?"

She thought a moment, then dropped her head back to his shoulder. "I can't believe she didn't tell me he was home."

He had to tread carefully here. "I'm guessing she wanted to settle the issue between her and your dad before she could bring you into it."

"Why? It's not like I still live at home."

"You're still their daughter. What happens between them affects you."

She sat up and swiped at her eyes, apparently done with crying over what had happened. "Well, that's for sure. Right now, I could cheerfully disown both of them."

He gave her hip a gentle slap. "Let's go. You need food."

She looked into his eyes, focused on him. "You came when I called you."

"You needed me."

A furrow formed between her eyebrows. "I've needed you all along. But you got so angry about the check..."

"That's because then you just *wanted* me to fit into a plan you'd made for how your life should go. When you phoned me this morning, you were..." He touched a finger just above her breasts in the pink T-shirt. "This woman, needing this man..." He indicated himself with his thumb. "Because you were hurting. I'll always be here for you that way."

SANDY, EMOTIONALLY BEATEN by her encounter with her father, winced as Hunter poured salt on her wounds with his admission that he could offer solace but never love. He was so good at being a friend she kept forgetting that was all he offered. Her emotions had been in hiding before he'd arrived in her life, and his kindness had made her feel safe, made her want more.

Inevitably, though, the reality of his careful distance surfaced to slap her down. It was as though a booming, unseen voice reminded her, *Not for you, Cassandra. Never for you.*

CHAPTER ELEVEN

"I HAVE TO CALL your mother." Sandy had finished a full order of Swedish pancakes with lingonberry butter, and dug in her purse for her cell phone. Food made her functional, if not necessarily better. "She has my girls. I should let her know where I am."

Hunter downed the last of a glass of orange juice. They'd been seated in a quiet corner of the restaurant, but the midmorning coffee break rush was now working toward them, table by table. He pulled out his wallet. "Okay. I'll wait for you at the door."

"Hi, Stella. It's Sandy." She reached for the last few sips of her coffee while Stella exclaimed at the sound of her voice.

"Sandy, I'm so glad you're all right! I heard you'd gone up the river, were in the big house, were getting tattoos on your knuckles!" Stella paused for breath and said more seriously, "Your mom told me what happened. Where are you?"

Why was her mother able to tell everyone else what was happening and bypass her own daughter?

"Hunter picked me up," Sandy replied. "He took me to breakfast, and now insists we're going to the beach."

"Well, you should take the day off. Just try to put all worries aside and…let the ocean renew you."

She tried to imagine what would renew her. There wasn't much.

"Sandy, try to remember that children don't always know what goes on with their parents. Give them some latitude."

She'd like to give them both whatever latitude ran through Abu Dhabi.

"I have a repairman coming at four this afternoon, so I'll pick up the girls and take them to my house. I'll fix dinner for all of us, how would that be? So when the two of you are finished with your day, just drive over to my place and you won't have to do a thing but drink a little wine and eat. The girls will be fine. I bought the new *Planes* movie related to the *Cars* thing. Should be good."

"Thank you, Stella."

"It's what I do. See you tonight."

Sandy put her phone in her purse and walked over to the counter where Hunter was accepting a plastic bag from the clerk. He handed the bag to Sandy as he went to the door and held it open for her. In a small vestibule with a bench and an ATM, Sandy put her purse down and reached into the bag. She pulled out a soft purple hooded sweatshirt with Astoria emblazoned on it in white.

She wanted to scold him for being kind, but that didn't make sense and she was too heartbroken, anyway. "Thank you," she said simply.

"It'll be chilly at the beach." He pointed out the window at the gray clouds. "You've had goose bumps on your arms since I picked you up."

She ripped the tags off the sweatshirt and put her arms inside the sleeves. When she emerged from the neck, he was studying her.

The man she was dealing with today was a little different from the Hunter she knew. This one had taken charge. That rankled a little until she considered what it could mean. She thought his feelings went deeper than even he realized. A friend indulged. A lover protected.

SEASIDE WAS AN old community that had had a funky carnival atmosphere just a few years ago.

The main street had been lined with souvenir shops, vendors of elephant ear pastries, curly fries and slushies. There had been arcades with air rifles and scores of games to keep a child busy for an entire day. She remembered spending Saturdays here with Charlie, enjoying the beach and the arcades.

Seaside's popularity as the Northwest's beachfront vacation spot eventually brought high-rise hotels that made the main street feel like a canyon. More elegant restaurants now replaced the vendors, and the souvenir shops had given way to boutiques and antiques stores. The world's largest amateur volleyball tournament was held here, and other events brought visitors from all over the Northwest.

Sandy supposed it was all a natural evolution of commerce, but she missed the Coney Island atmosphere she'd once enjoyed.

Hunter parked in a commercial lot behind the main street. The rain had stopped, but the sky was the same gunmetal gray as the ocean, and the air was cool. He locked the car and came around to take her hand. "You feel warm enough? Should we buy you a jacket?"

"Thanks, but I'm fine." She forced herself

to surface from the day's tensions. "Where are we going?"

"To walk along the Promenade. Check out the arcades. Drive the cars. Ride the Tilt-A-Whirl. But maybe save that until breakfast is digested." He squeezed the hand he held. "I know it isn't going to make you feel better, but it'll give you something else to think about until your brain and your body restore themselves and you can plot a course of action." He pointed toward the busy street. "What'll we do first?"

"The arcade? I used to be great at Whac-a-Mole."

"Good. Let's go."

The arcade was cavernous, with various games all over the space. Despite the weather, Seaside was filled with tourists enjoying the silly diversions. It was noisy and wildly kinetic, children running and jumping and shouting to one another, while parents abandoned all effort at control and simply stood back to watch. Hunter went to a cage at the back to buy the tickets that allowed play.

He handed her the Whac-a-Mole mallet. The game consisted of a series of holes through which "moles" popped up to challenge the player to strike them with the mallet and make them disappear, only to pop up again somewhere else. Sandy took the mallet in hand and waited for the first mole.

HUNTER WATCHED SANDY dispatch mole after mole with impressive skill and a serious expression. She had taken her hair down and combed it before going into the restaurant, and it now gleamed like red silk under the overhead fluorescent lights. It fell over her face as she whacked, and she tossed it back, taking a breath and aiming again.

He knew things weren't so simple, but he guessed she was working out the morning's demons as she struck at the evasive moles with power and vengeance in a way real civilized life didn't allow.

When the game was over, she played a second time. After that, she handed the mallet to a boy waiting behind her, dusted off her hands and turned to Hunter with a smile. He handed her the purse she'd asked him to hold and moved on to the air rifles.

"I supposed you're a good shot," she said, putting her purse down between her feet. "Having been in Iraq and all."

"Well, I got the training," he said, handing

the attendant their tickets and picking up a rifle. "But, I rode a desk for 18 months, so I haven't had a lot of experience firing a gun. And an M4 carbine is a lot different from this."

"No hunting experience?"

"No. You?"

"No. So we're on a level playing field. A sort of 'primal man against woman' thing." She challenged him with a sideways glance. "Let's see whether you're really better equipped to kill a mastodon than I would have been."

"That's not really a level field. You could have argued it to death."

She tried to turn her rifle on him, but the air hose wasn't long enough to allow it. "Wisenheimer. Let's see what you've got."

He raised the rifle to his shoulder, aimed and did a credible job of eliminating ducks, geese and many of the other critters that followed them across the target. He hit about seventy-five percent.

"All right! Not bad." Sandy applauded him while he took a bow.

"I believe that would have felled a mastodon," he said.

She raised an eyebrow to take issue with his statement. "A quarter of your shots missed."

He shrugged that off. "Well, yeah, but a mastodon is a bigger target than a duck. The shots that missed the duck would have probably hit the mastodon."

"Hmm." She sounded doubtful.

He leaned closer to watch her shoot. She lowered the rifle and turned to push him several feet back. "Don't want you to get messy," she said with a superior, playful tilt of her chin. "You know, mastodon blood-spatter and all."

Rolling his eyes, he suggested, "Maybe we should make a wager before you begin."

She frowned. "I had to pay for a cab to pick up milk and deliver it to the coffee cart while I languished in jail."

"Such drama. Okay, not a money wager." The thin, bewhiskered man behind the counter now leaned his elbows on it and watched them with interest.

"What, then?"

"You choose." He waggled his eyebrows. "You know what you can afford to lose."

"Big talk," she said. "All right, I want a kiss. Not a peck on the cheek, or a friendly buss on the lips. A kiss. A real, serious, kiss."

So. High stakes. She was deliberately challenging his resistance to a long-term relationship. "How does the wager work, exactly?"

"If I win," she said, "I get a kiss. A real kiss. If you win, you can have whatever you want."

All right. He had this sewn up. He shook her hand.

She shouldered the rifle, the target began to move and she veritably air-slaughtered everything that moved past her line of sight. When the targets came again, she got them again. Hunter listened in amazement as the dinging that indicated a hit filled the air with continuous sound, and she racked up a perfect score.

The man behind the counter bowed to her as she replaced the rifle, and gave Hunter an envious look. She told him to hand her prize to the boys standing behind her. Then she turned to Hunter with a straight face.

"I don't think I've told you about my three years in the Rifle Club at Portland State." She hooked her arm in his and walked him out onto the sidewalk.

"The Rifle...?"

She waved a hand dismissively. "I guess it never came up."

"And you forgot to mention it just now when we were discussing our experience with guns?"

"Oh, that would have sounded like bragging, and you know how reticent I am about..."

"Yeah. Reticent."

The rain had abated, though a mist hung in the air. It felt as though they were trapped in a cloud.

She faced him and smiled guilelessly. "Don't worry. It doesn't commit you to anything because I know we're done as far as lifelong love and all that, but...I want this kiss. Someday, when you change your mind and get married to someone else and the girls are living their own lives and I'm still putting on fund-raisers, I'd like to remember what it was like."

He glanced about. They had stopped in the middle of the sidewalk, and tourists and locals hurried around them, giving them smiles or raised eyebrows.

"You're okay with right here?"

"I am." Her eyes brimmed with challenge. He guessed she wanted him to see what he was missing. He put a hand gently around her waist, prepared to withstand all she had to offer. "Anytime you're ready," he said, the notion that this might not be his brightest moment registering as her lips reached up for his.

SANDY DIDN'T UNDERSTAND why she was suddenly afraid—not of him, but of kissing him. She wanted the touch of his lips against hers so much—probably because she knew she couldn't have it on a permanent basis. But she had the most unsettling feeling that having it now would make that loss even more difficult to bear.

His hand at the small of her back applied the slightest pressure. His head came down as she reached up so that their mouths almost touched, then he stopped, a sudden look of concern in his eyes.

She realized that he saw her confusion and wasn't sure what to make of it since she'd asked for the kiss.

He allowed her a moment to withdraw.

She wrapped both arms around his neck instead.

She kissed him with all the passion she felt for him. Always hopeful, she pressed the kiss while he resisted, and was about to give up, when he responded with a passion that equaled her own and exposed all the tenderness she knew him to have. For a moment, she forgot where they were, even who she was. The kiss had so much promise of love and longing that she no longer felt like the woman every man in her life walked away from. She was a full partner in a special moment that opened the future and promised forever.

HUNTER FORGOT HIMSELF and gave her everything inside him to try to make the point that it wasn't simple stinginess keeping them apart. He kissed her as though he were free of burdens, and in doing so, opened himself up to letting her feel how much he longed for her every day.

She kissed him back. That frightened look in her eyes when he took her in his arms had worried him enough to make him pause. But then she'd shaken it off, risen on her toes and looped her arms around him, waiting for the kiss.

He felt her silky hair under his hand, her soft, cool lips impressing themselves on his, one of her hands in his hair raising goose flesh on his scalp, the other flattened against his back, holding him to her as though she were afraid he'd get away.

There was some new fascination to having her wrapped around him. In the past, they'd always had her children with them, or their dates had involved shopping or errands. The moments together had seldom been just about them.

This time, he was just a man burdened with money issues he refused to share.

That honesty seemed to be making him over. His cautions were slipping away, and his arms were too full of her to catch them.

She finally freed his lips and, her arms still wrapped around him, held him with a desperation that made him want to reassure her. "You're going to be all right," he told her for the second time that day.

She nodded against him and expelled a little sigh. "Yeah," she whispered.

Dropping her hands from him, she caught one of his arms and leaned her head against his shoulder. When she looked at him again, there was something different about her that had nothing to do with what had happened with her parents.

She seemed curiously whole, not the needy young woman who searched for love with such urgency. Weirdly, he felt as though he'd lost something.

Sure he had. His head. Or was it his heart?

She pointed across the street. "Can we get some curly fries for lunch and sit on the beach?" She pointed at the sky, at a frail sun peeking out. "I think the rain's over."

"Sure."

He got a large order, loaded their take-out bag with ketchup packets and napkins and bought two cups of coffee.

"I have a blanket in the car," he said. Hand in hand, they walked back to the parking lot, retrieved a ratty red blanket from the trunk, then continued down to the Promenade.

They walked for a quarter of a mile past the summer homes that dated back most of a century, then took a broken-down stone stairway to the sand. Hunter spread the blanket in front of the low stone wall. There were tourists all over the beach, but most of them were down at the water's edge.

Sandy tore the paper bag down the middle, then opened several ketchup packets and squeezed their contents onto a corner of the bag.

"I love these," she said with enthusiasm. They sat side by side on the blanket, leaning against the stone wall. "I don't know what it is about the shape that makes them taste different from plain old French fries, but they do."

"They probably don't taste any different. You just relate to the curled, convoluted nature of the curly fry."

She bumped him with her shoulder. "You mean I'm twisted?"

"I was trying to put it nicely."

She ate quietly for a few minutes, then took a sip of her coffee and made a face.

"This is terrible," she said. "But it's so strong, it'll wake you right up."

He grinned at her. "The kiss already did that for me."

She smiled into his eyes. "Yeah. We'd be good together if there wasn't so much in the way."

He sipped from his cup. It *was* terrible, but it did get the blood flowing—probably in an attempt to get away from the coffee. "Someday, if you're still available..."

"Oh, I'll be a mistress of industry by then." She spoke airily, the intensity that was so her gone since the kiss. "Or, at least, the owner of a coffee cart chain. My mother says..." She stopped suddenly, apparently having forgotten, then remembering, that she was mad at her mother.

"She says what?" he prodded.

"That I'll own ten carts in no time." She twisted the bottom of her cup into the sand so the cup wouldn't fall over, and put another curly fry in her mouth. "But I don't want to talk about her. Her faith in me is misplaced, anyway. I couldn't meet all the bills this month, and I've been racking my brain for a plan to plump up income."

"The fridge set you back?"

"Yes." She crossed her ankles on the blanket and brushed hair out of her face as the ocean air gusted around them. "Daycare went up, business maintenance is costly, having employees is expensive, though very necessary. I hope they're doing okay today."

"Don't worry about that. Calli promised she'd get through the day and I believed her."

"I'm sure she will. She and Terri don't always get along, though. Different personalities. Working with someone you can't relate to is hard."

"People do it all the time. You're running a business, not raising a family—at least, not in the coffee cart."

"They're good employees." She was silent a moment, then said, "Addie loves her car."

"I knew she would."

"Your mom bought the new *Planes* movie

for the girls." She turned to him and said with mock seriousness, "Promise me you won't ever buy Addie a plane."

"I promise," he replied in the same tone.

She edged her hand under his to pinch his fingers. "You should get married someday. You'd be a good father."

He kept watching the horizon so she wouldn't see in his eyes that he'd known *her* father was home. "Seems to be a tougher job than it appears."

"Yeah. I guess the hardest part is staying when things go bad. Mine wasn't able to." She drew her hand away and ate curly fries until they were gone. She put a hand to her stomach and groaned.

"Time for an antacid?" he asked, leaning forward to peer into her face. "You look a little green."

She ignored his question as she watched the gray clouds moving along, uncovering small patches of blue sky, then covering them up again. "My mother lied to me," she said in an unimpassioned voice, "and my father hid from me. I apologize for belaboring the point, but..."

ouch, you know…I can't get over being angry. I mean, really angry."

She did look green, but he figured he'd have to help her with her emotional trauma before she could deal with anything else. "I don't think either of them meant to hurt you, Sandy. You have to get over being angry long enough to imagine their motives in keeping their secrets."

"Well, whatever his motives are now, he just left us. And he stayed away. The motive behind that has to be selfishness."

Maybe it was, but Harry Connolly didn't appear to be the selfish type. Unless life had changed him since he'd left his wife and daughter. "You'll have to ask him that, I guess. The best thing you can do about all this is talk it out. He seems to want to make things up to you now."

She turned to him, that suspicion from earlier this morning in her eyes. "How do you know?"

He resorted to this morning's easy shrug. "Why else would he be back? He had to know you and your mom would be furious with him, that he'd have to deal with a lot of angry accusations."

"And my mother. No wonder she didn't want

me to come by with food when I thought she was sick. She wasn't there. She was with him."

"They probably hoped to talk things out, or see if they could *work* things out, before getting you involved."

He had to stop offering opinions. She gave him that look again. It was a little stronger this time.

The shrug covered a multitude of half truths. "Well, doesn't that sound logical? If she told you he was back, but then they couldn't solve their problems, wouldn't you have been disappointed? Possibly a little heartbroken?"

She mulled that over, gave him one more suspicious glance, then settled back against the wall. "I guess. I just don't understand why you're on their side."

"Sandy, I'm on *your* side. And talking to them, figuring out what made your mother lie and your father hide, is the only thing that will resolve this for you. It might even explain the past."

She folded her arms and closed her eyes. "I hate it when you become the logical accountant."

"Sorry. I'll be quiet."

"Hunter?"

"Yeah?"

"I'm going to be sick."

CHAPTER TWELVE

"I'M MORTIFIED!" Sandy said to Hunter as she paid for toothpaste and a toothbrush at a Seaside drugstore.

"Relax. I belonged to a fraternity in college. I've seen lots of people throw up. And you had the grace to do it in a bag-lined trash can."

"It was as far as I could get." She'd made a mad dash for the Promenade, intending to run for the restrooms, then realized they were too far away, and settled for a nearby trash can instead. Afterward, Hunter had wrapped an arm around her for support to get her to the drugstore on the main street.

She took the bag with the items she'd just bought. "Well, that killed whatever mystery there might have been in our relationship."

"As a rule, you don't have a lot of secrets or private thoughts." He opened the door for her and patted her shoulder consolingly as she passed through. "Whatever's on your mind is pretty much out there. So, don't worry about it. Nothing lost."

Sandy excused herself to use the public restrooms in the parking area.

Nothing lost because it didn't really matter, she wondered, brushing her teeth? Or nothing lost because it *did* matter and he accepted her as she was?

She was too tired and felt too conflicted to give the question a lot of thought.

"Your mom was making dinner for us," she said to Hunter as he led her to the car. "I'm not sure I can eat anything."

"No doubt because of all those curly fries on top of that full order of Swedish pancakes. And the shock of this morning probably upset your whole system." He checked his watch. "We've got a couple of hours until dinnertime. We'll go to my place. You can relax on the sofa and enjoy some peace and quiet before meeting up with my mom and your girls. If you don't feel like eating anything, you can just tell her that, and I'll take you to Safeway to pick up your car, then make sure you get home."

She'd felt a strange sort of clarity since that kiss this morning. He didn't want to push her away any more than she wanted to be pushed.

He cared. She'd stake everything she had on it. Their relationship wasn't dead after all. That kiss had held serious affection, and he hadn't hesitated to come to her aid. He'd done it in friendship, true, but didn't he realize that friendship was an important part of love? Didn't someone quotable say love was friendship that had caught fire? Certainly, something could be built on that. Did that mean she was learning patience? "You're a good friend," she said.

When they reached his apartment, he encouraged her to lie down on the sofa, covered her with a blanket, and that was all she knew until she awoke with him leaning over her. His eyes showed indulgence. "You slept like a rock. Feel better?"

The sweetness about him stole her breath and made her heart beat a little faster.

She sat up to assess how her stomach felt. Still delicate, but considerably better. "I'm fine," she said with some surprise. "Are you okay? I got you moving kind of early this morning."

"I'm good." He glanced at his watch. "It's almost six. You go freshen up and I'll call Mom and tell her we're on our way."

Zoey and Addie were happy to see her, and

Sandy held them a bit longer than necessary, delighted that something in her life was familiar and steady.

The girls were thrilled to see Hunter, and hung on him as he wandered around the kitchen, helping his mother get dinner on the table. Stella had prepared a chicken casserole with rice and vegetables, which would likely be easy on her stomach.

"I'm so grateful for your help this week," Sandy said to Stella as she carried a basket of rolls to the table. "I couldn't have managed without you."

"I was happy to help. It's lovely to have children around."

"We saw *Planes*!" Addie said, bored with the adults' conversation. "And we made thumb cookies!" Addie help up her thumb as though she were hitchhiking. "I made the holes."

"Thumb*print* cookies," Zoey corrected knowledgeably. "Her thumb isn't very big, so Stella had to make bigger holes."

"We put strawberry jam in them!"

Hunter got up to investigate the cookie jar.

"They're on a plate on the counter," Stella said. "You want to dish up ice cream and bring the cookies? Use those green glass pedestal cups."

"Right. You girls want to help me?"

The girls ran to do his bidding.

"So, are you doing okay?" Stella asked, pushing her plate aside and leaning toward Sandy. "Hunter called me once today just to report in and he said you'd gotten sick."

Sandy shrugged off the episode. "I ate too much. Swedish pancakes and curly fries. Not a great combination."

"Yes. I eat when I'm upset, too. But usually pretzels and chili."

"Together?"

"For sure. They're delicious. Better than crackers or corn chips. Sometimes when life beats you up and takes away all your choices, it's fun to at least be able to decide what you want to eat."

A quiet moment followed, then Stella said in a rush, "Your mom's upset at the way things happened."

Sandy knew her mother and Stella were in touch all the time, but Sandy didn't want to talk about this with Stella—or with anyone. She nodded politely. "I imagine she is."

"She thought she was doing the right thing."

How could lying to her own daughter be the right thing? But Sandy kept that question to herself.

Zoey brought her a pretty cut-glass cup of vanilla ice cream with one of the cookies they'd made tucked into the side.

"Thank you, Zo."

"You're welcome." Zoey skipped back to the kitchen.

"And your father…well, obviously I don't know what happened, but Hunter thought he seemed like a good man. And he wants to do so much for Ast—"

Hunter thought he seemed like a good man. Something in those words wasn't right, but it took Sandy a few seconds to realize what it was. Then it hit her like a sledgehammer: Hunter had *met* her father?

Sandy felt all the strength the day had given her evaporate.

Stella stopped talking as she looked into Sandy's face. Sandy heard her own gasp and turned toward Hunter, who was still in the kitchen. She saw him looking at the table, before he closed his eyes in grim acceptance of his mother's slip.

"Hunter," Sandy said to Stella, forcing her voice to remain calm, "has met my father?"

"Well...your father...went to his...office." Stella appeared to realize she'd said something she shouldn't have.

Hunter walked out of the kitchen, his expression defensivc. "Sandy, don't get all upset." He held up both hands in a calming gesture. Zoey and Addie stood off to the side, sensing trouble.

Sandy stood, demanding quietly, "How do you know my father?"

"He came to the office to do business," he replied. "He's our mystery money man."

"What?"

"Yeah. It's a long story, one I'm sure he'll want to share with you."

She folded her arms, as though that would help her hold herself together. "You'd think so, wouldn't you? But, no. So, you knew my father was in Astoria and you didn't tell me?"

"I didn't know he was your father. His name was Connolly, your mother's name is Conway. She said she went back to her maiden name after he left. There was no reason for me to know. And he wanted his charity kept anonymous."

HUNTER THOUGHT THAT explanation almost put him in the clear. Sandy was measuring his honesty against what she knew. Then his mother added, intending to help, "Hunter didn't know until I sent him to your mother's to..." She stopped abruptly, realizing again when they both stared at her that she shouldn't have spoken. She gave Hunter a regretful look then dropped her face in her hands.

"You went to my mother's?" Sandy queried him, her tone cold and stiff. Her girls came over to her, sensing her distress.

"Mommy?" Zoey said. Sandy put a hand on each little girl's head and pulled her daughters close. "It's all right," she reassured them.

Hunter went for broke. "Mom saw your mother at Freddy's, and was a little worried about the man with her. She seemed to want to go one way and he another. Mom thought she might be with him against her will or something. She asked me to check."

He hoped that would pacify Sandy somewhat, but she simply regarded him darkly, waiting for him to continue.

"I was surprised to find Harris Connolly at your mother's, the man I knew as Astoria's benefactor. He was helping your mother pack. The rest—what's gone on with him since he left and why he's here, *he* should tell you."

"Really. So far, I'm the only one who knows nothing about him."

"Sandy…"

"And just when did you visit my mother?"

He tried to free his reply of all guilt, certain he didn't deserve it. "A couple of days ago." But he still felt guilty, and he knew she'd painted him all over with it, anyway.

She shot him one final, painful look that screamed betrayal, shouldered her purse, caught each girl by the hand and said stiffly to his mother, "Thank you for the lovely dinner, Stella."

"Sandy…" his mother tried to plead, but Sandy was already on her way to the door.

"You don't have a car," Hunter reminded her as he followed her.

She stopped, remembering, and leaned her forehead against the open door.

"Mommy," Addie whined, pointing to the kitchen. "We didn't get ice cream!"

Zoey, realizing something was amiss, shushed her little sister.

Hunter turned to his mother, who still appeared horrified over what her innocent remark had brought about. He gave her a quick hug.

"It's all right. You take her to her car, and I'll clean up while you're gone."

"I'm so sorry," she whispered, then grabbed her purse and hurried to follow Sandy out the door.

Sandy sat in the passenger seat, the girls in back in their car seats. Her teeth were clenched so tightly her jaw hurt.

Addie had begun to cry, upset about missing her ice cream and the cookies they'd made. Zoey was unusually silent.

Stella drove over the hill to Sandy's side of town and Safeway, missing a stop sign in her agitation and braking to a halt that would have sent them all flying forward had they not been wearing seat belts.

"Sorry," she said. "I'm sorry."

"It's okay, Stella. *I'm* sorry it's been such an awful evening."

After an eternity, they reached the Safeway parking lot. Early evening shoppers were everywhere. Sandy pointed to the spot near the carts where she'd left her VW.

Stella pulled in beside it and climbed out to help Sandy transfer the girls into the back of the Beetle.

Sandy thanked Stella for the ride home.

"Do you want me back in the morning?" Stella asked in concern.

"Stella, I know none of this is your fault. I'm not blaming you for anything. If you're available tomorrow, I'd be grateful."

Patting her hand, Stella said gently, "It isn't Hunter's fault, either, you know. I sent him to your mother's, and he said nothing because he was asked not to." Sandy opened her mouth to object, but Stella went on. "Yes, you're his dear friend, but he was in an unwinnable position."

Sandy opened the driver's side door, then smiled weakly at Stella, deliberately ignoring all she'd said. "Thanks for dinner and for the ride."

"Of course." Stella seemed to sink several inches. "See you in the morning."

Twenty minutes later, Sandy sat the girls at the kitchen table with bowls of ice cream and store-bought chocolate chip cookies. Addie was not happy, wanting the cookies she'd helped make, but when she tried to complain, Zoey gave her her cookie, too, and told her to be quiet.

Sandy felt as though she was trapped head to toe in a tar pit.

Hunter had lied. Hunter, who came to rescue her from the police station, overrode all her plans to go to work and took her away for a day, who played games with her at the arcade, then kissed her as though he wanted her desperately.

She poured herself a small glass of Moscato and drank it down. So, he lied. Their time at the beach today had been wonderful, despite how her day had begun, but he'd made it clear he had plans that didn't include her, and she didn't have time for him, anyway. She had to build a business.

Alone.

She went into the living room, out of sight of the girls, and sank into a chair, letting the tears fall. Hurt, betrayal and a simple anger came out in a little scream. She covered her mouth with both hands to stifle it.

Suddenly, a small, soft arm stole around her neck. It was Zoey. She held a box of juice in her free hand. "Drink this, Mommy," she said, in the comforting tone Sandy often used with the girls. "You'll feel better." Then she touched the box with her wand, a gesture that was uniquely her.

Sandy wrapped an arm around her and drew her close. She smelled of strawberry shampoo.

"Thank you, sweetie." She took the juice, straw already inserted in the box. Zoey knew Sandy always had trouble with it. Sandy had a sip. Icky sweet but somewhat restoring liquid trickled down her throat and into her stomach.

"Why are you and Hunter mad at each other, Mommy?" Zoey wanted to know.

Sandy struggled to simplify. "Oh…sometimes adults have trouble understanding one another."

"When Addie and I don't understand each other, you say we have to love each other anyway."

Sandy kissed the top of Zoey's head. "That works for little sisters, Zo, but not always for big people."

A rap on the front door interrupted Zoey's questions. Sandy hugged her again and pushed her back toward the kitchen. "Thank you for the juice, sweetie. I feel better already."

She went to the door, praying that it wasn't Hunter. Or her father. Or her mother. Considering all the people she *didn't* want to see, the odds were against her that the visitor would be welcome.

It was Hunter.

HUNTER SAW THE HURT and betrayal in Sandy's eyes and refused to let himself wince. Maybe he should have told her about her father, but it wasn't his place. And Harry and Loretta had said they were going to talk to her right away. No, it wasn't his fault.

Sandy looked as though she'd been crying. He steeled himself against feeling sympathy, determined to say what he'd come to say.

She stood in the doorway, her arms folded across her chest defensively. "I have nothing to discuss with you."

"Good. Then just listen!"

She gazed off as if she couldn't be more uninterested. He caught the front of her sweatshirt and yanked her to him to assure himself of her attention. Their faces millimeters apart, she was apparently too stunned to struggle.

"You've somehow convinced yourself we're all against you," he said. "I did not deliberately hurt you. What happened was an accidental order of events. I learn through no fault of my own that your father is back and I don't tell you because it isn't my place, and I'm out of the picture. Your father comes home to try to put his family back together, and without allowing him a chance to talk, you put him out of the picture. How many people are you going to throw out of your life? And how many times? You might give that some thought before I *do* marry someone else, your girls *do* live their own lives and all you *have* is your ten-chain coffee cart."

He lowered his head. "And think about this while you're at it." He kissed her hotly, angrily. His lingering mouth drew out her bottom lip when he finally did break the kiss, and left her mouth in a pout as he turned and loped down the steps to his car.

He wasn't sure what the point of that kiss was. He'd just wanted it.

SANDY BEGAN THE following day as she'd started all the others since she'd become owner of Crazy for Coffee. In her pink T-shirt, she hugged Stella goodbye, drove to work while mulling over plans for the Clothes Closet opening, climbed the steps and let herself into the cart, aromatic with coffee and all the wonderful flavors of syrup that lined the walls. She made sure everything was ready, then turned on her espresso and open signs, and greeted Dave with a smile.

Business was brisk. She hurried from window to window for an hour, until Calli arrived, followed by Terri. Sandy looked at the clock, then at her schedule. "You're an hour early," she said to Calli, then added to Terri, "and you're not scheduled at all."

Calli nodded. "Yeah. Terri and I are giving you a free day."

"A free day? I was off all day yesterday." And she couldn't afford to pay them for more days.

"Yeah." Calli waggled her eyebrows. "You were busted. We know all about it. My mom's a good friend of Stella's and they think you need another day off. And the free day means Terri and I are working for free. Just to be nice. 'Cause, you know, you're a good boss. So, go."

"No, Calli. You did yesterday morning all by yourself, and I…"

The door opened and Sandy paused in her argument as her father walked into the cart. Followed by her mother. All coherent thought fled and all she could do was feel. The small space inside the cart amplified her anger, but then she took a second look at their faces and her anger dissolved into something complex she couldn't identify.

"Please, Cassandra," her mother said softly. "We have so much to say to one another."

Her mother looked brighter, somehow, and Sandy thought she caught a glimpse of the woman Loretta had been before Sandy's father left.

Sandy didn't want to talk, but knew they had to. "Calli," she said. "Are you sure you'll be okay today? Terri?"

"Positive."

"Absolutely."

Calli's mother was a good friend of Stella's. Sandy detected collusion in the way this day was progressing, but she had to deal with it.

"Fine." Sandy reached for her purse.

Sandy hugged her staff and followed her parents out. The three stood apart on the pavement.

"Where shall we go?" Loretta asked.

"My place," Harry said with a reluctant smile. "I have a feeling there'll be a lot of yelling. Come on, Sandy. You're riding with us."

Loretta pointed to Sandy's car. "But she has her…"

Harry nodded. "But she might decide on the way over to do something else today." He opened the rear door of a silver Lexus and gestured her in. It reminded her of the old days when she rode in the back of her parents' car on shopping trips and other drives. Though their car then hadn't been this elegant.

She climbed in, admiring the red leather upholstery and the French stitching. She guessed her father was no longer a sous chef in some little restaurant. Of course. Hunter had said he was the mystery money man. If nothing else, hearing how that had come about would be interesting.

In ten minutes, Sandy was climbing out of the car and following her parents into the lower level of a structure that leaned out over the river and housed her father's condo. They stepped into an elevator and rode up several floors. She felt a stab of memory, of the time before everything had gone bad. She'd just turned thirteen and they'd spent all day celebrating her birthday.

They'd gone to breakfast, then to buy her a new outfit for school, and after a picnic of burgers and shakes at the park, they'd gone to the movies to see *You've Got Mail*.

They'd trooped into the house after driving home, Sandy carrying her leftover popcorn. Her mother was telling her about the New England boiled dinner she'd made, Sandy's favorite meal, and the chocolate birthday cake with sour cream frosting.

Though she hadn't thought about that day in years, Sandy remembered her happiness then, the pleasure she'd felt in their simple, happy lives. A year later, everything would be different.

Her throat constricted and tears scratched the backs of her eyes. Emotion billowed inside her, taking her completely by surprise. How feelings of love and sadness could overtake her when she should have a head of angry steam going was mystifying.

Her father unlocked the door and stood aside to let her and her mother go in. The place was elegantly simple, with a view of the river immediately visible from the door. Her mother turned left into a moderately sized kitchen. Sandy glimpsed granite counters and pine cabinets.

Sandy's father, walking in behind her, pushed her gently toward a square living room in subtle shades of brown and cream, with a brick-trimmed fireplace on one wall, neutral Berber carpets and sliding doors leading out to a small patio. The day was stormy and dark clouds crowded together over the purple hills of Washington.

He looked a little more comfortable, as though being in his own surroundings gave him an edge.

"Please. Sit." He went back to the kitchen. "I want to talk to you first, Lorrie."

Sandy heard that, and while she wondered suspiciously what it was he wanted to discuss with her mother first—ground rules for their conversation, probably—she remembered that no one called her mother Lorrie but him. Sandy had the oddest sense of reeling backward through her life.

She took one corner of her father's wide sofa and sat primly, waiting while her parents disappeared into the bedroom to talk. She'd waited this long to learn what had happened all those years ago; she could wait a little longer.

Admiring the view, she spotted a pot of fuchsias on the patio, her mother's favorite flower. Clearly her parents had reconciled.

Still, she heard the sounds of an argument coming from the bedroom. If they had reconciled, it apparently wasn't without some disagreement. She heard her father's "That isn't necessary!" in a voice intended to be quiet but failing, then her mother's firm "Yes, it is!" The two of them finally emerged from the bedroom, and her father and mother sat down side by side on the other end of the sofa.

Being here felt so strange. The three of them hadn't been together in almost sixteen years and it was all her father's fault. Yet, maintaining anger was difficult when her mind was crowded with old memories and many unanswered questions.

Her mother now appeared tired, frail, as though she was about to burst into tears. She drew a deep breath, blew it out like some extreme athlete and turned so that she faced her daughter. She reached a hand out. Sandy was forced to move closer to take it. She could feel the tension in it.

"You're going to hate me," her mother warned. "I mean, more than you already do."

"I don't hate you." Sandy heard herself deny that before her brain even formed the words. She'd wanted to be cooler about this situation. "I don't hate you," she repeated, "but I would like to know what happened—and what's happening now."

Her father gently rubbed her mother's back. Such a small gesture, but it reminded Sandy that she was an outsider in what went on between them.

"You don't have to," her father said softly.

Her mother's voice was firm. "Yes, I do." Then she faced Sandy and said intrepidly, her voice breaking, "Your father left because I…I cheated on *him*."

CHAPTER THIRTEEN

SANDY REPEATED THE WORDS to herself because they didn't make sense. Her mother had been the ultimate housewife, though she'd worked long hours, too. Meals were always on time and special. Laundry never fell behind, lunches were always made. Of course, good housekeeping wasn't the definition of a faithful woman.

Sandy sat still to absorb that information. Her mother tightened her grip, grinding Sandy's knuckles together, but she was only dimly aware of that pain because the startling revelation was so much more painful. Her *mother* had cheated on her *father.*

"It was a rough time for us." Her father leaned backward to catch her eye behind her mother's stiff body. "You know there's never been a fortune in restaurants, unless you're a celebrity chef or work for a big house in a big city. We'd both had our hours slashed. You remember. The mill that had supported the restaurant closed down and business was cut in half. I got two other part-time jobs, one of them at night, and I was tired and grumpy all the time. It got to where we could barely talk to each other without shouting."

"That was no excuse," her mother said thinly, "I understand that, but he wouldn't talk to me about it, wouldn't go to counseling, slept a lot or just kept to himself when he was home, and I felt old and unloved. When a patron at the restaurant paid attention to me..." Tears fell down her pale cheeks as she continued, "I was foolish."

"It was my fault," her father insisted. "She was my wife. The two of you were my family. No matter how bad things were, it was my job to keep us together. I should have been stronger. But when I found the two of them, I was so hurt, so compromised as a man, that it was either run away or murder both of them."

He shook his head regretfully, apparently the intervening years and acquired wisdom having changed him. "It didn't occur to me that *I'd* been a jerk. All I could focus on was the betrayal of the woman I'd loved so much and for whom I'd worked three jobs."

He sat forward and reached around Loretta

to put his hand on top of hers and Sandy's. "I didn't think I could explain my leaving in a way you'd understand. And you had to be better off with your mother than with me. I worked in a dozen little cafés across the country on my way back home to Fairhaven. Then I got a job in a great little restaurant where the owner liked me, wanted to add new items to the menu and appreciated my ideas. Still, I was just getting by. And then he retired, gave me easy terms for buying the restaurant, and I developed a new whoopie pie recipe." He smiled, squeezing both Loretta's and Sandy's hands. "Remember when your mom and I were working on developing a new flavor?"

She thought back. It wasn't difficult. She could recall the two of them in the kitchen, excited, working side by side, struggling against the laws of culinary science that allowed one part of a recipe to come through perfectly while causing another to fail. She recalled being their taster.

"You couldn't get the cherry juice quite right, or something," she said, able to close her eyes and taste it. It had been wonderful, but her father had wanted a stronger, truer flavor. She hadn't thought about that in years.

"Yes!" Her father seemed thrilled out of all proportion that she remembered. Her mother smiled; the first smile Sandy had seen on her today. Her father went on. "I perfected it. I went to a cherry liqueur rather than juice. The pie became my restaurant's most popular dessert, then Mrs. Walter's Whoopie Pies bought it from me for a lot of money."

He appeared to be waiting for her to be elated. And she was—for all the nonprofits that would benefit from his generosity. But the loss of their family could not be put right for her by any amount of money.

She made herself revisit everything she'd just learned. He'd left because her mother had cheated on him. It hadn't been his fault. Well, it had been, because he'd left, but he'd had a pretty substantial reason. Still, he'd stayed away a long time.

No wonder her mother had gone into a decline. Even as Sandy thought about that, her mother patted the hand she held with her free one. "I had a hard time functioning for so long when your father left because I knew *I'd* brought it on all by myself. You were so upset, hated him so much and turned all your efforts to trying to help us survive, and *I* was responsible for all the woe."

She leaned forward to wrap Sandy in an embrace. "I'm so sorry. I should have told you the truth, but you were all I had left and I didn't want you to hate me."

Sandy was at a loss for words, an unusual circumstance for her.

Her mother sat back, tears falling freely. "For such a young girl you set a strong example of survival. You worked so hard, were fearless of the obstacles, so determined to get us through."

In the moment of silence that followed Sandy wondered if her life would ever be in balance again.

"You can tell us what you're thinking," her father said. "And you're free to be completely frank." He grinned briefly. "Not that that's ever been a problem for you."

She needed a few seconds to collect her thoughts. Her anger was completely gone in the face of their honesty, but some hurt feelings and a few questions remained.

"That was a long time to be gone without a word," she said finally. "Never a note or a phone call?"

"You're absolutely right." He accepted the rebuke. He sat up a little straighter and she saw her mother reach for his hand. "And the really awful, unforgiveable truth is that I don't have a reason for it that I expect you to understand. It took me a year to realize how prideful I'd been and how much I missed both of you, but every time I thought about some sort of reconciliation, I remembered your mother with another man and I…I wasn't strong enough to overcome the anger and resentment. I just worked and built the restaurant into a really great little place and tried to take comfort in that. But, finally, that wasn't enough. I did come back a few years ago. I took a cruise to Astoria, planning on using the day in town to talk to your mother and you, but when I got here and went to your mother's, her neighbor told me no one was home, that Loretta's daughter was in the hospital having a baby—Addie. I couldn't bring myself just to walk into the middle of that, so I returned to the boat. I think I was so…deranged by being unable to talk to you that I fell down the stairs on the way to my cabin and broke my leg. The kindness Astoria extended to me when the ship had to leave me behind and move on is the reason I want to repay this city."

He didn't have a good answer. That was reprehensible. But somehow she thought his honesty was better than a lot of excuses or pleas for understanding.

"Dad." The simple word held a wealth of empathy and all her confusion. She saw her father's eyes react to it. He began to reach a hand out to her, then stopped himself. She guessed he wanted her to make the first move. She felt sympathy, even forgiveness, but the adoration she'd had for him as a child couldn't be retrieved.

"Our nonprofits will be so excited," she said, her voice unsteady. "But, Dad…" He sat up straighter, waiting for her to go on. "Addie is four. Not a moment in all that time that you couldn't have gotten in touch?"

"Oh…" He ran a hand over his face and shook his head. "I took that roadblock to seeing your mother and you as a sign that maybe I should just stay out of your lives. The two of you seemed to be doing well. I found you on LinkedIn, and you had a good job and all kinds of skills. I researched you." He smiled with obvious pride. She swallowed, emotion about to overtake her. "It amazed me and made me proud that, as difficult as life must have been for you, you became a remarkable person.

I found out about your fund-raising for various causes in Astoria, and how much your friends and coworkers love and respect you. You're a remarkable woman, Sandy." He gripped Loretta's hand tighter, proud of how their daughter had turned out. "When your mother was still working, I saw that she won second place in the Good Eats Daring Desserts contest. I wanted to call then, but just remaining silent seemed the better part of valor. Then I got this windfall and I wanted so much to share it."

"Why did you think money would make a difference?" she asked. Her voice held no anger, only surprise.

"Because it wasn't just a little money—it was a lot of money. I didn't think it would necessarily change how you felt about me, but I thought it might at least make you listen to me. Even if you don't want me in your life, I want to try to make yours better."

Sandy stood, feeling again as though she was about to lose it, and she simply couldn't do that to her father two days in a row. "Okay, I've listened. I understand what happened. That is, I want to, but I'm finding it hard. I have compassion for both of you, and…" She gasped, groping for words. "And I love both of you. But my life is fine, and I…can't imagine the three of us fitting right back into the Connolly Family slot." She looked down at her mother. "Are you two getting back together?"

"Yes," she said.

"Will you live here?"

"Yes." Her father stood. "Will you be able to forgive me?"

"And me?" Her mother stood, too. "I'd so like your father to get to know his grandchildren."

Sandy bent to pick up the purse she'd placed at her feet when she sat down. She looked from one parent to the other, her father's face older but so dearly familiar. She gave each parent a quick, stiff hug, then took a step back.

Apparently encouraged by her conciliatory gesture, her father said quickly, "I can pay off all your accounts payable, buy you a nicer cart. Put…"

The anger she'd thought she was rid of reared its head again. "Dad, I don't want you to pay off anything, or buy me anything," she said, her voice growing louder. "I want you to regret that you walked away from us! Mom's a bigger person than I am. I want to put all that aside, but I can't just forget that you left us."

"It's easy for me to be a bigger person,

Sandy," her mother told her in a small voice. "It was all my fault to begin with."

Sandy was starting to lose it. Warring emotions made her woozy. "I don't know what to say anymore. I'm going home, but I'll call you tomorrow."

She let herself out into the hallway and was halfway to the elevator before she realized, once again, that she didn't have her car.

Her mother called to her from the hallway. "Wait in the parking area. Your father's phoning Hunter to take you back to work."

"Don't phone him. I'll walk!"

Sandy hurried off, her purse over her shoulder, just as rain began to fall. She made a rueful face at the sky as traffic rushed by. Walking on Marine Drive always made her feel she was *in* the traffic, a body without protection against the cars passing just a few feet from her. That was a good metaphor for life, she thought. The unprotected Everywoman against the threatening traffic of the universe.

Hunching into the collar of her jacket, rain pelting her head, she played her father's and her mother's revelations over and over in her mind, as well as how easily each had forgiven the other for all the intervening years. She wanted to be that generous, but found it hard.

She continued to hurry toward her coffee cart. It was becoming her refuge—the scents of the coffee and the syrups a sort of aromatherapy for her.

Hoping her mother had heard her say not to call Hunter, she stopped at the driveway to Stephanie's Cabin, a popular restaurant, to let a city truck pull in for lunch, windshield wipers working hard. Behind the truck was Hunter's BMW. He pushed the passenger side door open in invitation.

She ducked to look inside. He wore a white cotton sweater and his handsome work persona. "Thank you, but I'm almost there. And I'm not talking to you."

"You're still half a mile away," he disputed. "Get in. And you don't have to talk to me. I'll just toss you out once we're there."

When she hesitated, he added, "I'm buying coffee for the office, so hurry up. If I take too long, they're all over me."

She got in. At this point, she couldn't afford to discourage a customer, even the lying Hunter.

CHAPTER FOURTEEN

"THANK YOU." Hunter thought Sandy's voice was decidedly ungracious, despite the words of gratitude. But, contrary to her threat, she *was* talking to him. "I told my mother not to phone you."

"Your dad called me, and asked if I'd intercept you. He seems to feel you need me."

Her belt fastened, she faced him. "Why would I need a liar?"

"I think you think you don't need anyone. But your father said this morning was hard for you—for all of you. He and your mother have each other now, but he didn't know what you'd do for comfort. Your best friend is still out of town."

"I'd take comfort in the Urban's chocolate cake and ice cream, but it only makes you fat. It doesn't help you forget anything. And booze is too expensive."

"True. Then I guess I'm it."

She was quiet while he pulled into the left

lane. Her coffee cart was now just a short distance away. As he pulled into the lot the cart stood on, she asked completely out of the blue, "Did you know my mother had someone else and that was why my father left?"

"Ah…no. I didn't. How would I know that?"

"I don't know. Everybody appears to know more than I do. Well, not anymore, but you all knew it earlier."

He edged into a spot near a fence at the back of the lot and stopped the car. Rain drummed rhythmically on the roof. "I remember Loretta trying to speak several times when I visited her, and Harry cutting her off. It's possible she was trying to tell me then, but your father kept stopping her."

"He's assuming the blame. They were arguing in the bedroom before we talked. He didn't want her to tell even *me*, but she insisted. She fell for someone else because he wasn't there for her during a difficult period." She delivered that information unemotionally then added with sympathy in her voice, "My father had three part-time jobs and he was exhausted. Still, he made her feel unloved, invisible."

Hunter wanted to ask Sandy if that meant she'd forgiven them, but he was guessing that if that was the case, she wouldn't be wearing that grim expression. He unfastened his seat belt.

"He offered me money." She spoke quietly, but it was easy to see she was completely offended. "Do you believe that?" she asked. "What is it with you guys? Why does it all come down to money?" She freed herself from her belt and frowned at him.

He considered his reply carefully. He didn't want to sound sarcastic, but she was missing an important point here.

"Sandy, don't you recall offering *me* money?"

Apparently, she didn't see the parallel. "You need it to pay your debts."

"Maybe he's thinking that starting out in business, there's a lot *you* could do with extra money."

She ignored that and rested her arms on the large purse in her lap. Her lips trembled and she grabbed a tissue from the box in the console. "What a mess!" she said. "I haven't cried this much since high school."

He put a hand to her knee in comfort. "Sandy, I'm sorry. I know how hard your life has been, but it could go really well from here. Harry seems like such a good guy—apart from the past. Maybe he's wised up and just wants his family back together."

Noisy sobs issued from her but Hunter went on intrepidly. "Think about it. You're no longer the girl whose father walked away when she was 14. You're the woman whose father came back to reclaim her and her mother. Sure, your husband left, but he sounds like a jerk anyway. So you're reborn, sort of."

Her tear-filled eyes gazed into his while she thought through his words.

"Zoey and Addie get a grandfather, and your mother has her entire life restored to her. It's a win-win, Sandy."

"I want to be generous, I really do. I'm sure I'll get over the shock and we'll all deal with one another civilly, but I'll never feel that... that adoration for my father that I felt before he left. Or my mother. I mean...she cheated on him with another man. That's shocking to me."

Sandy saw that a line was forming at the coffee cart and she opened her door. "I've got to go."

Hunter got out of the car and walked around to take her hand and help her out. Rain quickly soaked his shirt. Her jacket became drenched. Still, he had things to tell her.

"You know," he said, "adoration of parents is for children. I figure you aren't a worthy offspring unless you can know all sides of your parents, good and bad, and love them anyway. Mostly, they do their best for us, and all they want is that we love them and remember, when they're old, that they did what they could for us. Your father left—that was bad. But when he stayed away, it was because he simply didn't know what to do. Haven't you ever felt like that?" That notion seemed foreign to her, so he smiled inside and changed tack. "Don't try to find him worthy of your adoration before you let him back into your life. Love him for what he is—a flawed human being like the rest of us. He just wants to be your dad again."

She considered that, then made a face at him. "You know, half the time, I try to avoid you. Then, invariably, something happens that puts you in my path. I want to shake you because you're so kind and charming, but you keep this distance that's hard to bridge. But, every once in a while…" She sighed and hesitated as rain continued to pour down on them. "You make sense, and I hate that I can't get you to see how great it would be to be…us."

It would. But, then, he'd be hijacking the

future she'd worked hard for, and he wouldn't do that.

She wanted him to confirm that he understood. Instead, he turned her toward the cart. "You'd better go." Horns were honking. "Your customers sound impatient."

DEFLATED AND DEMORALIZED, Sandy ran up the steps and let herself into the cart. She was completely surprised to find mild chaos and major hostility. Terri and Calli shouted at each other as each made drinks, took money, counted change.

"I'm the one who invited him to have a mocha." That was Terri. Sandy concluded she must be talking about Ryan.

"Well, it isn't my fault that he came to the window I'm working, is it?" Calli responded. She'd lost her usually adult cool in teen sarcasm.

"You didn't have to hang out the window to make sure he *saw* you."

Terri's emphasis on *saw you* suggested Calli's more impressive proportions. "We don't usually drop our customers' drinks on their heads. I just reached down to put it in his hand."

"We had customers lined up and you were running off at the mouth."

Momentarily stunned by the goings on, Sandy watched the two girls bump into and bounce off each other as they reached for the right product. Usually when they worked together, their moves appeared choreographed. Neither girl had noticed Sandy was in the cart.

"I wasn't. He asked me when rehearsal was and I told him."

"You've been trying to get him away from me…"

"Terri, you don't *have* him. Ryan and I both love drama, and because we're both in community theater this summer we've discovered that we have a lot in common. He likes me. You'll just have to deal…"

"He doesn't like you. You just push yourself on him, and when he can't get away, you tell yourself he likes you."

The awkward dance of coffee production stopped as the girls confronted each other. Terri went on. "How could he like you? You're…" Gesturing toward Calli with a cup of raspberry syrup, Terri groped for the right word.

"What?" Calli demanded, her face reddening. "Fat? You think he couldn't like me because I'm overweight? Guys are getting smarter than that. *He's* smarter than that." Calli held a sixteen-ounce cup of Snickers Frost, complete with whipped cream, and threw the entire thing in Terri's face. There was a screech, a quickly penitent "Oh, my God!" and both girls stood still, hands to their faces.

Sandy sprang into action. "That's enough!" she whisper-shouted. "Everyone out there can hear this childish argument. Calli, remake that frost right now. Terri, wash your face and clean up this mess. The three of us are going to have a serious discussion about this as soon as the lineup clears. Do you both understand me?"

"Yes."

"Yeah."

Being the mother of little children paid off. A strong voice replaced a lot of action.

Another hour and a half of frantic coffee making ensued, and then the midafternoon slump gave them a few minutes' respite.

Terri sobbed while she continued to clean like a maniac, and Calli burst into tears the moment she handed a simple cup of decaf out the window and faced Sandy. Without a car in sight, Sandy turned to the sobbing girls and wondered how to successfully arbitrate a fight over a boy. Then she remembered that wasn't her job here. She just had to make sure this never happened again.

"Okay," she said calmly. "I want both of you to take a deep breath and come down off the ceiling. Whatever caused this, we can talk it out, but I don't ever want to see this kind of behavior in here again."

"I'm sorry," Calli wept.

Terri said something tearfully unintelligible.

"We had cars lined up at both windows while you argued. Does that mean I can never schedule the two of you together? And this was your idea, wasn't it? How did such a nice gesture deteriorate into a catfight?"

Terri pointed to Calli. "She's trying to steal Ryan."

"I'm not." Calli dabbed at her eyes with a napkin. "He just asked me what time rehearsal was for community theater." Large tears fell down her cheeks. "And she called me fat."

"I did not," Terri denied, sniffing and regaining her composure in her need to clear herself of that charge. "*You* said fat. I was going to say *bossy* because you are."

"That's because you always talk instead of work."

"Well, that was you this time, wasn't it? And I didn't call you fat."

"She didn't," Sandy corroborated. "I heard that part of the conversation. Listen to each other when you're talking, then you won't misinterpret what's being said. Maybe Ryan likes both of you as friends."

Terri sighed. "He does like her better. He's nice to me because he's just nice all the time. I hate that. I wanted him to want *me*."

Something in Terri's tone reminded Sandy of Addie. She could just imagine the state of her own sanity during her youngest daughter's teenage years.

"Okay. So, we don't always get what we want when other people are involved because they want what *they* want and sometimes that isn't us." Right. Even profound.

Terri accepted that with a moody exhalation of air.

"Why don't the two of you take the rest of the day off and mellow out. Boys are great, but they're not worth losing girlfriends over. And thanks for covering for me this morning."

"How did it go?" Terri asked. "Your dad's back, isn't he?"

"Yes. It went fine. It'll just need some getting used to."

Calli reached for her purse. "That's nice. My dad died in Iraq. I wish he could come back."

Terri slung her purse crossways over her chest. "You want to get some onion rings?" she asked Calli grudgingly. "I've got my mom's car."

Calli replied in the same tone. "I would, but I'm broke."

"Here, I'll buy." Sandy took a bill out of the register and handed it to Terri. "Oh! Almost forgot." She quickly threw together a familiar order and handed Calli a drink carrier, and a paper bag with the delivery address on it. "Would you make this delivery for me, please, before you guys stop to eat? Tell them no charge."

AT THE OFFICE Hunter hung his jacket on the back of his chair to dry off, grabbed his cup from his desk and went into the kitchen to get coffee. Nate was there, adding creamer to a steaming cup. He stepped out of Hunter's way so he could have access to the coffeepot.

"Everything okay this morning?"

Hunter held the pot of murky brew. Nate must

have made it; it poured like black honey. "Sure. Why?"

Leaning a hip on the counter, Nate replied, "Because you didn't bring back our coffee order. And I know Connolly called you just before you ran out of here. Is Sandy okay?"

The coffee order. "Sorry. I'll go back."

"Not necessary. We're all just concerned about you and hoping...nothing's wrong."

"Nothing's wrong."

"Because you'd tell me if there was anything we could do. Say, if you wanted to reconsider the loan..."

Hunter threatened him with a look, then realizing Nate was just being a friend, relented and smiled. "Thanks, but no. I'm working on it."

Arching an eyebrow, Nate said, "Happy to hear that. With your customary backbreaking payment every month, or is there a new twist to the plan?"

Hunter frowned at him. "Mind your own business."

"I know." Unaffected by Hunter's rudeness, Nate grinned. "I used to live and let live until I met Bobbie. She claims she was that way, too, until she met Sandy. Sandy's involvement in helping everything and everyone has infected our lives. So, spill."

"Let's just say life could be simpler, and money is only some of the problem."

"Money and the eternal mysteries of how to save it, what to spend it on and what to do with the extra keeps food on an accountant's table." Nate took another sip of coffee. "Unless, of course, someone forgets to pick up the scones..."

"Here they are." Terri, one of Sandy's staffers, walked into the kitchen holding a paper bag and a carry box of coffees. "Sandy said you forgot these." She handed them to him with a smile. Each cup had an initial on it. "Scones are in the bag. Sorry the order's late. We were slammed."

Nate dug into his pocket and handed her a bill. She pushed it away. "Sandy said this round was on her."

Nate took her hand and put the bill in it. "Tell her that her accountant says it isn't. She can't give product away and expect to stay in business. Thanks for the delivery. Here's something for you." He handed her another bill.

She beamed.

When the front office door closed behind her,

Nate delved into the bag for a scone, then said to Hunter, "Last thing I'm saying on the subject."

Hunter rolled his eyes.

Ignoring him, Nate walked slowly backward toward his office. "Money doesn't have to be a problem. Give me the word and it's yours. We can set up whatever payback plan you want. You could pay off your debts with it and reimburse me a hundred a month. Think about it."

"At a hundred dollars a month, Nate, you won't live long enough to collect!"

"I'm in love. It's the Fountain of Youth. Really. Think about it." Nate turned and went to his office.

SANDY CLOSED UP at six and climbed into her car, grateful that Stella had been able to stay a little later with the girls. After the morning with her parents, and the afternoon with Terri and Calli, Sandy was eager to get home and recharge. Her brain was a muddle of new discoveries she found hard to believe.

"Hi," a voice beside her said.

Sandy cried out in surprise and jumped an inch. She put a hand to her racing heart.

"Mom!" she complained. "What are you doing here?"

Her mother pointed to the sunny sky beyond the windshield. "Sun's out again. I walked. Sorry I frightened you. Got a minute to talk?"

Her mother was once again drawn, pale… without her usual sparkle.

Sandy probably had a minute, but she didn't want to talk. "My staff was having a problem, so Stella stayed late to allow me to close up. I have to stop for groceries…"

"Ten minutes?" her mother pleaded.

Resigned to a talk, Sandy turned the key in the ignition. "Fine. If you think you can explain a lifetime of lying to me in ten minutes, I'm game. Where do you want to go?"

"How about that bench near the Maritime Museum. Isn't that your favorite place?"

It was. But that was where she went to get *away* from problems, not to discuss them. She drove over anyway, parked and walked with her mother the short distance to the bench that looked out on the river. Seagulls dove among the several freighters anchored there. The sky was mostly gray, with small patches of blue fighting for space. A harbor seal breached the water for air.

Unwilling to look at her mother, Sandy stared at the hills of Washington on the other side of the gray water.

"I'm sorry," her mother said, her voice quiet and matter-of-fact. "Your father and I should have come to you days ago, but… We were excited to make it right for each other, but we knew there was no way to make it right for you. So we delayed. Your father didn't know how to explain to you why he'd stayed away so long, and I didn't know how to tell you what I had done. So, you found out by accident that he was back. That shouldn't happen to anyone."

"Well, it did." Sandy folded her arms, the low clouds making even the June air cool. She was wishing she had the sweatshirt Hunter had bought her. "I'm just not sure where we go from here."

"Can I explain what happened?"

"Yes." Even to her own ears that reply had subtext: "If you think you *can* explain."

Her mother put both hands to her face and said, almost to herself, "Yeah." She dropped her hands, cleared her throat and began. "You must remember what life was like for us then. Your father was working three jobs. I was kept on because the chef claimed to need me, but my hours were cut and I waitressed a couple of nights a week for extra money." She paused. Sandy nodded, still not looking at her. She did remember that time. She'd missed a class trip to the beach because she hadn't had the money students were asked to bring, and she hadn't been able to buy a yearbook or a dress for the Christmas Dance. She'd acquired a bosom since the Freshman Dance and couldn't wear the same dress. Yes, she remembered.

"We were all mad at each other because we couldn't do much to change the situation."

That had been the beginning of her sophomore year. Sandy had had a poor attitude, herself. A usually good student, she was finding geometry impossible to fathom, and her plumpness and red hair socially unacceptable. The fact that her parents quarreled constantly worried her and made her entire life feel unstable.

Sandy's mother caught her hand. "You were at that stage where I couldn't do anything right, and your father's attitude convinced me that he'd rather be with anyone but me." She dropped Sandy's hand and made a helpless gesture with her own. "Bill Ferrara was a bachelor who ate at the restaurant a couple of evenings a week. He had inherited his family's flower shop down the street and I don't think there was much else in his life."

Turning to face her mother, Sandy felt her own anger diminished by the look of misery in her mother's eyes. "He noticed me," she said. Her voice held surprise, as though she still could feel what she'd felt then.

Sandy remembered that her mother had been noticeable. Beautiful and talented, vulnerable at that time, she must have been attractive to a lonely bachelor.

"I always tried to steer him toward the best thing on the menu, the best dessert. He began bringing me flowers, and once, when your father fell asleep and forgot to pick me up, Bill took me home."

"Did he know you were married?"

"Yes. But, sometimes, when you really need someone, and you find him, and he seems perfect...you forget all the other things in your life that make it wrong—a husband, a daughter, a belief system that doesn't allow for that sort of thing."

Sandy gazed into her mother's face, saw the depth of her private pain, and felt her own heart break. She'd seen something like that expression on herself in the mirror lately. It didn't have that same depth of drama attached, but she, too, had longed for what she couldn't have, and found it hard to face the fact of it.

"One afternoon," her mother went on, "your father was working and you stayed overnight with a friend, Bill took me to his place." Her fingers knotted and unknotted and finally, afraid her mother would break one, Sandy put a hand over hers to stop her.

"He was gentle and kind and everything I needed in that moment. Until it was over, and I realized what I'd done. That was the only time, but still, it happened, and I'll be wrong forever."

"Mom..."

"Bill took me home. We were parked behind the house, sure it would still be hours before your father returned, and Bill kissed me the way a man kisses a woman he's just made love to. Your father got home early." She drew a breath with a sob caught on it. "I'll never forget the look in his eyes. He knew we'd shared more than that kiss. And I understood in that instant what I'd done to us—to all of us. Your father had been horrible to live with, but it was because he'd been exhausted and felt diminished by his inability to provide. And while he was working three jobs for us, I'd had time to be with another man."

The last word emerged as though ripped from her. Sandy wrapped an arm around her mother, not knowing what to say.

"I realized the marriage was over. We fought all night about what had happened, and he was gone the next day."

"When I asked you why he..."

"I know. I told you that he couldn't cope anymore and was heading back home to Massachusetts."

"But that made me hate him, Mom. How could you have done that?"

Her mother stared at nothing, or perhaps she was staring at the memory. Then she said flatly, "I had to save myself at that point, or I couldn't have gone on. If you had known what I'd done, you'd have hated me, too." She refocused to look into Sandy's eyes, apparently seeing something that allowed her to smile understandingly. "You never hated your father. You were hurt, but hate just isn't part of who you are. Although you do have a right to hate *me*."

For Sandy to say that she did would have been satisfying, but she couldn't. She had an inkling of what her mother had felt. The circumstances were hugely different, but someone refusing to love her, Sandy, was now part of her experience. Nothing hurt quite so much, or made someone feel such desperation.

"So...he's been able to put that aside?"

Sighing, her mother sat up a little straighter and admitted sadly, "Yes. He says it doesn't matter now. We've both been through a lot and can just walk around all the things that hurt so much before. He'll never really forget it and that hurts me every minute. When he first came back, I didn't want to reconcile because I was sure that the first time we hit a rough patch, the past would come up again. But, your father says we have to forgive ourselves, or we'll lose the life we can have together now."

That did not sound like the attitude of a selfish man.

"Well, I think he's right."

Her mother wrapped both arms around her and wept. Sandy held her and cried with her.

"We want you in our lives, Sandy." Her mother straightened and dried her eyes, handing Sandy a tissue out of her pocket. "And the girls. This new chance won't mean anything if you're not part of it."

"We'll figure that out, Mom. For now, we'll all just go easy on one another, okay?"

Her mother appeared exhausted. "Okay."

Sandy drove her mother to the condo, then decided to forego grocery shopping and drove home. She sat in her car for a minute, feeling just a little beaten up.

The saddest part of all was that she couldn't call Hunter for comfort. Oh, he'd offer it, but as a friend. She didn't want that.

Forcing herself to deal with her life as it was, Sandy climbed her porch steps and prepared to walk through the front door with a smile for her girls. But there was a note from Stella taped to it.

"Hi," it read. "Taking the girls to Dooger's for dinner, then on to Fred Meyer to shop for Hunter's birthday present. We won't be too long."

Hunter's birthday. In all that had happened recently, she'd forgotten that Stella had once told her his birthday was in July. What was the protocol for gift giving in their situation?

Letting herself into the house, she wondered why Stella hadn't simply called her cell to tell her about her plans with the girls. Maybe her mother had told Stella about their meeting tonight and Stella hadn't wanted to interrupt.

Happy to have a little quiet time, Sandy dropped her purse and keys on the coffee table and walked into the kitchen. A woman walked out at the same moment and they collided, screaming in alarm until they recognized each other.

"Celia!" Sandy said sharply, leaning against the doorframe. "What are you doing here?"

Her tenant yanked ear buds out of her ears and stuffed them into the kangaroo pocket of her sweatshirt. Then she patted her heart with one hand, an extended duster in the other.

"Sandee. I'm sorry. Your mother paid me to clean for you. She said you would be away for a while."

Sandy dropped into a kitchen chair, grateful for a strong heart. This day had been too full of stress and startling moments.

"What can I get for you? Do you have wine?"

"Yes, in the refrigerator on the door. I'll get glasses."

Celia looked firm and pointed to her. "Do not move. I will get them." She opened a cupboard door and snagged two juice glasses, then retrieved the bottle of Moscato. Sandy poured as Celia sat opposite her.

"Who's with your children?" Sandy asked.

"Mando is home. He left me here, then took the girls for ice cream."

"That's right. I forgot I was later than usual."

"Your mother said you were having a difficult day and she wanted to do something to help. Thank you." She accepted a glass and toasted Sandy with it. *"¡Viva la Vida!"*

Sandy attempted to translate. "Live life?"

"Long live life. It reminds us that death will never win."

Okay. Sandy liked that and returned the toast.

Celia pointed to a cardboard box in a corner of the kitchen. "That has the coats and jackets I have fixed. We will come and help to prepare to open the Closet."

"Thank you, Celia. We have lots of stuff to put out."

"I am happy to help you." She stared into her glass, then looked up, her dark eyes troubled. "Where is your man? The *cazador*?"

"You mean, Hunter? He isn't my man, Celia. He doesn't want to be." Her friend's sympathetic gaze encouraged her to add, "He keeps pushing me away."

"Ah. *Si.*" She nodded thoughtfully. "When Mando was in jail, he wanted me to divorce.

He did not want me to be hurt by what he had done. He tried to push me away. But I did not let him."

"Yes, but Hunter isn't in jail."

"He is in *deuda*. In English—ah—money owed?"

"Debt."

"Yes, debt. It is jail of another kind, no?"

It certainly seemed to be.

She patted her friend's hand. "What time is Mando coming?"

Celia glanced at the clock over the stove. "Oh, no. Now! And I am not finished." On time, a horn sounded in front of the house.

"Just go," Sandy said, pushing away from the table. "I'll finish whatever isn't done." She glanced around the spotless kitchen. "It looks better in here than it has in weeks."

Celia ran to the utility closet with the duster and grabbed her purse from a shelf. "The sheets are still in the dryer."

"That's fine. I'll remake the beds." Sandy walked her to the door and waved at Mando and the girls in a battered white Chevy. "Thank you, Celia."

"Thank your mama. I did not want her to pay

me, but she began to cry. She looked like she had been crying already. Is everything okay?"

Sandy nodded. "It will be. You keep that money. You can't do everything for free."

"*You* do."

Sandy watched Celia get in the car and lean over to kiss her husband. The small gesture was so ordinary yet so intimate.

Was having that too much to ask for herself?

CHAPTER FIFTEEN

"BUT, I DON'T WANT a shot!" Zoey complained as Sandy led the girls through Columbia Memorial Hospital's glass doors the following Monday. Zoey held her wand and Addie wore her tiara. Their expressions were very unprincesslike.

"We'll go somewhere fun for lunch," Sandy promised. "We'll have hot chocolate and go grocery shopping. How's that?"

"Let's do that *without* the shot," Zoey bargained.

"You're going to kindergarten, Zo." With a firm grip on both girls' hands, Sandy walked down the hallway to the right, where the doctor's offices were located. Their pediatrician was at the very end of the hall. "You have to have all your vaccinations before you can go. You don't want to stay home, do you?"

"I like daycare. I'll just go there."

"But they can't teach you all the things you'll learn in school." Actually, they came pretty close, but that wouldn't help her argument. "You'll get to meet new kids, make new friends, and the school has that double slide you like so much on their playground."

"The shot's gonna hurt."

"Just a little, and for just a second."

"I want to go to school," Addie said, an uncharacteristic whine in her voice, "but I don't want a shot, either."

"You're too little to go to school." Zoey was starting to drag her feet. Sandy pulled a little harder.

Addie, having heard all her sister's complaints, stopped in the middle of the hallway. She said her favorite word. "No."

Sandy did her best to consider their feelings in most things, even those that were inconvenient for her, but in matters of their health and welfare, she was firm.

"We have to do this, Addie," she said.

"You said I was too little for school."

Good argument. "But we have to keep your shots up, too. Come on. Let's just do it, and after lunch and groceries, we'll help set up the Clothes Closet." They were less than enthused.

"You're going to give them our coats," Zoey complained.

"Because Grandma bought you new ones. And some girls and boys don't have coats at all."

Addie's arms were folded resolutely, but the man who ermerged from the door to her right momentarily distracted her. Sandy was surprised to find her father mere inches away. Not that he noticed her. He was staring at his granddaughters with amazement.

"Hi, girls," he said quietly, carefully getting down on his knees.

"Hi." Addie pouted. "I don't want a shot."

Zoey nodded. "Me, either."

He tore his eyes away from them and looked up at Sandy. His manner was hesitant.

"Hi." She smiled, a lot still unresolved between her father and her, but unwilling to expose the girls to conflict. "We're getting their back-to-school vaccinations. Zoey starts kindergarten, and Addie has to get them just to keep up. We're going to go shopping and have hot chocolate. Girls," she said, "this is your grandpa, Harry."

He seemed inordinately pleased that she'd introduced him. He smiled into the girls' pouty little faces.

Sandy had discussed their lack of a grandfather a few times with the girls. She'd told them he lived across the country, though she hadn't been sure where he was. She appreciated that he didn't smother them with hugs and kisses. He simply smiled warmly and looked them over as though he couldn't get enough of the sight of them.

"I thought you were far away," Zoey said, touching a small finger to a round zipper pull at the collar of his jacket.

"I used to be," he replied, "but I heard you two were getting so tall and pretty that I had to come and see for myself."

"Did *you* get a shot?" Addie asked.

"No, just a test. Now *I'm* going to get a hot chocolate. You know what?"

"What?" they asked simultaneously.

He dug several bills out of his pocket and extracted two tens.

"Dad," Sandy warned.

He gazed up at her, his eyes soft with affection; he was apparently too thrilled that she'd called him Dad to notice the warning note in her voice.

He gave a bill to each child. "This is for being brave about getting your shots. When you and your mom go shopping, you can buy yourselves something fun!"

The girls grinned from ear to ear, then looked to her for approval. "Is it okay?" Zoey asked.

"Yes, it is," she said. "Tell Grandpa thank you."

They singsonged in harmony. "Thank you, Grandpa!"

He was a happy man. He studied them an extra moment, then had a little trouble getting to his feet. Sandy put a hand out to help him.

"Thanks. Old age," he joked. "Getting rickety."

"We have to go." Sandy checked her watch. "Our appointment is right now."

"I'm so glad I ran into you. Call your mother. She's worried about you. Oh, and we want to make plans to distribute the money to your nonprofits. Will you set it up?"

"Sure."

"Great." He waved at Zoey and Addie. "Bye, girls." They waved back as he walked away.

"Okay. Are we ready?"

They nodded, each clutching a ten-dollar bill, avarice a powerful motivator. Then they skipped off down the hall. As Sandy moved to follow, her eyes caught the name on the door of the office her father had exited. It was the name of an oncologist.

She stopped, a cold finger of concern running down her spine. An oncologist. A score of alarming possibilities ran through her mind. As the girls pushed their way into their pediatrician's office, she temporarily put her concerns aside and hurried to catch up.

ZOEY AND ADDIE were heroic about their shots then prowled the toys at Fred Meyer, looking for just the right thing to spend their money on, while Sandy paced, wondering about her father. She leaned against a display of stuffed animals and called her mother's cell phone.

"Hi, Sandy," her mother answered.

"Mom, the girls and I met Dad this morning at the hospital."

Her mother hesitated. "Yes?"

"He was coming out of an oncologist's office? Is he okay?"

She hesitated again. "We're waiting for the results of some tests."

She had it on the tip of her tongue to ask why no one had said anything about tests, then she remembered that during their past few meetings, there'd been little time to talk about anything but their family problems.

"Okay, listen," she said.

"I always do, sweetheart."

"Dinner at my house, Sunday. 2:00." The girls had made their selections and were running to her, Zoey waving a child's umbrella with flowers on it, and Addie carrying a plastic Jeep. Conversation would be difficult from here on out. She straightened away from the stuffed animals. "See if you can get Dad to make the new whoopie pie. Bye."

That anvil was back on Sandy's chest. She could barely breathe past it, and almost couldn't speak. But she'd promised the girls lunch at the Coffee House to practice their social skills and they were behaving well. Once there, she ordered them hot chocolate, and sipped at a soft drink while waiting for their fish and chips.

Was it possible, she asked herself, that her father could finally be restored to her, then taken away again? She really didn't want to follow that thought to a conclusion.

After lunch, she drove home and collected all the clothing she'd received for the Clothes Closet. She put the girls into their car seats first, then packed trash bags of clothing around them and under their feet, while they giggled. Since they were enjoying it so much, she added blankets on their knees and hats on their heads.

She headed for the Food Bank, housed in an abandoned church on a hill overlooking the river. Volunteers had spent months of their spare time converting the old parsonage next door to the Food Bank into the Clothes Closet.

She parked in front of the church, and gave the girls hats and socks to carry, then gathered up as much as she could of the bags. Winter clothing was heavy. A helpful volunteer pushed up a shopping cart next to her.

"Oh, thanks!" she said without paying attention to who it was, concentrating on hefting the bags into the cart. "I also have a dozen blankets in the trunk if you don't mind helping with those."

A large hand took one of the bags from her. Recognizing its strong, lean lines, she glanced up. Hunter stood there in a paint-smeared gray sweatshirt and old jeans. He looked wonderful.

"Do you *ever* stay in the office?" she teased to hide her delight at his presence.

"We closed right after lunch. The whole office is here helping. That's what happens when your boss is on the Food Bank Committee. And, speak of the devil."

Nate appeared with another shopping cart, Addie in the child seat and Zoey inside. "We've got the kids helping Bobbie make signs to mark categories of clothing. They're in the basement of the church. Is it okay if these two *artistes* help out?"

"Please, Mommy!" Zoey loved working with Bobbie. Addie had picked up a small plastic fire truck somewhere and would have happily gone anywhere with it. "Sure. Is it okay that Addie has that?"

"Yeah. We've got all kinds of toys to sort through as well as clothes. I'll make a donation to cover it." Doing *vroom, vroom* noises, Nate pushed the girls toward the church.

"You take the cart," Hunter directed Sandy, "and I'll get what's in the trunk."

Several trips back to the car were required to transfer all the items into the Closet. They spent hours sorting clothing by type and size, and placing them in areas designated for men, women and children. Eventually, everything was hung on rolling racks the recently remodeled Fred Meyer store had donated.

The store had contributed bins as well for

stockings and socks, hats and mittens, and scarves.

Mando Moreno, who'd painted a lot of the space, touched up a closet that would be used as a dressing room, while Celia folded baby clothes.

Blankets hung on pegs all around the Clothes Closet, several opened out for decoration. Sandy had received a donation of umbrellas from a rain shop in Portland, and Hunter suspended one by its handle from the ceiling.

He shouted to Sandy from the top of the ladder. She looked up from organizing socks by color in the bin. "Yeah?"

"How's the umbrella? Do you want the others in a straight line down the middle, or randomly throughout the room?"

She knew climbing up and down a ladder a dozen times was no pleasant feat. "What's easier for you?"

He grinned down at her. "Usually, whatever you'd like done. Less backtalk from you that way."

She acknowledged the playful slam with a smiling nod. "That one's great. How about randomly, wherever you can set up the ladder without breaking your neck? Although, breaking your mouth is acceptable."

"Ha, ha." He climbed down to move the ladder.

In late afternoon, Bobbie came with the children to place their signs. The day after Bobbie returned from visiting her father, Sandy phoned to tell her about the Connolly family drama. That had been before Sandy had seen her father coming out of the oncologist's office. She didn't have the emotional energy to share that news today.

Bobbie now came to give Sandy's shoulders a squeeze. "You doing okay?" she asked softly.

"Of course."

"Good. You will prevail. You always do."

Sandy smirked. "Yeah, right. I'd like that on my tombstone. Or does the tombstone invalidate the whole notion of prevailing?"

"Aren't you funny."

Someone ordered pizza, and everyone went back to the Food Bank basement to sit on the outdoor-carpeted floor and eat. When they'd finished, the children played with a small bowling set someone had brought along to donate, and the adults lingered over the soft drinks provided with the pizza.

Nate and Bobbie and their boys, and Hunter and Sandy and the girls stayed to clean up. Addie stood on the broad broom Hunter pushed across the floor, while Zoey helped Sandy and Bobbie throw away paper plates and napkins and other remnants of the volunteer crew's meal. Nate and his boys carried chairs across the yard to the Closet so that shoppers would have an opportunity to sit while trying on shoes.

Sandy held the trash bag so that Hunter could empty the dustpan into it. Addie headed off with the broom to do unnecessary sweeping while Bobbie and Zoey put away the supplies they'd used for making signs.

"You all right today?" Hunter asked Sandy as he took the bag from her to tie a knot in it and heft it onto his shoulder. He waggled his eyebrows in theatrical seduction. "Want to come to the garbage cans with me?"

She didn't think she had any laughter in her, but she did. She shouted at Bobbie that she was taking out the trash. Bobbie waved to let her know she'd heard and would keep an eye on the girls.

Sandy followed Hunter up the steps to the main floor of the Food Bank and out a side door. It was dusk. Trash cans lined the back of the building. He deposited the bag in a can, then reached for her hand and led her around the building in the other direction.

"Where are we going?"

"Around the garbage cans isn't the most comfortable place to talk. Everybody's left the Closet. There's a glider on the front porch of the parsonage."

They climbed the parsonage steps and sat side by side on a two-person bench. From there they could see Washington on the other side of the river and the headlights of the traffic on the Astoria-Megler Bridge in the distance. Hunter propelled them slowly, rhythmically, back and forth with his foot. "You still haven't made peace with your parents?" he asked.

"I have, sort of." She wrapped her arms around herself. A light breeze had whipped up the hill from the river.

"What do you mean, sort of?"

Her throat hurt suddenly and she had to swallow and start again. "You know, for most of my teen years, I wanted the solid family some of the other kids had. So many times I longed for a father who would go to bat for me, handle our money problems, deal with household issues.

Just to feel strong arms around me that let me know I had someone to turn to."

Hunter put an arm around her. She wondered if he was trying to offer comfort or warmth, then decided it didn't matter. She leaned her cheek against his chest and accepted the offering.

"Anyway..." she went on "...I've come to terms with what happened and decided you were right. Adoration is for little children. We all just do the best we can and that's all we can expect from the people who raised us." She pushed away just a little but he kept his arm around her. She loved how that felt. His expression was grave, sympathetic.

"I was beginning to think that after all these years we were going to be a family again." She drew a deep breath. "But the girls and I ran into my father as he was coming out of an oncologist's office. My mother says they're waiting for test results."

He put both arms around her now and made a sympathetic sound. "Sandy...I'm sorry you're worried, but you don't really know that there's cause yet, do you?"

"I guess not. But that would be just like life,

wouldn't it? To give me everything back with one hand and take it away with the other?"

"Hey. You're usually the optimist."

"I know. Anyway, I'm tired of being mad, so I invited my parents to Sunday dinner. Is that crazy?"

"No. In their confusion and pain they hurt you, but now, instead of running away, or hurting them back, you're reacting with kindness. You'll provide them with the loving family they took away from you. That's *big*, Sandy. It'll be good for the girls, good for you, too."

She wrapped an arm around his middle and felt her breath rise and fall with his. Life, hope flowed through her. This wasn't the behavior of a man who didn't care about her.

"Would you want to join us for Sunday dinner?" She knew asking him was taking a chance, but she did it. She waited breathlessly, her cheek against his heartbeat. When an answer took longer than it should have, she realized that no matter how it felt to her, his arms around her meant nothing more than the friend in him responding to her need for a friend. As he'd told her the morning she'd bawled in his arms in the Pig 'N Pancake parking lot.

Hope died. Life, however, flowed on. She

had things to do and she would have to do them without him. At least, without him loving her the way a man loved a woman.

Hunter felt the change in her from soft and pliant to tense, removed. He hated himself. "I volunteered to do an audit for the public radio station on Sunday," he said finally, forced cheer in his voice. He was sure it didn't fool her. "I'm sorry. Your first dinner should probably be just family, anyway."

She didn't lift her head. "I understand." She said the words quietly, but he got the feeling that meant she thought he was lying.

Darkness had fallen. Hunter could feel Sandy shivering against him and pushed her away so he could pull off his sweatshirt.

"No," she protested, "you'll be cold."

"Well, if you'd worn the sweatshirt I bought you…" he chided, forcing the neck hole over her head then holding each sleeve out as she groped for them, finally pushing her arms in. "There. Better?"

Her eyes shone in the dark. He saw clarity in her gaze and pain, which had supplanted all her passion in their relationship.

They heard the Raleighs come out of the

Food Bank building next door, and her daughters shouting for her.

She pushed away from him and answered their call. "We're coming!" she said.

"Long trip to the garbage cans," Nate teased, meeting Sandy and Hunter at the bottom of the parsonage steps. "You guys want to stop by for ice cream?"

Sandy refused with a weary smile. "Thanks, but I've had a rough day. I'm exhausted."

"Yeah, me, too. But, thanks."

Everyone said good-night and went to their cars. Hunter took a yawning Addie in his arms and put her in her car seat, while Sandy secured Zoey.

"I'll follow you and help you get them in the house," he offered, holding the door for her to get in the driver's seat.

"No, thanks, I'll be fine." She smiled, but her eyes were filled with sadness. "I do it all the time. Except now, thanks to you, I have light in the garage. Then she added, "One more thing before you go."

"Yeah?"

"My father's ready to distribute the money. I'm setting a meeting up for Monday and Nate says we can do it in his conference room. Can you be there?"

He shook his head. "I'll still be at the audit. I just provided information, you're the daughter of the benefactor. You don't need anyone else."

"Okay, then." There was a remoteness about her now. "Bye, Hunter."

She uttered the two words softly but they sounded final. He opened his mouth to answer—and couldn't think of anything to say. He waved instead.

SANDY HAD NEVER seen a group of nonprofit managers so happy or so hopeful. Her father had simply broken his donation into ten equal shares because all Sandy's and Hunter's analyses proved was that each group accomplished remarkable things with what they had. She told them he preferred to remain anonymous, and presented the gifts from "someone who appreciates Astoria's giving spirit and wants to help it continue." The *Daily Astorian* photographed the delirious smiles, and noted words of gratitude and promises to make certain every penny served a good purpose.

Everyone shook her hand, and the group bestowed flowers on her. They asked her to give the flowers to their mystery benefactor with their heartfelt thanks.

She did that afternoon. It was a bright, beautiful day and she sat with her parents on their deck while the girls watched the Disney Channel.

"You did it," Sandy said to her father. "You've accomplished all the goals that brought you back to Astoria."

He held the large bouquet of stargazer lilies, roses and daisies, then presented them to Loretta, who sat beside him.

"The primary reason was your mother and you," he said, a small break in his voice. He coughed. "And that's worked out even better than I'd dared hope, and is much more than I deserve. So, it's wonderful that the nonprofits are happy and can continue their work, at least for a while, without having to strain for every dime."

Sandy's parents were radiant. She finally had part of what she'd wanted so badly when she was fourteen—her parents back together and in love again. They were good people whose lives were shaken by hard times, and though maybe they'd coped badly then, they were doing their best to restore their family now. She was happy about that.

"I have more happy news." Her father smiled widely. "My tests were negative. I was sent to the oncologist in error. I've got a simple infection antibiotics can handle."

Sandy stood to wrap her arms around him, relief flowing through her. "I'm so glad. We should celebrate."

"We will. After the Clothes Closet opening when you have more time."

"That's a promise." She made to leave. "I've got to pick up some things for the cart, then drop off a donation at the Closet. Stella's partner in the yarn shop sent us even more things."

Her mother stood, too, arms filled with flowers. She looked ten years younger, Sandy thought, and a lifetime happier. "You want to leave the girls here again," she inquired, "and we'll take them to daycare in the morning?"

Sandy went inside to ask the girls if they wanted to stay. They peered around her to watch the television while she explained the plan. They nodded without even glancing at her.

She indicated their stares to her mother. "I'd say it's okay."

"Bye, sweetheart." She gave Sandy an extra

hug at the door. "Thanks for bringing the flowers. You've always done that, you know."

"Done what?"

"Brought the flowers. Provided the finishing touch, the bit of beauty that pulls everything together and makes it right. I love you."

Touched, Sandy said simply, her voice thin. "I love you, too, Mom."

THERE WAS A certain advantage to being without a man in her life, Sandy thought as she stood on a ladder and strung lights along her coffee cart early Monday evening. She had more energy for other things. She would probably love Hunter Bristol forever, but it really was time to give up on him. It was against her nature to surrender to anything, but she had to save herself.

Her family dinner had gone well. She and her parents were on wonderful terms, Zoey and Addie loved spending time with them. Letting the anger and resentment go was liberating. She felt reborn, despite the underlying sadness over Hunter.

He was the one who'd told her that adoration of parents was for children.

She felt suddenly very adult. Most of her life, she'd been forced to take charge, to work hard and be strong, but inside, she was always the sad young girl who'd lost so much. Now that she'd let that go, she felt like a woman.

Bobbie, standing on a ladder on the other side of the cart, peered over the top at her. "Hey! Wake up. Toss me the end of your string and we'll connect it in the front. Is this roof strong enough for me to climb on?"

"Yes, but don't you dare. I'll do it."

"I will." She cast Sandy a grin. "I'm lighter, just in case you're wrong."

"Hey. I've lost twelve pounds since I bought the cart."

Bobbie had already climbed up. She strung the lights on the hooks already in place, and connected the two strings in the middle. "There!"

Off the ladders, they walked around the cart to make sure the strings were straight, all the bulbs aimed in the same direction.

"Okay. Ready to see how it looks?"

"I am." Bobbie stood aside, arms folded, and watched as Sandy plugged in the cord to the inside power source. The lights came alive, brightly outlining Crazy for Coffee. She applauded. "It looks wonderful."

It did. Sandy was pleased.

Bobbie put an arm around Sandy's shoulders as they stood back to admire their handiwork. "So, things are not too bad. Business is going well?"

"Right."

"Sunday dinner as a family went well? The girls like him?"

"Yes. I was just thinking that I finally feel grown up."

"How so?"

"I've given up longing for what I can't have in the future, and I've forgiven and forgotten the things that hurt me in my past, so...the present is good."

"Are we talking about longing for a future with Hunter?"

"Yes. I invited him to family dinner and he wouldn't come." Sandy hesitated, pushing down the emotion that filled her chest. "His refusal took me by surprise, you know, because he'd been so great all afternoon at the Closet. He was witty and wise and comforting and I thought... Well, I always figure I can make things turn out right. I guess *I'm* just not right for him."

Bobbie squeezed her shoulders. "I think you are. But, if he doesn't, it's his loss. Come on, let's go home."

"Let me just make sure the cart door's locked."

"What did you do with the girls?"

"They're at my parents'. Mom will take them to daycare in the morning." She climbed up the portable steps, tugged on the door then, finding it secure, leaped off the steps. "She's going to start watching them again in the mornings. I told her she didn't have to now that my father's home, but she insisted. He's going to come over with her."

"You want to have dinner with us if you're alone tonight? I can put a few of those twelve pounds back on you."

Sandy grinned as they climbed into her VW. "Do you know how long it's been since I've had a quiet evening to myself?" Before Bobbie could hazard a guess, she said, "Since before I married Charlie. I'm going to put my feet up, pour myself a glass of Moscato and watch the Hallmark Channel."

"That does sound heavenly."

Since Bobbie had married Nate, given up her dreams of painting in Italy and acquired two young boys to care for, Sandy wondered if she regretted the loss of her single life. "Do you miss evenings on your own?"

Bobbie thought a minute and shook her head, appearing almost surprised at the question. "No. Oh, occasionally I'd like a long enough silence to think a thought through, but for the most part, considering I once looked death in the face, I am so happy to hear laughter and arguments and television and all the other sounds of life. I'm here and I don't care if it's noisy."

Sandy leaned across her gear shift to wrap Bobbie in a hug. "I'm very happy you're here, too."

She dropped off Bobbie, then drove herself home, eagerly anticipating the solitary evening she'd planned.

HUNTER STOOD ON the viewing platform atop the Astoria Column, at the peak of Coxcomb Hill, as dusk began to overtake evening. He was searching for perspective and had hoped to find it by looking down from a great height. The hill was six hundred feet high and the tower, patterned after Trajan's Column in Rome, was a hundred and twenty-five feet tall.

So far, his strategy wasn't working. The view was breathtaking—the ocean, the Columbia River, Youngs River and the Lewis and Clark River, all the freighters at anchor in the Columbia resembling toys in a beautifully situated bathtub. He just continued to feel small and out of sync with his environment.

He didn't know if Sandy was changing, or if he was, but he thought about her constantly. He was impressed with her response to her father's return, and proud of what she was accomplishing with Crazy for Coffee. Word was out that it was *the* place in town. She'd made insightful recommendations for the distribution of her father's money and Nate told him she'd been gracious at the presentation.

So, what did he do now? He wanted to spend the rest of his life with her, but that life stretched out ahead of him burdened with debt. It would be cruel to invite anyone into it.

He should live as he had before she'd come into his life. Focused. Determined. But knowing her had changed everything—including him. He now wanted her more than anything.

His cell phone rang. It was his mother.

"Hunter, can you stop by the house?"

He was tired and confused, and sometimes being in her company only exaggerated those feelings. But she sounded oddly anxious. "What's wrong?" he asked.

"Are you at home?"

"No, I'm at the Column. What's wrong?"

"What on earth are you doing at the Column?"

"I'm...thinking."

"Well, can you come and think over here?" She hesitated a moment then added, "I want you to meet...someone."

He wondered why everything had to be shrouded in mystery with her. "Who, Mom?"

"Derek McNabb."

"And who is that?"

"He's...a detective."

Mercy. "Which one of your friends is keeping company with a suspicious man this time?"

"Hunter, he's found Jennifer. Would you please come over?"

Unable to answer for a minute, Hunter looked out at the magical view of the confluent ocean and rivers and wondered if his life was finally coming together, too. Not that he wanted Jennifer back in his life, but he could sure use the money. "I'll be right there," he said.

He flirted seriously with death as he drove down the circuitous road from the Column in three minutes, then made it to his mother's in another five.

Hunter's mother and the detective sat at her

kitchen table, the light on above it. The man had a laptop open in front of him and stood to shake Hunter's hand.

Derek McNabb was probably in his late twenties and had a craggy Tommy Lee Jones kind of face and a Humphrey Bogart voice. Had Hollywood cast him in a film as a detective, he wouldn't have been more perfect, unless he'd been ten years older.

"Nice to meet you," he said. "I think I've finally got some answers for you."

Hunter sat opposite him and focused on the laptop's screen as Derek turned it toward him.

"Found her at a hotel in Cozumel on the Yucatán Peninsula."

Hunter leaned on his forearms to study the photo of a youngish, dark-haired woman in the uniform of a maid. If he hadn't known Derek was showing him a photo of Jennifer, he'd never have guessed it was her. She was skinny and the pretty face that had smiled often was now set in hard lines as she clutched a stack of towels to her, intent on her destination in what was probably a hotel corridor.

Hunter narrowed his gaze. "You're sure that's her?"

Derek leaned over to advance the photos.

Now Jennifer looked directly into his eyes, clearly unaware she was being photographed. It was indeed her face, dark eyes, slender nose, hair that once had been glossy and free now pulled back against her head, probably knotted into a bun in the back. She looked like merely the wrapper that the woman he'd known had come in. The same outside, but empty inside, without the spirit and intelligence that had been there.

"The boyfriend left eighteen months ago," Derek said. "Took off with a waitress in the hotel bar. Jennifer's been alone since then, rooms with one of the other hotel maids. I'm afraid the boyfriend made off with what was left of your money."

Hunter sat back in his chair, still staring at the photo as Derek went on. "I can try to find him, but I'm betting the money's gone by now. You've still got a good criminal case, though, and I'm in if you want to pursue that. The local police in Cozumel are keeping an eye on her for me until you tell me what you want to do. I'm guessing she'd roll on the boyfriend, since he left her for another woman."

His mother placed a hand on Hunter's arm.

"Both of them would likely do time," Derek

said. "That was a substantial amount of money, you were forced to close your business, you..."

Hunter waited for angry resentment, cruel disappointment to overtake him. But they didn't. The simple truth was—and he couldn't believe he was thinking this—it didn't seem to matter anymore. *It was only money.*

He said that to himself again. It was only money.

His fiancée had been important, of course, though he'd obviously not been important to her. She was clearly no longer the woman he'd loved—or maybe this was who she'd been all along.

In any case, that part of his life was over. Finished. He didn't have to think about it anymore. Jennifer's expression conveyed an emptiness more complete than his had been when she'd left him.

He still had bills to pay, but he was doing that.

"Shall I call the Cozumel police?" Derek asked.

Hunter shook his head. "No. I'm not going to press charges. She looks like she's suffered enough."

"Hunter!" his mother said in complete exasperation.

"We've got a good case," Derek persisted, frowning at him.

"Thank you for what you've done." Hunter turned to his mother with a reproachful expression. "Though I didn't know you were doing it. It would serve no purpose to send her to jail. Having the money back would have been nice, but since that's not a possibility, I'd just as soon put the whole thing behind me."

"What if she does this to somebody else?" his mother asked.

"Hopefully, everyone else is more clear-sighted than I was." He stood up to shake Derek's hand. "What did all this cost?"

Derek shrugged. "I had another case in Mexico, so I worked on this one when I wasn't otherwise occupied. And your mother has a deal going with my aunt, who owes her some money. Nothing for you to worry about."

Hunter was concerned. "So, your aunt will pay you?"

"Yes. She pays me off in bakery goods, scarves and socks, fix-ups with pretty young women who take her classes." He grinned. "I'm doing okay."

Now Hunter understood. He grinned, too. "Your aunt must be the famous Glenda Barrows."

Derek closed his laptop and gave Hunter's mother a hug. "You're pretty good. Any time you want to join my agency..."

Hunter walked him to his car. "Seriously, thanks. I don't want to press charges, but I am happy to know what happened."

"I understand." They shook hands again. Derek got into an old Chevy truck and drove away.

Hunter's mother waited for him in the doorway. "I'm so sorry," she said again. "I wanted this to turn out differently for you."

He hugged her tightly. "It's all right, Mom. It took looking into Jennifer's face for me to realize how far I've come from that time and place. It's too bad the money's gone, but it's only money."

She blinked, then leaned closer as though she hadn't heard him. "Say that again."

"It's only money."

"Does that mean you'll let me give you some?"

"No. It just means I won't belabor the loss of it. I'm moving on."

Now she was smiling. "Really. In which direction?"

He kissed her cheek and ran out to his car.

WEARING A YELLOW fleece robe in which, so Zoey had told her, she looked like a Peep, the yellow marshmallow chicken sold at Easter, Sandy sat on the sofa with a chocolate bar in one hand and a glass of Moscato in the other. She was living tonight's dream of happy isolation when the doorbell rang. She looked at the clock. It was after ten.

She put the wineglass down but held on to the chocolate as she went to the door. Hunter stood on the porch in jeans and his black leather jacket, a watermelon under his arm. He seemed indefinably different. Still gorgeous, but different.

"Hi," she said warily. "On your way to a barbecue?"

"No, actually. I'm here to see you."

That was a surprise. "You are?"

"I went to Safeway for flowers, but they were out, so the produce guy told me that in Asia, a watermelon is considered an excellent hostess gift."

"I didn't know that. But this is Oregon."

"Yeah. Can I come in?"

"No." She hated to admit this, but she had to say it. "Hunter, I don't understand. And that's okay, because I don't get you half the time. You like me, you push me away, you invite me closer, you push me away again. I can't do that anymore. Just tell me what you want."

He nodded grimly, then suddenly smiled, as though he couldn't help himself. Now she really didn't understand.

"Remember the day you knocked over the apples at Safeway?" he asked. "When we were on our way to Seaside, you said if you'd knocked over the watermelons instead of the apples, you could be 'doing hard time by now,' I believe your words were."

Who could forget that day? "I remember."

He transferred the watermelon to his other arm. It had to be a twenty-pounder. "I was wondering if you'd want to do hard time with *me*."

What was he talking about? "You're asking me to go to jail with you?"

He looked heavenward in supplication. "You're usually sharper than this, Sandy. No, to the *altar* with me. Will you marry me?"

Stunned, Sandy stared at him in disbelief for a full five seconds, opened her mouth to speak and seemed unable to. Then she did what she'd never done before. She fainted dead away.

SANDY AWOKE WITH a fish on her face. At least, that was how it felt.

"Sandy! Thank God."

At the sound of Hunter's voice, she raised her head and a wet washcloth fell onto her chest. She was lying on the sofa, a pillow behind her head. It took her a moment to focus on Hunter's features. Now he looked different, gorgeous and worried.

He helped her sit up and sat beside her, tossing the wet washcloth into a bowl on the coffee table.

"Did you come to my door with a watermelon?" she asked, struggling to bring her world back into focus. Because the other thing she thought she remembered couldn't possibly be real.

"I did," he replied. "It's in a couple of pieces at the moment because I dropped it when I caught you. It's still on the porch. Now that I know you're all right, I'll go get it."

"Wait!" She grabbed the sleeve of his sweatshirt as he stood. He sat down again and smiled into her eyes. His smile worked like a xylophone mallet on every vertebra she possessed. "Did you ask me…to marry you?"

"I did. But you fainted before you answered me."

Breath whooshed out of her lungs. "I may faint again. What *happened*?"

HUNTER TOLD HER about Derek McNabb and all he'd uncovered, and about his own decision not to file charges against Jennifer.

"Why not?"

He was loving this. "Because it's only money," he said.

"Okay, now I know I'm hallucinating." She put a hand to her head in amazement, then seemed to realize that her hair had that octopus quality again, and that she was wearing a giant robe over—possibly—nothing. "Oh." She pulled the robe more tightly around her and tried futilely to smooth her hair. "I can't believe you proposed to me when I look like this!"

He wrapped both arms around her and leaned back into a corner of the sofa, taking her with him. "I proposed because I love you in whatever you're wearing, and I'm tired of your indecisive, wishy-washy, can't-make-up-your-mind approach to having…"

She giggled at his teasing. "Hunter, are you absolutely sure? You've been resisting me for so long that I'm finding this hard to believe."

"I'm as sure that I want to marry you," he said, catching one of her hands and kissing it, "as I am that the sun will rise tomorrow, and that taxes will be due on April fifteenth. I don't know how to make myself clearer."

"Oh, Hunter." She got up on her knees to pin him to the back of the sofa and kiss him senseless. "I love you so much. I can't believe this! I thought we'd end up going our separate ways and you'd marry some corporate accountant and I'd be that redheaded divorcée doing charity work to fight off loneliness, with one daughter in the Senate, and the other one on the NASCAR circuit."

"So, your answer is yes?"

She made a face at him. "Did you really think I'd say no?"

"Honestly, Sandy, I never know what you're going to say or do. Which is part of your charm, I guess, but I'm not sure my sanity will survive a lifetime of it, so we might put something in our vows about continuity and predictability."

She kissed him again. "That from the man who proposed with a watermelon."

He returned the kiss. "I thought it was an edgy gesture. Very unaccountant-like. My mother told me to stop being a bean counter and start counting flowers and stars. As much as I'd have loved to bring you a star, even when I'm feeling invincible I have my limitations."

Sandy lay against him, finally feeling the reality of his proposal. He loved her. He wanted to be with her.

They continued to hold each other, talking about dates, churches, reception venues, when to tell family and friends. Then an alarm sounded from Hunter's jacket pocket.

"Is that some protection you've installed," Sandy teased with a straight face, "against falling in love and getting married?"

"Cute. No, it's my cell phone." He took it out of his pocket and held it up. "It's to remind me to go back to the office. Clarissa Burke needs business reports by morning. It'll be easier to get them done when no one is around."

"Is she refinancing?"

He shook his head and pushed Sandy gently away. "Sorry. Accountant/client privilege."

"Is there really such a thing?"

"Well, we don't call it that, but yeah."

"Well, what about proposer/proposee privilege?"

"You've got it. I'll take you and the girls to dinner tomorrow night. We can even take your parents and my mother and tell them what's going on."

She walked with him to the door. "Wow," she breathed.

"Wow?"

She lifted a shoulder. "I'm hearing trumpets and feeling confetti on my face."

"You know what?" He leaned down to kiss her and hold her tightly one long minute. "So am I. Go to bed. You'll never be able to get up at 4:00. Good night. I love you."

CHAPTER SIXTEEN

HUNTER WAS WRONG. Sandy was up at three-thirty. She jumped in the shower, shampooed and blow-dried her hair as though she was going to a ball rather than to work. She couldn't help herself. She felt beautiful. Glancing at herself in the mirror before she left the bathroom to dress, she laughed. She didn't *look* beautiful, she just *felt* it.

After a bowl of yogurt, fruit and cereal, she retrieved art paper and pens from a stash Bobbie had once given her, and made several signs to post around the cart. They advertised that fifty percent of the sales made during the opening weekend of the Clothes Closet would be donated to the Closet to buy boots and shoes.

Signs and extra paper tucked under her arm, she grabbed her purse and left for the coffee cart. She lit her open and espresso signs and fixed Dave's white chocolate caramel mocha;

then, in the dark now lit by the lights strung around the cart, she taped her signs outside near the service windows. She stepped back to see if they were noticeable and clear enough. Satisfied that they were, she ran back into the cart just as another customer drove up.

The pace was busy until five-thirty, then she had a moment to restock cups and lids and make up a few carry boxes. She stood at the north window to do so and noticed the traffic on the bridge in the pale dawn. A light rain had begun and she thought worriedly of the signs she'd just put out. The markers were waterproof, but that wouldn't help if the paper didn't hold up as long as the lettering. Fortunately, she'd brought supplies with her.

A squeal of brakes drew her attention back to the bridge. There she noticed a small car pull as far to the left as possible to get out of the way of a semi bearing down on it.

She watched, transfixed, as the semi screamed along the straightaway, barely made the turn off the bridge, then screeched into another turn that would take it to the highway.

Her heart pounding, a little scream on her lips, she then watched as the truck careened through the red light and across the highway, headlights coming straight at her at a terrifying speed.

HUNTER AWOKE SHORTLY after five-thirty in the morning. He was surprised he'd gotten even four hours' sleep considering he felt as though his body's operating system had suddenly been equipped with a turbo booster. He wondered if that was love or simple exhaustion. He'd emailed Clarissa's reports after midnight, gone home and spent the next hour sitting in the dark, remembering the look in Sandy's eyes when she'd realized he had proposed. To be loved, to be wanted that much, was humbling.

He microwaved a breakfast sandwich and thought about how thankful he was that she still loved him after all the distress in their relationship. He couldn't wait another moment to see her. She was working, but hopefully she wouldn't be too busy to hear again that he loved her and was taking her to buy a ring this weekend.

He grabbed his sandwich, jumped in his car and headed for Crazy for Coffee.

Traffic was light, but he got stuck behind a utility truck, its equipment hanging out the sides. He sat a little taller in his seat, trying to see beyond the truck, looking for the lights outlining Sandy's cart. But all he saw were blinking and rotating lights on what appeared to be emergency vehicles.

He slowed down and frowned at the road ahead, straining to see. The truck in front of him was diverted to the right lane at the intersection by the Pig 'N Pancake, and Hunter followed it.

Apparently there'd been an accident. Then he saw a semi stretched across the left lane, the sidewalk and the paved area where… "Oh, my God!" He heard his own voice reverberate inside the car.

Not until he saw what appeared to be kindling under the giant wheels of the truck did he realize what had happened. A semi had run over Crazy for Coffee!

Hunter turned left with a squeal of tires into the parking lot of a little shop just beyond the cordoned off area. For an instant, he couldn't move, couldn't think. Then he was out of the car and running toward the semi and the pile of rubble that had been Sandy's coffee cart. This could *not* happen to her—or him—after all they'd waded through to get their lives together. No!

He leaped over the tape and ran around the front of the semi, and noticed that Sandy's red Beetle was accordioned between the semi's bumper and the bulging cyclone fence. A gasp in his throat, he raced to the ambulance pulled up beside the semi.

"Sandy!" he shouted, peering inside. Two paramedics were settling a tall man into the back. "Where's the woman who owns the cart?" he asked one of the paramedics.

The young man shook his head. "Don't know. Ask Richardson."

Scott surfaced from inside the cab of the truck. "Hey, Hunter," he said, holding up the backpack he'd retrieved. "Excuse me. Driver wants his pack." He handed it into the ambulance. The doors closed and the vehicle sped away.

"Where's Sandy Evans?" Hunter demanded, his breath coming in short bursts. "Did they take anyone else away?"

"No. She's okay. She saw the truck coming and got out."

Hunter waited a minute for his lungs to catch up with his emotions. "Where is she?"

Richardson pointed to a low concrete wall that bordered the property. Sandy sat on the farthest corner of the wall, her arms wrapped around herself. Hunter pulled off his jacket as he ran toward her.

"Sandy!" He sank to his knees is front of her, threw his jacket around her, then pulled her into his arms. "Are you okay? What happened? I just about had a stroke when I saw…"

He realized she lay inert in his arms except for a formidable trembling, and wasn't saying a word. Of course, he'd been firing questions at her. He held her away from him and looked into her eyes. In the early morning light her cheeks were white, her brown eyes enormous. Her face was smudged with dirt.

"Did you have to dive for cover?" he asked gently.

She nodded.

"Are you hurt? You're sure you haven't broken anything?" He ran his hands along her arms, touched her knees.

She shook her head. "I jumped out of the cart when I saw him coming," she said faintly, "and ran for the grass. He broke his leg."

"The driver? The ambulance just took him away."

Now that she'd found her voice, words began to tumble out of her. "His name's Bud. He lost his brakes coming off the bridge and ran right through the light, then..." She pointed a shaky finger at the kindling that had been her coffee cart.

"Yeah," he said. "I'm so sorry."

"What time is it?" she asked.

She looked very unlike herself. Of course, why wouldn't she? But she was worrying him. He glanced at his watch to answer her question.

"It's 6:17."

"It was twenty minutes ago. I looked at my watch just before I ran. I thought I was going to die."

"You're fine, Sandy," he told her, rubbing her back. "You're okay. You're sure nothing hurts?"

Her lips trembled. "Nothing hurts. I called 911 and sat with Bud 'til the ambulance came. He told me he'd just bought the truck from a private dealer and wanted to become an independent contractor."

"Yeah?" That was a lot of information to garner from an accident victim, Hunter thought. Particularly one who'd just decimated your livelihood.

"Yeah. He doesn't have insurance yet." Ah.

So that was why it was so important. Then another possibility occurred to him. He continued to hold her, afraid to ask the question. She answered it before he could.

"I DON'T HAVE INSURANCE, either," she said finally.

Hunter held her away from him to look into her face. "You don't have insurance," he said in disbelief.

"No."

"Sandy..."

"I know." She couldn't stop shaking. Every time she glanced at the semi still blocking the lane, she remembered her panicked race to the door, her leap from the stairs, her run for the grass while the deafening collision occurred behind her and pieces of things flew around her and over her head. Hunter loved her, she had her family back and her father wasn't going to die—but maybe she was.

"Should we be watching for money in the cash register when they remove the debris?" Richardson came over to ask.

She shook her head. "I make a deposit at the bank every night, take home the cash advance for the register and bring it back with me in the morning." She indicated the purse on her shoulder. "Fortunately, my purse was on top of the counter and I grabbed the bag when I ran."

Hunter and Richardson went off to talk for a few minutes, then Hunter returned to her. "Okay, then." He drew her to her feet. "Let's get you home and we'll figure out what to do."

She looked up into his face in the gray light and saw… She wasn't sure what it was. Not judgment, but maybe disappointment in her lack of business smarts.

"What?" he asked.

"Nothing." She wasn't shaking anymore, but some strange darkness was overtaking her. Actually, it wasn't strange at all. It was self-condemnation. She hadn't bought insurance!

Her life had finally gotten to where she'd always dreamed it would be. And now it was all going *away* because she'd made a stupid mistake.

"You will survive, Sandy," Hunter said, rubbing her shoulder. "I know it doesn't feel like it now, but we'll find a way to get through this."

At his car, she drew away from him, unwilling to climb inside, needing air, room to move. The enormity of what she'd done had her by the throat. She strode to the end of the parking strip, all the shops still closed, the occasional passerby slowing to see what all the lights and vehicles were about.

"Sandy Evans was stupid!" she wanted to shout at the gawking traffic, but her throat was constricted with self-blame.

Hunter tried to catch her hand. "Sandy."

She pulled away, began walking in an aimless circle, infuriated by what she'd done. "I will get through this! But *I'll* do it!"

He stood apart from her, seeming to realize she was dangerously volatile. "I know you will. I just said that."

HUNTER DIDN'T LIKE the turn this was taking, but he couldn't quite figure out what was at work here. She didn't have insurance, and neither did the other driver. The accident was the perfect storm of bad luck. He understood she was probably upset with herself and the situation, but not why it suddenly shifted the solution to the accident from something he and Sandy would tackle together to something she would do herself.

"So...you couldn't afford insurance?" he probed gently.

She took a few agitated steps away from him,

then back as the morning breeze blew her hair around her face. "First there was all the start-up stuff, licenses, taxes, all those things. Then the fridge failed and I had to replace it and all the product that was in it, then daycare fees went up and..."

He opened his mouth to say something supportive, but she shouted at him, "I *know* insurance is important, but *everything* was important."

"I was going to say that you can't control all events. Rotten things happen. But if anyone can figure a way out of this, you can. And I'll help you."

"No!" She said the word so vehemently that if he'd been a weaker man, she might have blown him down. Fortunately, he was the progeny of a tough cop, and a woman who had no fear. And yesterday, he'd had an epiphany. He was invincible. She repeated more quietly, "No. I did this. I will deal with it."

"Maybe you should have some breakfast first."

"I just want to go home."

"All right. I'll fix you some—"

She folded her arms and looked at him directly. "I want you to drop me at home. And leave me there."

"Okay, why?" he asked as directly. "I understand this is devastating to you. You've lost everything. I get that. What I don't get is why you're pushing me out of the picture when we were finally getting ourselves together."

A scary calm came over her. Finding the woman he knew in that unimpassioned, level stare was hard. "Because I'm responsible for this. And it's going to take me down for a while. You're just getting your life back. There's no reason for you to be involved in my mess."

"Really. Not even my being the man who loves you? The man you just promised to marry?"

She pivoted away from him and walked toward the end of the parking lot again. He followed her, caught her arm and turned her around. Her eyes were miserable but her face was set. "This isn't the place to argue this," she said.

Seeing where this was going, he was determined to stop it.

"Why not? Is there a good place to tell me you're backing out?"

Her bottom lip quivered and she yanked away

from him. He caught her again and held her in place with both hands on her shoulders. "If you're telling me that you're going to let making a thoughtless mistake kill us, you can darn well look me in the eye when you do it."

She went slack under his hands and her head fell back for a moment. Then she sniffed and straightened and did exactly what he asked. "It wasn't just a mistake," she said, her voice shaking as she met his stare. "It was a devastating error in judgment. I took pride in attending to every detail of life for myself and everyone else, then failed to do something so…so elementary."

"So you're not perfect. Who cares? Nobody is. You're smart and capable, a wonderful mother, and an all-around fine person when you're not acting insane. We'll be good together. You know we will."

"Hunter, I have other things to do now. I can't afford to rebuild. I've got to find a job. I don't have time to love anyone."

"Sandy." He gave her a small shake. "Your dad would help you. You know that. And love doesn't take time, it just takes dedication."

"Try to understand what I'm telling you, Hunter. My father worked hard to make what he has now. He's donated all that money and he and my mother want to travel, to..." Her eyes changed focus suddenly and she looked in danger of losing the calm she'd acquired.

"Okay, I'm done arguing with you." He took her arm and led her back to the car. "We're going back to your house, I'm going to fix you something to eat, then we're going to assess the situation and come up with a plan." He put her in the car, then slipped into the driver's seat.

"There are women who love the masterful male," she said in annoyance as she buckled her belt, "but I'm not one of them."

"We're of a similar mind. I'm not wild about the bossy woman, either, but I'm stuck with you."

"You're not *stuck* with me—that's what I'm telling you! You're free to go. It was a nice dream, but we're now suddenly very much awake."

He started the car with a weary glance at her. "Oh, stow it, Cassandra. Awake or asleep, I'm in love with you and I'm not leaving you."

"YOU'RE AFRAID THAT if you leave, even though I want you to," she said coolly, trying to push him away, "I'll dissolve into a puddle, unable to go on. Well, I'm made of stronger stuff."

He shifted in his seat to see her and jabbed her shoulder so she would look at him. She ignored him.

"You're made of crazy, noisy stuff, but that's not what I'm afraid of. Look at me."

There was that tone in his voice she never quite knew how to read. She just knew she didn't trust it. She turned her face toward him, careful to keep her expression neutral.

"First, I'm not *afraid* to leave you—I don't *want* to leave. But I think you'd like it if I did, because then you'd have an excuse to get angrier, tougher, take over everyone and everything to prove to the world that you're the survivor. You can do anything and everything alone because you're so big and scary."

She rolled her eyes and turned back to the windshield. "That's ridiculous. You're an accountant, not a therapist. I want you to leave because getting out of this mess is something I can do better by myself." Then she added for effect, knowing it would anger him and push him away, "You wouldn't let me help you, remember? Well, I have to do this by myself. You should understand that."

He laughed mirthlessly. "I understand that you can't believe you've done something so wrong. You think you're losing control of what you manage, and that somehow diminishes you. Well, it doesn't. You're not Wonder Woman. Get over yourself. You screw up just like the rest of us. Life can beat you up, no matter how prepared you think you are. And you need other people, just like the rest of us. Not just so you can give to them and shore up your woman-in-charge identity, but because *they* can help *you.* I can help you. Just relax and let yourself need someone."

She was going to lose it, and she didn't want to in front of him. She'd cried in his arms before, but only because things had happened to her over which she'd had no control. This could have been avoided. Well, the loss it would bring could have.

"Would you drive me home now?" she asked the windshield. "Or should I walk?"

He groaned and started the car again. "I wish I was the kind of man who could let you walk."

Ten minutes later he pulled up in front of her house and reached past her to push open the passenger door.

She looked into his eyes one more time and memorized the shade of blue, the glint of wit and intelligence, the glimpse of contrariness and—God—under it all, the love. "Goodbye," she whispered. Her voice had no volume. She closed the car door behind her and ran for her porch.

The moment she was inside, the door locked, she bellowed her despair. Throwing her purse aside, she sank onto the sofa and cried her eyes out.

SHE INTENDED TO call her parents at a reasonable hour, but apparently the accident had made the Portland television news and they were at her front door before she could. She stepped aside to let them in.

"Why didn't you call us?" her mother demanded, going into the kitchen as she always did when she visited, to fill the kettle and rummage for tea.

Her father smiled fondly after her as he followed, sharing an empathetic look with Sandy. "I'm sure she was going to." He eyed the soup spoon stuck in the carton of blueberry cheesecake ice cream that Sandy held to her chest. "You think if you put on a few pounds, you can better tackle the situation?"

"I haven't paid my power bill," she said, then spooned ice cream into her mouth. "They'll turn it off eventually, so I'm not wasting the ice cream. Sit down. I'll pour you some coffee. Want a scone? I always bring a few home from the cart." Realizing she wouldn't be able to do that again, she paused to deal with the huge lump of emotion in her throat. "Well...I used to."

"No, thanks. We just had breakfast." He sat down at the table and her mother poured him a mug of coffee. She retrieved another cup and waited near the stove for the kettle to boil.

Sandy pointed her to the table. "Sit down, Mom, I'll watch the kettle."

"Is it true you didn't have insurance," her father asked, turning a chair away from the table and straddling it. "And the truck driver didn't either?"

"Yes." Admitting it was getting easier every time she did it. She waited for a paternal lecture on good business practices. Instead, her father said, "I want to set you up again with another cart. Or whatever else you want. What are you going to need?"

Sandy moved her worries about the future to the back of her brain and replied firmly, "I need a job that pays well, and for you to not worry about me. I'll figure it all out. I was the one who stupidly waited to buy insurance until I could better afford it, so I'm the one who's got to fix the mistake."

Her mother shook her head at her father. "She is so much like you. It's a miracle I'm not in the loony bin."

"Sandy…"

Before her father could begin to recite a litany of reasons she should let him help her, she asked about the girls. "Did they do all right last night? Did they miss me?"

"They did fine," he replied blithely. "Your name never came up. We ate, we watched movies, we wrestled around on the floor, then they went to bed. We had just dropped them off at daycare and were having breakfast at the Wet Dog when we heard about the accident. Where's Hunter?"

"He was stopping by to see me at the cart early this morning. He got there right after it happened. My car didn't fare very well, either; it now plays oompah music. So he drove me home. I sent him away. I have to call Calli and Terri."

"Why?"

"Because they no longer have jobs."

Her mother rolled her eyes. "I mean, why did you send Hunter away?"

Though that dream of being his wife had lived such a short life, it had been so bright, so life-altering. But now that Hunter had finally put Jennifer and the embezzlement in the past, she wanted him to be happy, not to have to pay her debts as well as his. She almost hated to tell her father the truth.

"We broke up," she said matter-of-factly. The kettle began to sing. She poured water into her mother's cup and placed it in front of her.

"Cassandra Elizabeth," her mother said, leaning toward her, "what did you do?"

"Why do you presume it's my fault?"

"Because he's absolutely besotted with you for all his teasing ways. It had to be you. Why? What could he possibly have done that you disapproved of?"

While she tried to formulate a reply that her mother would buy, she noticed her father studying her face and nodding, as though he saw something that provided an answer.

"He's trying to pay off his old debts," he said, his eyes still on her, "and she's kicking herself for having operated without insurance and losing everything. So, she can't be of help to him now, and God forbid she let anyone be of help to *her*, so she broke it off."

Sandy folded her arms, and eyed him back. "A little brutal, but mostly true."

Her father studied her another moment, then crossed his arms on the chair. "Your mother said that you refinanced this house to get enough money to help him pay off his debts so the two of you could get together."

"Yes." Her answer was hesitant because she was unsure where he was going with this.

"And the two of you broke up then, because he'd told you more than once that he didn't want your financial help. He had to pay off his creditors on his own."

Now she saw it coming. "But he..."

"And you got mad because he was too proud to accept help." He let that sink in. "Remind you of anyone?"

"It's not the same."

"Why not?"

"It just isn't."

"Okay...so I'm thinking that with your positions reversed, you probably have a much clearer picture of what motivated *him* to refuse *your* help, and how pride is sometimes detrimental to clear thinking."

She opened her mouth to dispute that and found that she couldn't. She said instead, "That's in the past. I have to deal with the here and now."

Her father shook his head and said to her mother, "She is so much like you."

Leaving her parents to decide which one of them was responsible for all her bad qualities, she went to telephone her staff and tell them what had happened.

CHAPTER SEVENTEEN

IN HER PERSONAL tradition of getting on with her life, Sandy dressed the girls in their prettiest summer dresses for the Clothes Closet opening. All invited guests tonight were bringing a piece of warm clothing or a financial contribution to celebrate the realization of such a necessary service.

Hunter would not be there. Nate had told her that Hunter and his mother had gone to Wheeler, an artistic community farther down the coast, for a couple of days. "He's talking about house-hunting. He finally took that loan from me."

Sandy smiled at that. That was good. Had she been a little smarter about managing her affairs, she might be house-hunting with him.

She felt heartbroken and painfully alone. It was hard to feel alone with her parents behaving like a couple of teenagers and so, so happy together, but while the daughter in her was happy, the woman in her felt broken by the absence of Hunter in her life. And he was house-hunting in Wheeler.

Still, she was thrilled that his life was finally working out for him. She loved him enough to be happy for him, even though his new life couldn't include her.

Sandy put the girls in her mother's car, outfitted with child seats since she'd been babysitting. Her parents were using her father's Lexus until Sandy's car insurance came through. Zoey held her wand out of the way while Sandy secured her belt. "Is Hunter coming?"

"Hunter and Stella have gone away on a little vacation," Sandy said, clearing her throat to hide a break in her voice. "But Bobbie and Uncle Nate, and Dylan and Sheamus will be there. And Crystal and Elena."

"Okay." Zoey lowered her wand, her reply distracted. Apparently all her usually favorite people couldn't make up for Hunter's absence.

Fighting off depression, Sandy got in behind the wheel, and drove to the Clothes Closet.

The converted parsonage was already filled with people, and the bin placed near the door to collect donated clothes was already half full. "And we've got a couple of thousand dollars,"

Bobbie told her, drawing her and the girls toward the back where the Raleigh boys tested items on the treats table. "We can give clients certificates to buy shoes. That's something we didn't get much of in donations."

The Morenos were there with their girls, and all the children gravitated toward the basketball hoop in the backyard visible through the open door.

"They'll be fine out there," Bobbie said. "Glenda brought her granddaughter along to help keep an eye on the kids. She says she met you the night you and Hunter…"

Sandy turned to her. Bobbie gazed into her face and stopped abruptly. "Don't look like that," she scolded. "You sent him away. Heard anything from him?"

"No." Sandy didn't want to talk about Hunter, yet words seemed to keep coming out. "Not since the day of the accident. I said goodbye. He took me literally. That's what I said I wanted."

"Do you wish you hadn't said it?"

"No. His life is in a good place now, and I'm the one who's scrambling to figure out what to do. He doesn't need that."

"Your father told us he wants to buy you another cart."

"He does, but I want him to save his money for all the things he and Mom hope to do."

"You're doing to everybody," Bobbie noted gently, "the very same thing you hated Hunter doing to you."

"So everyone keeps pointing out. Have you seen my parents? Dad told me they were coming early."

"No, not yet."

"Didn't Stella drive over with you?"

"Yes, but she and Nate went off to do something. I don't know. Something about the…the… you know, the thing that regulates the heat."

"You mean the thermostat?"

"That's it!" Bobbie waved at someone behind Sandy and made a hasty departure. "Got to go. See you later."

Sandy attributed Bobbie's odd behavior to studying online for her license in art therapy. She'd been working late into the night.

"I was going to tell you that I'm off to check out the Toad and Frog stuff," she muttered, "but that's okay. I'm kind of a lone wolf these days anyway." She stuck her head out the back door to make sure the children were all right and that Belinda really did have her eye on them.

She did. Dylan Raleigh appeared to be suffering from a major crush on her.

Sandy went to the east wall, where all the blankets had been hung on a laundry line run from the back to the front of the room. The display was colorful and impressive. Sandy wandered along, looking for the throw that Hunter had liked so much, thinking she would get it for him for his birthday and ask Stella to give it to him. She saw a similar blanket in different colors that she didn't remember seeing before, but not the one Hunter had admired.

She spotted Glenda and was delighted that she'd brought with her the woman who'd made the blanket. Tonight the woman was without the knitting needles in her bun and wore a homemade snood over it instead. She looked elegant if a little lost in time.

Glenda saw Sandy and reached for her hand with a wide smile. "Sandy! You're just the woman we want to see."

They drew her into a little island in the sea of clothing where they'd placed two chairs. The area smelled of yarn and potpourri, and the fragrances of all the ladies who'd worked on these projects. Before Sandy could protest, Glenda sat her in one of the chairs and placed a plastic-wrapped package on her lap. Through the plastic, she saw the familiar, colorful squares of Hunter's blanket.

"Oh, Glenda! This is just what I was looking for." She smiled at the other woman, whose name escaped her.

"I'm Florrie," she said.

"Florrie! My…friend fell in love with this blanket, remember? He mentioned it at the meeting."

Florrie blushed again, as though Hunter stood there, praising her work. "I remember. I want you two to have it." She pointed to the new blanket Sandy hadn't seen before. "I put a different one up in its place."

Sandy dug into her purse. "That's so sweet of you, but I can't take…"

"I *want* you to have it."

"Thank you, Florrie. It's beautiful. I thought I'd buy it for my friend for his birthday. Please let me…"

"Then, you're back together?" Glenda looked hopeful.

"No. I'm going to ask Stella to deliver it to him. He's out of town today."

"But I saw…" Florrie nodded toward the back of the building.

"The point is," Glenda said, pushing Florrie into the chair beside Sandy, "that this... disagreement between you won't last forever. You'll figure out that you should be together and..."

Sandy was about to ask her how she knew, then stopped herself. As Stella's business partner and good friend, Glenda knew most things. "It's not a simple disagreement, Glenda. My life is filled with big messes, and his is finally..."

Glenda raised an index finger that rendered Sandy silent. "Florrie thinks it's appropriate that this particular blanket appealed to Hunter because she makes them for a special reason. You explain, Florrie."

The plump little woman took one of Sandy's hands in hers and held it on top of the blanket. With her gentle eyes and her sweet smile she reminded Sandy of the grandmothers of long ago who were gentle and sweet with spines of steel.

"This is a patchwork blanket," Florrie said. She unfolded the plastic and pulled out about a six-inch length of the beautifully made squares. There were several shades of blue, a muted pink, soft yellow, a little green. "Now look at it closely." She indicated a green block and covered the two blocks on either side of it with her hands to isolate it. The block took on a strangely different look. The color was an odd shade. "All by itself, it isn't even pretty. It's leftover yarn I hated to throw away." She moved her hands. "But the pink block and the yellow one give it a glow it doesn't have on its own."

"You mean," Sandy asked, "that I'd be prettier if I was standing next to Hunter?"

Florrie swatted her hand punitively. "No. You couldn't be prettier if you tried. I mean that our lives are filled with all kinds of things. Good things and bad things. Fun people and not so fun people. Good memories and things we wish hadn't happened. Things we're proud of and things we'd like to have done differently. If we put the bad things all together, they're ugly, but if we accept them into our lives with all the good things that usually outnumber the bad, they make up a pretty pattern we can live with. One that keeps us warm. And makes us real. Young couples have to be reminded of that. Life is art, and art is never perfect."

Sandy remembered all the times Bobbie had said that very thing.

Florrie folded the blanket back into the plastic and looked at Sandy over the top of her glasses. "I'm not sure who it was, but somebody said,

"Life is patch, patch, patch. This goes wrong, you fix it. That goes bad, you fix it. You don't run away, and you don't cut yourself off. You fix it. Patch it. Marry that man, put this on your bed and remember what I told you."

Her brain trying to follow that simple reasoning with its complex implications, Sandy wanted to sit still for a moment and absorb all Florrie had told her. But a group of young women were remarking over knitted sweaters for children, and Glenda and Florrie went to answer their questions.

The evening was under way. The room was filled and the noise level was high. Sandy went looking for a place to be alone for a few minutes, Florrie's words nagging in her brain. Patch, patch, patch. Pretty colors make the bad ones glow.

On her way toward the back of the room, she was conscripted by Bobbie to help hang all the new clothing brought in. "You look peaked," Bobbie said, putting a hand to her forehead. "You're not coming down with something?"

I might be, Sandy thought. Could someone come down with love? With sense?

Their conversation was interrupted by the mayor, who was standing in the middle of the room and telling the assembly how proud he was of his city, that the community worked so hard to meet the needs of its people. "And I was asked to announce that we're short of slippers and boots, if anyone has those to donate."

A pianist and a violinist from the high school provided background music while everyone nibbled from the treats table and talked with friends they were too busy to visit with unless a community function brought them together.

Still trying desperately for a moment alone to think, Sandy noticed Kate Loughman, her customer with the alcohol problem whose husband had died in Afghanistan, and remembered there was something she'd intended to do tonight. She crossed the room to Kate and gave her tall, dark-haired friend a quick hug. "Where's your son?"

"Spending a week with my brother and his family." Kate held up her paper cup of coffee and made a face. "They need you here desperately, Sandy. This stuff is terrible. I'm sorry about the cart. What are you going to do?"

Sandy hooked her arm in Kate's and led her across the room toward the bins of hats and gloves. "I'm not sure. I'm looking for work. I'll think of something. But I have somebody I'd like you to meet."

"Oh?"

"Another customer of mine." And there he was, just where she'd noticed him when she'd left Glenda and Florrie. "Brody!" she called. He turned, a not-so-tall but well-built man in his thirties. That smile he always had ready early in the morning was still on his face. "Kate, this is Brody Benson. Brody, Kate Loughman. She teaches a Yoga class. Kate, Brody was in construction before the economy tanked. Now he's taking classes at the college. Oh, hi, Clarissa!"

Sandy left her customers talking and grabbed Clarissa as an excuse to leave Kate and Brody alone. She'd intended to excuse herself to Clarissa, but the woman pulled her into a group of four couples who were talking about how good the room looked, how organized it all was. Sandy sloughed off their praise and mentioned all the volunteers who'd helped paint and set up.

Then she spotted Stella over Clarissa's head. Her heart lurched. For an instant, everything froze. Hunter must be back.

She saw him, his blond head bent to hear what Jill Morrow had to say. Jill stood very near his shoulder, her eyes blatantly seductive as they gazed into his. He'd always said in the past that Jill made him crazy, but he looked interested in whatever she was saying.

Sandy felt the world tilt. She'd begun to realize that she'd have to live without him, but it hadn't occurred to her that he might find someone else—and not in that distant future they'd talked about when she'd have one daughter in the Senate and the other in NASCAR but *sooner.* Maybe even tonight. Of course, Jill probably didn't want all the things Sandy wanted from him—love, permanence. That would make it easy for him to find her interesting.

Time began again. She excused herself and went to the small closet Mando had painted for use as a dressing room. She'd stashed her purse and the blanket there while she'd helped Bobbie hang the new donations. She drew the blanket out of its bag and splayed her fingers over the beautiful squares stitched together and trimmed with several rows of blue yarn and then fringed with a darker shade.

Stuff happened, she thought, forcing her brain to explore new avenues. And maybe, even if you brought the bad stuff on yourself, it wouldn't be too awful if you let it live beside the good things that happened. Perhaps stubborn self-sufficiency wasn't always the right answer to everything. Her father came back, her parents forgave each other, Hunter accepted Nate's loan, she loved and was loved by a lot of people.

She clutched the blanket to her, Florrie's rose scent still lingering on it, and turned to the door to…to… She forgot what she'd intended. Her mind went blank. Hunter stood in the doorway in a long-sleeved, dark blue T-shirt. His hair had been forced into order, but whatever that was in his eyes had not.

SANDY WORE A purple cotton sweater over jeans and her hair was piled up in a messy knot. Her eyes went over him with a definite hunger that seemed to match his own. She was clutching something to her, and gulped back a sob as she looked up at him. He stepped into the room and pulled the door closed behind him.

"What are you doing?" he asked.

She took a step back, her eyes widening. "I'm…ah…"

"Yeah?"

She stammered for another moment, then thrust the object in her hands toward him. He accepted it and saw the blanket with the knitted squares, which he'd so admired. He looked into her eyes. "For me?"

"I…thought you might need that for…your bed." She folded her arms, avoiding his eyes. "There are never enough blankets when it gets wet and cold." She was flushed and in a complete dither.

"It's July," he said.

"Well, it won't be July forever." She gave him a look that reminded him of the more familiar Sandy.

"True. Thank you."

"And Happy Birthday. I'm sorry I don't have a watermelon."

She pushed her hair behind her ears, put her hands on her hips. "Well, I didn't buy the blanket. Florrie sort of gave it to me. The lady who made it. You should thank *her*."

"She gave it to you and you're giving it to me?"

"She gave it to me to give to you."

"Well, that's just in time," he said. "I put earnest money on a house today. Four bedrooms and a spectacular view."

HE WAS MOVING to Wheeler! A dark, sinking feeling pushed aside the frail hope Florrie's words had brought Sandy just a moment ago. He'd foresworn her and him. And who could blame him.

Wheeler was only an hour away, but she wouldn't see him every day. He'd go somewhere else for coffee— Of course, he'd have to. She no longer had the cart. She couldn't think clearly.

A little gasp caught in her throat. "A view of what, Hunter?"

"Pardon me?"

"You said a spectacular view. Of what?"

"The river."

"What river?"

His frown narrowed. Tension pulled so tightly inside her that it took her breath. She opened her mouth to speak, but nothing came out. She tried again. "What river? The Nehalem?"

He studied her in concern. "Where would I be that I could see the Nehalem?"

She wanted to scream at him to just tell her where the new house was so that she'd know whether she had a chance of getting him back. But she was done with ugly-colored blocks in her patchwork blanket—at least, of being the cause of them. Even if she couldn't have him, she wanted to remember their parting as that soft pink or the pretty blue.

She lowered her voice. "Did you buy a house in Wheeler?"

He studied her, as though trying to see what she *wasn't* asking. "No, I'm looking at a house near the college. One of those old Craftsman style places up Seventeenth Street." He placed the blanket on a nearby shelf and took a few steps closer to her. "Mom and I drove over to Wheeler because Glenda's thinking about opening a shop there. Florrie's moving to be near her daughter and would run it for Glenda. Mom wanted me to look at the space. I have no intention of moving to Wheeler." He took one more step. She could feel the heat of his body, his breath stirred her hair. His blue eyes were steady. "I'm not leaving you, Sandy. Not even when you act like a crazy person. I'm staying right here until you realize that you want me. And you need me."

If she drew a breath, their bodies would touch. She was afraid of that. Keeping a clear head was already so hard. He wasn't leaving. He was buying a house here? She might have misheard him. Her ears were ringing. "You're staying."

"Yes."

"Because of…Jill?"

"Who?"

"Jill. Morrow."

He put a hand to his forehead, apparently offended by the thought. "What is wrong with you? I'm staying because you're here. I love you, I'm going to marry you, and we're going to raise your kids together and be happy. Do you hear me?"

THE SOUND OF his raised voice made Hunter groan. Sandy stared at him in disbelief. No wonder. That was not the sweetest proposal ever made, and that even counted the first one made with a watermelon. But in his defense, she drove him nuts. Now desperate, he dug into his slacks pocket, withdrew the jeweler's box he'd wanted to save for a romantic moment later tonight, and snapped it open to reveal the smallish but brilliant round-cut diamond on a simple band.

"What I meant was," he said, a little worried because her complexion was now white, "I love you. I need you. I would love to be a father to your girls. I know you've already answered this question once, but you did change your mind about it. So, I'm asking again. Will you marry me? I will..."

He'd been prepared to promise all the things he knew she wanted in her life, but that didn't seem necessary. She was already in his arms, sobbing, making her own promises. He put the ring on her finger, then wrapped his arms around her before she changed her mind.

She was telling him something about the blanket, and he knew that only because she pointed to it. Most of her words were unintelligible because she was talking too fast and through her tears. She rambled about ugly colors and pink and blue. He had no idea what she was talking about, but she was holding him tightly and he wasn't going to do anything to stop that. He had to pretty soon, though. He had to get her to the new corporation's meeting.

SANDY HELD HUNTER, feeling his warmth and his solidity smooth away all her concerns about the rest of her life. He was here. She'd made a terrible mistake, reacted like a lunatic, and sent him away. And he was still here. She spread her palms against his back and let that reality flow between them.

She finally raised her head and gazed into his eyes. He looked happier than she'd ever seen him.

"I finally took the loan from Nate," he explained, "and paid off all my bills. Your dad gave me enough for earnest money. In exchange I'm going to help him with investments, set up a set of books and do his taxes. I'm going to pay Nate back as quickly as I can."

"Dad didn't say anything to me about your arrangement."

"You sent me away, remember? I asked him to keep it to himself. So, if you have time tomorrow, we can go look at the house together, see if you approve."

He wanted her to look at the house. It was still all hard to believe.

He seemed to read her surprise. "It'll be hard to be married if you're living on Fifteenth Street, and I'm in the new house. The bedrooms are big, the girls can each have a room, and there's a big backyard for Addie's car, a basketball hoop, a swing set..."

She was so filled with joy there was little room for air. When she began to gasp, Hunter pushed the door open and drew her out of the small space. "Please don't faint on me again," he said. "Want some water? Some coffee? Something to eat?"

Drawing a deep breath, Sandy noticed that almost everyone had left. Kate and Brody were now leaving together. Only Glenda and Florrie remained, refolding their donations.

The intake of oxygen made her brain begin to function again. That made her remember Belinda and the children.

"I haven't checked on the kids!"

"I went out there with Nate. They're fine. The girls might be a little dirtier than you'd like. The boys were playing a little one-on-one, then taking breaks to let the girls do granny shots."

"They're letting the girls play?"

He made a face at her. "Can you keep Addie out of anything?"

Nate and Bobbie appeared beside them suddenly. "There you are!" Hunter exclaimed. "Were you…kissing in the closet?" Nate pointed to the open door. "Clarissa said she saw Hunter follow you in there. Honestly," he teased. "Have you no sense of decorum, no—"

Bobbie put a hand over his mouth. "The committee's having a quick meeting to go over…" She hesitated and looked to Nate.

"Um…finances," he said. "Yeah. Finances. Right over there in the furniture department."

Sandy arched an eyebrow. "We have a furniture department?"

"Well, somebody brought a small kitchen table and some chairs tonight."

"Did you fix the thermostat?" Sandy asked Nate.

He appeared confused. "What thermostat?"

Before she could answer, Bobbie bustled across the room. Sandy followed her through the maze of bins and racks to the table and chairs set up near the treats table. She was surprised to see her parents around the table; Mike Wallis, who owned the Wine Cellar and rented Nate the office space upstairs; Clarissa Burke, the Morenos, Stella. Many of the people from Sandy's neighborhood stood around the table: the Jensens, the Crookhams, the Wedells, the Johnsons, Alan Berg and Irene Wolfgram. Calli and Terri were there.

She nodded at them, delighted to see them, but surprised as well. They weren't part of the committee.

Hunter pulled out a chair for her and she realized with a niggle of alarm that everyone was looking at her. They were smiling, so she had no reason to be frightened, but her heart began to race all the same.

Nate went to the other side of the table so that he could smile into her face. "Sandy. Welcome to the first meeting of the SS Dancer Savana Corporation. We've gathered here to form this entity to get your savvy self back in business. As your friends and neighbors, we've all decided to put our faith and trust in you into practice by pooling our money and resources and handing them over to you to do your magic. Many of us have worked with you on community projects often enough to know your work ethic and your nimble brain. Your neighbors know you to be brave and resilient and eager to help anyone who needs anything. So, we're helping *you*."

She put a hand over her mouth to prevent blubbering. There'd been no problem with the thermostat. There was no discussion of finances—except for the loss of her business. Hunter held firm hands on her shoulders, and her mother caught her hand and squeezed it, tears starting to fall.

"Only problem is," Nate went on, "the funds invested are too much for a simple coffee cart. You might want to consider three carts, or even a restaurant."

Her father pointed a finger at himself and then her mother. "You have a sous chef and a pastry chef right here."

"I have waited tables," Celia said.

Mike Wallis raised his hand. "I'll be your wine supplier and I have access to tableware."

"If you decide to do this," Clarissa added, "I can uniform your staff."

"And we'll do whatever you need," Calli said, speaking for herself and Terri.

There was sudden silence. Completely overwhelmed with everyone's kindness and support, Sandy struggled to clear her mind so she could express how touched and grateful she was. For a moment all she could see in her mind were the colorful blocks of Hunter's blanket.

She wanted to say that she couldn't possibly accept their outrageous generosity, but she couldn't do it. These people had stepped out in faith because they believed in her, trusted her, wanted to help her.

She had to accept.

"I…I can't imagine why you are so generous and so kind, but I'm happy to be a part of…what was it again?"

"The SS Dancer Savana Corporation," Nate supplied with a grin. "Blame Bobbie. You try to make a new name out of the letters in Cassandra Evans and see what you get."

"I've done Bobbie one better," Hunter said.

"I'm going to turn Cassandra Evans into Cassandra Evans Bristol."

There were squeals and shouts as the room erupted with congratulations. Handshakes and hugs were exchanged and Clarissa told Sandy she wanted to give her her wedding dress.

Wedding dress. Sandy allowed herself a moment to absorb the words.

"The law requires," Nate said, breaking her spell as people began to gather up jackets and purses, "that we meet twice a year. We can do that in the conference room at my office. We'll email next—" he calculated "—January to see what date works for everybody. And, of course, as plans finalize for whatever Sandy decides to do, we'll let you know."

A general goodbye followed as the SS Dancer Savana Corporation streamed out the door, Sandy's parents and Stella promising to be in touch tomorrow.

Blin appeared with the six children, every one of them absolutely filthy.

Celia gasped as she drew her dusty girls to her. Mando, stocky and smiling, shook his head. "I tell you over and over that boys don't get as dirty as these two girls."

"What did you do?" Bobbie asked, her eyes

going over the boys' dirty faces and their smudged and rumpled clothes. Their appearance refuted Mando's claim. She pulled a leaf out of Dylan's hair and a candy wrapper out of Sheamus's collar. "I didn't realize basketball involved rolling around on the ground."

"We were rolling down the hill!" Zoey announced with a giggle. "It was fun." She touched each of the Raleigh boys on the shoulder with her wand and declared, "Clean!" She did the same with the Moreno girls.

Addie, wearing her tiara like a bracelet, said, "We only did it once 'cause Blin said no."

Blin apologized guiltily. "I was watching them, then the ball got away from Sheamus, he fell while chasing it down the hill and rolled the rest of the way. All four girls thought it looked like fun and followed, then Dylan was right behind them."

The girls' pretty summer dresses were probably ruined, but Sandy found it impossible to look into those smudged and happy faces and scold them. She was too happy, anyway.

Zoey suddenly noticed Sandy's ring. "Mommy!" she said. "Where did you get that?"

Sandy held her hand down so the girls could see it. "Hunter gave it to me."

"Wow. It's more sparkly than my wand."

Celia and her daughters closed in for a better look.

"That means he wants to be your husband." Crystal leaned over it so closely she was cross-eyed. She refocused on Sandy's face in excitement, a small clone of her mother. "There's going to be a wedding?"

"Yes."

"Do we get to come?"

"You do. In fact, you're all going to be in it."

Mando appeared concerned. "All of us?"

Nate turned to him. "If I have to wear a monkey suit, you do, too."

"No tuxedos," Sandy said. All she and Hunter had talked about the night before the accident with her cart flooded back to her. She'd been so sure those dreams would never come true. "Casual but elegant. The church, then the Red Building for the reception."

Zoey tugged on her mother. "Do we get to wear floaty dresses?"

"You do. Purple ones." The four girls jumped up and down like wild pistons. Even Addie, the grease monkey, was excited.

"Purple?" Nate asked.

Bobbie waved the question away. "It's a girl

thing. All little girls love purple. And make it floaty, and they're in heaven."

"Brunch at our house on Sunday," Bobbie said, "so we can talk about this. I'm going to design your wedding invitations, so I'll need time. You're not planning to get married next week, are you?"

Sandy leaned into Hunter and felt his arm inch around her. She could have died a happy woman at that moment. "We talked about early October. Fall flowers. And you and Celia in pink and plum, the guys in gray."

Hunter squeezed her shoulder. "Okay, Nate and Mando and I are going to have to go look at a car engine, or put on boxing gloves or something. The estrogen's getting a little thick in here."

"We'll pick this up on Sunday." Bobbie shooed everyone toward the door. "You guys go home. We'll lock up." She caught Sandy's arm and gave her a final hug. "Thank God!" she whispered. "I thought you two would never wise up."

"Really. As I recall, you were heading off to Europe when Nate was trying to talk you into marriage."

"Yeah, well, some of us are a little slow.

But how cool is this? College roommates who end up in the same town married to friends, so that we get to live out our lives together. Great, huh?"

There had to be a bigger word than great.

Hunter helped Sandy put her girls in the car.

"If you marry Mommy," Zoey said, "you'll be Daddy."

"Right." He cinched the belt on her car seat.

"And you'll live at our house."

"Yes. But we're going to have a new house. We'll go see it tomorrow."

Worried blue eyes gazed back at him. "You mean, move to a different house?"

"Yes. Where we'll have a swing set and room for a puppy."

The worry turned to delight. "A puppy? Addie, we're going to get a puppy!"

When Hunter leaned out of the car, Sandy's brown eyes questioned him. "A puppy? Really? Hunter, we..."

"She looked worried. I didn't want her to worry."

"We have to discuss these things. You can't just..."

He pinned her to the driver's side door and

kissed her. She surfaced breathlessly. “Well played. We were about to have our first fight.”

“You’re wrong there.”

“We’re not going to fight?”

“Sure we are.” He laughed. “But this would be number 672.”

* * * * *